Follow Your Heart

Heartfelt Romance

Book one: *Runaway Romance*
Book two: *Follow Your Heart*

Follow Your Heart

BY MIRALEE FERRELL

Follow Your Heart
Published by Mountain Brook Ink
White Salmon, WA U.S.A.

All rights reserved. Except for brief excerpts for review purposes, no part of this book may be reproduced or used in any form without written permission from the publisher.

The website addresses shown in this book are not intended in any way to be or imply an endorsement on the part of Mountain Brook Ink, nor do we vouch for their content.

This story is a work of fiction. All characters and events are the product of the author's imagination.

ISBN 978-1-943959-98-3
© 2020 Miralee Ferrell

The Team: Miralee Ferrell, Nikki Wright, Cindy Jackson, Alyssa Roat

Cover Design: Indie Cover Design, Lynnette Bonner Designer & American Cinema International

Mountain Brook Ink is an inspirational publisher offering fiction you can believe in.

Printed in the United States of America

Dedication

To Susan Marlowe, who has championed and encouraged me through this entire journey from book to movie.

Acknowledgments

First and foremost, my gratitude goes to the Lord Jesus Christ, my friend and savior who made all of this possible. Again, you'll see the amazing sequence of events that only HE could have brought about, when you visit the Author Note.

Second, I owe so much to Chevonne O'Shaughnessy and director George Shamieh, who God brought into my life. They are not only professionals and experts at what they do, they are amazing people who I've come to call friends. And of course, a huge thank you goes to the entire ACI team who helped bring this movie to the screen, as well as the actors and actresses who lended their talent to the production. Thank you all for helping to make my dream come true!

Susan Marlowe is a cherished friend I met at an OCW conference not long after both of our first books had released with Kregel Publications. We had an almost instant friendship and have stayed in touch over the years. I wish she wasn't at the topmost part of Washington state while I'm at the southernmost part. She is truly my sister in Christ. When I was first approached about doing a movie, she was ready and willing to jump a jet with me on a whirlwind research trip to Virginia. That book/movie didn't come to pass, but she's been available whenever I picked up the phone, whether I needed to share exciting news or moan about something taking longer than I'd anticipated. Thank you, Susan, I love you!

I so appreciate my family who encourages and

blesses me each step of the way. I came home one day, knowing I needed to write, but also knowing the house needed help. Allen had vacuumed, loaded/unloaded the dishwasher, and scrubbed the countertops. I asked him one time if he'd like to take over the writing, and he decided vacuuming occasionally might be more his speed.

My critique partners, Kimberly Rose Johnson, Vickie McDonough, and Margaret Daley, have been a blessing on several of my books, working through them and offering suggestions. They were only able to get through a little over half of this one, but I still treasure the time they were able to give me. I basically wrote it too fast for them to keep up, LOL!

And of course, I'm blessed by each person who reads my work and shares their excitement and enthusiasm with their friends. If it wasn't for you, there would be no movies or books. Please keep sharing—it's such a blessing when you do!

Chapter One

KATHY YODER STEERED HER LEXUS AROUND a slow-moving car on the busy Los Angeles freeway, wanting nothing more than to be home, curled under a light throw on her couch and reading a novel. It wasn't quite noon, it had been unseasonably cold, and she was already tired.

If it was only a lack of sleep for a night or two, she could deal with that. But this went deeper, all the way into her core. If she could get off the merry-go-round of traveling and writing travel books—even for a month or two—maybe she'd get her perspective back. She looked at her iPhone clipped to the dashboard. Maybe Evelyn would cancel their appointment.

She almost groaned. Fat chance of that happening. Her manager who doubled as her agent was nothing if not punctual and rarely agreed to skip a meeting. Well, she could hope, couldn't she?

As though on cue, her phone rang, and Kathy hit the answer button on her steering wheel. Her Bluetooth kicked in, and Evelyn's voice sang through the speakers. "Hey, girl! I've got your flight booked to Kenya next week. I'm afraid it's a twenty-three-hour jaunt."

Kathy groaned. "Seriously? You couldn't get me something better than that? Seriously, Evelyn, I'm twenty-seven, not seventeen. You know I have a hard time sleeping on planes. My body will be destroyed by the time I arrive."

"Ha! You can do twenty-three hours standing on your head. Remember Istanbul, when they rerouted you through half of Eastern Europe?" Evelyn's laugh followed, but it didn't bring a smile to Kathy's lips.

"Unfortunately, I do remember. It still gives me nightmares." She reached toward the cupholder, plucked out the large glass of iced coffee, and took a sip. "Are you sure we can't get a better flight? That's going to be torture, especially if you expect me to hit the ground running."

"Hey, look at it this way—it's a free trip to Kenya."

Kathy set the cup back in the holder and sighed, half hoping Evelyn would hear and at least show a little sympathy. She loved her zealous agent, but sometimes the woman seemed heartless. Wasn't she supposed to be the boss and Evelyn her employee? Probably not quite the case. Of course, she did land contracts for her and pretty much order her promotional life, so maybe Evelyn was the boss. She smiled. It certainly felt that way most of the time. "It may be a free trip, but it's not a vacation. It's a working trip. Did you at least get me business class so I can rest?"

Evelyn's laugh bounced through the car. "You write travel guides for college kids who love to travel cheap. You're lucky they're not strapping you into a jump seat."

This time Kathy made sure Evelyn could hear her sigh. "At least that way I'd have enough legroom. Hold on, Evelyn, I need to park." She flipped on her blinker and pulled into the valet parking at one of the most expensive hotels and restaurants in this section of town. Even after six years of this life, the way people spent money like it didn't matter still amazed her. If she'd had her choice, she'd have found some little mom and pop café with hand-formed burgers and homemade pie. She transferred her call back to her phone and switched off the ignition.

Sliding out of her Lexus, she handed the valet her key fob, then reached into her backseat and pulled out a well-worn backpack, covered with decals from the various countries she'd visited. She slipped her arms through the shoulder straps. Her laptop, notebook, and other important items didn't leave her possession when she handed her car over to someone else. They were her livelihood, and she liked to keep them close.

"You haven't forgotten our lunch meeting, have you, Kathy?" Evelyn never sounded annoyed, but there was something in her voice Kathy couldn't quite put her finger on.

"No. I'm walking into the hotel right now. I'll be to the restaurant in a minute or two."

"Good. See you when you get here. We have a lot to talk about and plan for this upcoming trip."

Kathy's shoulders sagged as she trudged across the opulent hotel lobby and headed toward the restaurant. "Hey, I'm here checking in. I've got to ask—do I really need to go on this tour? After all, I've been putting out four travel books a year. Isn't that enough? I'm not sure I can keep up with my writing with so much time away. Honestly, Evelyn, I'm tired."

If only life was a little simpler. She couldn't help but compare the past few years to her time growing up, but she couldn't go there. Not now. Not when things had lined up with her career. She'd wanted this for what seemed like forever, hadn't she? Stopping at the hostess's desk, she gave her name, scanning the restaurant for Evelyn. The hostess directed her toward a table next to a window.

"You can rest later," Evelyn said. "Right now, it's time to focus on your career. Besides, it's the fifth anniversary of *Broke Girl's Travel Guide*. We need to milk that for all it's worth. Hanging up now, darling, I see you walking my way." The phone went silent against Kathy's ear.

The hostess wove through the dining area ahead of Kathy, the room complete with crystal chandeliers, large windows overlooking the ocean, and plush but understated appointments. Evelyn Arnold stepped out from behind a large potted plant hiding part of her table. She waved her ring-bedecked hand, diamonds glittering on three fingers. As always, Kathy's pencil-thin agent was dressed impeccably in a designer jumpsuit with her Coach bag sitting in the chair next to her. "Darling. How good to see you. Look who agreed to join us!" She waved across the table at the man who swung around and stood, right as she spoke.

Jacques Burly, Kathy's close friend and sort-of boyfriend, took a step toward her and enveloped her hand in both of his. His warm brown eyes sparkled, and a dimple showed in his cheek, belying the otherwise rugged looks. He leaned over and kissed her cheek, then gazed into her eyes. "Kathy, my love. It's so good to see you."

A light fluttering hit Kathy's heart at his warm smile. She slipped her arms around him and gave him a gentle hug, then stepped back. "It's always wonderful to see you, Jacques."

Evelyn arched one perfectly manicured brow. "Look at the two of you. You're so adorable I could swoon." She waved at the chair between herself and Jacques. "Sit. We have a lot to talk about."

Jacques shot Kathy a private, sweet smile, then held her chair as she sat. "Surprise, my love. I hope you don't mind that I came?"

"Not at all. So there's no business meeting then? Just lunch?" She could hope. What would it be like to only have lunch with two good friends and not have to worry about her career? Somehow, she doubted that would be the case. Nothing happened with Evelyn that wasn't centered around work.

"Not a soul coming but the three of us, darling." Evelyn leaned forward and patted Kathy's hand. "We're celebrating *The Broke Girl's Guide to South Korea*. It made *The New York Times* Best Seller list. Aren't you excited?"

Kathy gave Evelyn a tight smile, then picked up the menu. "Of course. Who wouldn't be? But I'm also starving."

"The meal is on the company expense account." Evelyn waved at the menu but didn't pick hers up.

"Have you already ordered?" Kathy looked from Evelyn to Jacques. "This is so much better than a business meeting with my editor or publisher. Thank you for this break, Evelyn."

"We ordered right before you arrived, but we told the waiter to bring everything together. Since I know your favorite dish here, I ordered for you." She beckoned to the hovering waiter, who hurried over and brought their drinks. As soon as the man left, Evelyn leaned back in her chair and a catlike smile tugged at her lips. "Speaking of business, Jacques's agent called me with a very interesting proposal."

Kathy's stomach lurched, and she suddenly wondered if she'd be able to eat lunch. "Do we have to talk business right now? Let's eat and enjoy the meal and the company. You said this was a celebration, not a meeting, right?" When had she become so averse to talking business? She used to love all the details surrounding her career. Every new piece of information was an event in her life. She chased them with determination and purpose, wanting nothing more than to grow in her writing and pursuit of the life she'd always dreamed of. *Dreamed.* That was the definitive word.

When had that changed? She'd grown up chafing at all the restrictions of her life. What a conundrum. Born Amish and now living fully in the *Englischers'* world, as her childhood community called it. All she'd wanted as a teen was to leave the plain, simple life and stretch her wings—learn how to fly and explore the vast world that she'd seen so little of. Now she'd done it—she'd traveled to a number of exotic countries, but somehow, she hadn't quite found the fulfillment she'd hoped to find.

"Kathy?" Jacques's voice brought her back to the table at the same time the waiter set her steaming plate of stir-fry vegetables and chicken in front of her. The mouthwatering aroma rose from her plate, and she suddenly realized she could eat. Quite a lot, in fact.

The old habit of wanting to bow her head and give thanks almost had her doing so, but the nudge from Jacques turned her toward him. "Sorry. You were saying?" She took a bite of her food and savored the flavor. Delectable. If only she could cook this well.

"I think you'll want to hear what Evelyn has to say." He picked up his own fork and took a bite of his salmon before moving to his strawberry and walnut salad.

Kathy narrowed her eyes. His tone held something different—a hint of mystery, perhaps? Maybe this wasn't anything that would pull her down. She could use something intriguing in her life. She turned to Evelyn and tipped her head to the side. "Okay, I'm listening."

Evelyn dabbed at her lips with the linen napkin, then spread it back on her lap. "As you know, *Jacques's Voyages* is wrapping up its umpteenth season on Traveler Network. While it's all been going well, the format is getting a little—" She shot a glance at Jacques, who smiled.

"Stale." He lifted his cut-glass goblet and took a sip of water, then set it down. "We're losing viewers and our ratings aren't as high as they once were. I blame streaming and the large variety of shows to choose from currently on the market."

Evelyn jumped in, her dark brown eyes sparkling with excitement that only something career-changing could bring. "When the network found out about you two lovebirds, the execs went crazy!"

Kathy still didn't get it, but this didn't seem to be going in a direction she could get enthused over. Besides, Evelyn was always raving about her and Jacques being in love, while Kathy didn't quite see it that way. "And?"

Jacques leaned forward, folding his slender hands on the table in front of him. "They want us to co-host a show ... together! Just think, you and me, traveling the world. Chasing adventure. Just like we've always talked about."

Kathy blinked, not sure she was hearing him right. They had talked about it in the early days of their relationship, and at the time, there was nothing Kathy would have wanted more. But now? Now she wasn't so sure. She didn't want to keep chasing adventure and traveling the world. There had to be more to life.

"So, what do you say?" Evelyn's eyes bored into hers. "You're excited, right? You should be thrilled at this amazing opportunity."

Kathy bit her lip. She loved Evelyn. The woman had done so much to train her and had given her career more than one boost over the past few years. The last thing she wanted was to disappoint her or seem ungrateful. "It sounds ... very interesting. A unique idea. But why me? I'm a writer, not a travel aficionado."

"You're a writer now, but this could change your trajectory." Evelyn waved her hand. "You could be the next Padma Lakshmi. I mean, she's an actress, model, and the host of her own cooking show. If she can do it, so can you." She practically gushed over the final words.

"I'll think about it, Evelyn." Kathy hunched a shoulder. "I'm flattered, but I can't make a promise now."

"I understand. Take all the time you need." Evelyn shot a look at Jacques, and something seemed to pass between them.

He reached over and squeezed Kathy's hand, letting it linger in his for a few moments.

Evelyn picked up her wine glass and held it out toward Jacques. "To Kathy's big trip, her bestseller, and..."

"The TV show." Jacques moved his water goblet toward Evelyn's and Kathy followed suit, clinking the sides of their glasses with hers. Kathy smiled. "Thank you, guys. I appreciate your support."

"And love." Evelyn gave a teasing smile and tossed another glance at Jacques.

He gave a firm nod. "Absolutely and always."

Kathy's heart lurched, but she wasn't sure if it was due to pleasure over Jacques hinting he loved her or nervousness that he might be stating something she wasn't ready to reciprocate.

Evelyn took a sip from her glass before setting it down. "There's one other surprise."

Kathy stiffened. "There's more?"

"I know you've been tired lately, and you've got that big trip coming up, so I wanted to pamper you. And this isn't on the expense account, this is from me." Evelyn lifted her purse onto her lap, drew out an envelope, then handed it to Kathy.

She took it and perused at it for a moment before slipping the flap open and withdrawing what appeared to be a gift certificate. "A spa treatment? Here at the hotel?"

Evelyn's smile widened. "Yes. For the full weekend. That's why I wanted to meet here. Since you gave me a key to your apartment a couple of years ago, I took the liberty of stopping by while you were gone and packing you a weekend bag with everything you could need. You're already checked in and ready to be waited on hand and foot."

Jacques held up an identical envelope. "She gave me one too." His expression was almost sheepish, like he wasn't quite sure what to think of the promised pampering.

Kathy stared from Evelyn to Jacques and back to her friend and agent, not sure how to respond. Evelyn better have gotten the two of them separate rooms.

Evelyn took one look at her face and burst out laughing. "Chill, darling. There's nothing immoral about this. You have rooms on separate ends of the hall in the spa area."

Kathy glanced at the certificate again. It might be nice to have a weekend to relax and not be on her laptop or in front of a camera or podcast mic. "Are any treatments included?"

"Yes, you're getting massages, facials, hot stones, aromatherapy, the whole works. If you're not relaxed by the time you walk out of here, I'm asking for a refund. I'm not going to pretend. I want you to take this weekend, relax, think about the show, and by the time you walk out of this door, you'll be rested and ready to sign the papers before you leave for Kenya. Sound good?"

Chapter Two

AN HOUR LATER, KATHY AND JACQUES walked a few yards from the restaurant to the spa reception desk as Evelyn headed to valet parking. She had explained they weren't just hotel guests, they were spa guests, and as such, they would follow different protocol. In fact, there was a small dining room, sitting room, game room, and more that only the spa guests could access. About the only time they'd be in their rooms within the spa wing was at night. There was a full regimen planned that was guaranteed to relax anyone willing to pay the steep price to experience it.

Kathy gave her head a slight shake. She was grateful for the gift, but at times it still floored her that people would spend money the way Evelyn did—like there was an unending supply that would keep flowing like a spring bubbling out of the ground. Maybe it would, as long as Evelyn was careful who she signed as clients. But maybe it wasn't luck or even being careful. Her agent had a knack for spotting potential, as well as a gift for helping to develop that potential into something very salable.

"Miss?" The hostess behind the desk brought her back to the present. "I'd like to welcome you both to Tranquility Spa. Your bags are already in your rooms, and you're ready to begin your weekend. But before we go over all of the amenities we have waiting for you, we would like to collect your cell phones and any other electronic devices."

"My what?" Kathy closed her hand over her phone and held it against her chest. No way was she giving up her phone. She looked at Jacques, certain he'd have the same reaction.

He simply arched his brows.

Kathy wasn't going to give up so easily. "What if there's an emergency?"

"Evelyn obviously knows where we both are, as does my agent. If anyone from your publishing house or my director's office needs us, they know to contact our agents. I'm sure we'll be fine." Jacques shrugged.

The hostess gave them a look that said she'd heard all the excuses and questions a thousand times. "If you need to call any family or friends first, please feel free to do so. But we don't allow cell phones or laptops for the time you're here. We've found it increases your stress level, and most people find it difficult to relax if they're always checking for updates."

Kathy muttered under her breath. "How about my stress level if I can't check anything?"

Jacques bumped her shoulder with his. "She's probably got a point. We won't miss them for two days. What can go wrong in that amount of time that we would need to know about?"

Kathy mustered a weak smile. "I suppose." She slowly released her hard grip on her phone and laptop case and laid them on the counter. Her fingers itched to snatch both back and march out of there, but she somehow controlled the urge and stepped away from the counter.

The hostess scooped them both up, put them in a plastic bag with a label, and placed them in a safe behind her. "You're signed up for the serenity package, which includes a hot stone massage, a facial, a mani-pedi, time in the sauna and jacuzzi, and you can choose two of our classes." She withdrew two sheets of paper and slid them across the counter to Kathy and Jacques.

He read his then glanced at Kathy, his eyes sparkling with laughter. "Hmm. Well now. Maybe the relaxing to gentle music class and the stretching class?"

The hostess pointed to the sheet. "You could try one of our more popular classes. Astrocartography or Soul Journey."

Kathy blinked. "Uh. What are those?" They had a foreign sound that didn't quite hit her right.

The hostess smiled. "We can help you gain insight on issues such as love, career, health, wealth, travel, and spirituality through astrocartography, a locational astrology system. Or ... we can teach you to have a higher level of consciousness, awareness, and understanding through the use of imagery, music, and breathing."

"Okay." Kathy nodded at Jacques then turned her attention back at the hostess. "Sounds ... interesting ... but I think I'll stay with the two that Jacques picked, as far as classes."

A slight frown pulled at the woman's lips, but it quickly disappeared and was replaced with a bright smile. "Whatever you say. We want our guests to be happy and relaxed, after all." She waved a hand toward a glass door etched with pictures of planets. "Right through this door. Let's get you started on your journey to rest and relaxation."

Sunday morning, Kathy sat across from Jacques, feeling more rested and relaxed than she had in months. His good looks, charismatic grin, and perpetual good mood always drew her. She'd rarely met a man as upbeat as Jacques. She hadn't seen him as much as she'd thought she would, since they hadn't taken part in all of the same things, but from what she could tell, he seemed rejuvenated as well. "To be honest, I wasn't sure about this place, but now I want to stay here forever. It's hard to believe we have to go back to the real world tomorrow."

Jacques took a sip of his coffee, then smiled. "I hear you. I slept better the last two nights than I have in a long time."

"I fell asleep during a massage. It was a really peaceful sleep even if it was for only an hour. There's something about not having access to my phone or tablet that's refreshing—although part of me is beginning to wonder what I've missed." She gave him a rueful smile. "Bad, huh?"

Jacques set his mug down on the table and leaned forward. "So ... now that you're rested and relaxed, what do you think about the show offer? I hope you spent at least a little time considering it."

"I suppose I'd be crazy to say no." She held up her hand when Jacques's eyes brightened and he seemed about to jump in and celebrate. "Wait. I didn't say I'm in full agreement. While it's an amazing opportunity, it's also a big change. Traveling ten months out of the year is hard enough, but then add a camera crew to the mix, and it doesn't feel like there'd ever be any privacy or down time. I'm not sure I'd enjoy that."

"I get that, Kath, seriously. But we'd be together. Right now, the majority of our time together is texting or FaceTime." He reached across the table and took her hand in his. "I've never met another woman who shares my passion for adventure the way you do. Admit it—you're a restless soul, exactly like me."

Kathy smiled. "'Not knowing when the dawn will come, I open every door.'" She loved that quote, but somehow, she didn't expect it would impact Jacques the way it did her.

As she expected, he raised a brow, his expression neutral.

"Emily Dickenson. I've always loved her work." Kathy took a sip of her coffee, then let her breath out. "I'm sorry I can't tell you what you want to hear right now."

He squeezed her hand. "I might not be able to say it like Emily, but I want us to be in the same time zone. Don't you?"

No fluttering of her heart or increase in her breathing as his thumb stroked the top of her hand. That fact both relieved and bothered her at the same time. "I ... yes, sure. I mean, it would be great to see you more often. I do miss you when we're separated by a continent or two."

Jacques released her hand and seemed to stiffen. "I guess I'd hoped you'd be as excited about this opportunity as I am. Not only for us, but for your career."

"I am excited. But I'm not sure yet. I haven't had enough time to weigh all the pros and cons." She spread her finger and thumb an inch apart. "There's a small part of me that's still unsure, and I can't commit if I'm not in one hundred percent."

He nodded, and a warm smile spread across his face. "I get that, and it's a fair point. By the time we go home, you'll be certain it's the right decision. I can guarantee that one hundred percent."

Kathy saw something between excitement and worry warring in his expression. She wanted to reassure him and not add to his concern. This new show possibility was important to him, and it would be a boost to both of their careers. She wasn't sure why she couldn't jump in with both feet and agree, but something kept holding her back. "That sounds good. We'll talk about it again later." She rose from her chair, leaned over, and gave him a quick kiss on the cheek. "There's no rush. Even good things can wait while we learn to slow down and just breathe again."

The next morning, Kathy exited the foyer of the hotel with Jacques by her side and handed her parking slip to the valet as she listened to her phone messages. She glanced to the side and saw Jacques doing exactly the same thing. She smirked. So much for lasting peace and tranquility. The minute they retrieved their devices from the front desk, they'd both immediately checked texts and voicemail.

He met Kathy's eyes as he tucked the phone into his pocket. "I don't think I missed it too much while we didn't have our phones, but now it seems like it's been forever since I checked in anywhere."

She nodded and held up her finger. She'd noticed a voicemail from a number she didn't recognize and almost hadn't checked it. However, since it could be industry related, she'd decided to listen before she put the phone away and got in her car. After a pause, a poor-quality message started, and Kathy's heartbeat increased at the familiar Pennsylvania Dutch accent coming through the line. "This message is for Katrina Yoder. This is your sister Miriam. It is my responsibility to tell you that our father has gone to be with *Gott*. His service will be held on Monday at ten a.m. in our home church, should you feel the need to attend."

The line suddenly went quiet. Kathy pulled the phone away from her ear. Could that be all? Nothing more? A cold message from a sister she hadn't talked to in several years, saying *Daed* had died? She hit replay to make sure she hadn't missed anything. Her mind had been wandering, after all, to all the things she needed to take care of now that she'd reentered the real world. She listened again for the full fifteen seconds it took for Miriam to leave the message, then nothing. She wanted to stomp her foot and demand Miriam tell her more. A cold wave washed over her body. *Daed* was gone? How could that be? She hadn't had a chance to say goodbye. To kiss his whiskered cheek one last time. To let him know she was sorry...

She startled as Jacques touched her shoulder. "Kathy? What is it?"

"My *daed*. My father. He's dead. That was my sister. She left a message." She waved a hand in the air. "I shouldn't have been here. The service is..." She glanced at the face of her phone. "Right now. Ten o'clock. And I'm not there."

"I'm so sorry." His attention swung from Kathy to her car as the valet stepped out, walked around, and held out the key fob to Kathy.

She barely registered what she was doing as she took the fob and handed the valet a tip. "Thank you." She turned to Jacques. "I shouldn't have let them take my phone."

"I understand, but he'd still be gone. That wouldn't have changed anything."

A stab of irritation hit her. "I get that, but I would have been there. I didn't even know his health was poor. I should have been there before he ... left." She choked back a sob trying to escape her throat. "I should be at that service right now, not standing in front of a posh hotel after being pampered for two and a half days." She turned away and walked to her car.

"Kathy? Are you going to be okay?"

His voice tugged at her heart, but she pushed the feeling away. She slipped into her car and rolled down the window. "I have no idea. I'll talk to you later. I'm going home."

"Home? Your apartment, right?" He took his keys from the valet who'd arrived with his car.

She didn't take the time to answer. She rolled up the window, gave a quick wave, and pulled out into traffic, her foot itching to hit the accelerator and drive as fast as she possibly could to Cave City, Kentucky.

Chapter Three

SARAH STOLTZFUS HUNG THE LAST SHEET from her laundry basket on the line and watched with satisfaction as the linens moved in the warm breeze. It wouldn't take them long to dry with this temperature. Now to see how the produce was doing in her garden.

The tomatoes appeared like they'd give her a bumper crop, and the zucchini was growing so fast she'd have her hands full picking those, if she could keep the squash bugs away. Saturday market should be a fruitful day. She'd already picked three flats of raspberries, and satisfaction swelled in her heart at the blackberry patch and the apple tree with their ripening fruit.

The phone in her outdoor work area rang, and she set the basket down and trotted over to pick it up before the person gave up. "Hall-o? This is Sarah."

A soft voice that Sarah couldn't quite put her finger on came through the line. "Sarah. Hi!"

"*Ya?* Who is this?"

"Hey, it's Kathy." The voice was quiet, as though giving Sarah time to remember who Kathy might be. "Katrina Yoder. Your cousin."

"Katrina! I haven't heard your voice in so long, I didn't recognize you. I'm sorry." She put her fingers over her lips as she remembered. "Forgive me, dear cousin, for not recognizing your voice. And I am so very sorry about your *daed*. It was a wonderful service. Very solemn and appropriate—exactly what he would have liked. I understand you must be very busy with your new life and couldn't come."

Katrina was quiet for so long, Sarah wondered if she'd lost the connection. "Katrina? Are you still there?"

"Yes. I'm here." She cleared her throat. "I have a favor to ask." She drew in a hard, sharp breath. "Would you allow me to stay at your inn?"

"Of course. Any time. When were you thinking of coming?"

"Um. Today? I'm on the road now and I should be at your house in an hour or two. I should have called ahead, but I decided to come this morning after I got a message from Miriam about *Daed*. Are you sure you don't mind? I know I never took my vows with the church, so I wasn't shunned, but I can't believe most of the community will welcome me."

"*Ya.* Some will, and some might look away. But those who matter will open their hearts to you again. I will prepare a room for you. Will you come straight here, or do you plan to stop to see Miriam, or possibly Hazel? You two cousins were close as children—even closer than you and Miriam, I think."

"Sarah, I can't remember a time Miriam and I were ever close. I never measured up. I could never make her happy or do any chore right."

Sarah shook her head, then realized Katrina couldn't see her. "*Nein.* That can't be true. I remember she used to boast to me that your quilting was some of the best in our community. Surely, you've only forgotten the good times? They will return when you see each other again. You've been gone too long. All will change when you return and find your place among us again."

"Um ... Sarah?" Katrina's voice was hesitant, careful.

"*Ya?* Is all well, Katrina? Something is bothering you, *ya?* I hear it in your voice."

"I'm not coming home to find my place again. I'm coming ... well, honestly, I'm not sure why I'm coming. Miriam left me a message about *Daed*. She sounded ... hostile. Brittle. Like she hates me. Or like a complete stranger leaving a message that she was obligated to leave. There was no warmth at all. Just ... facts. That's all. If my own sister feels that way about me, I can imagine the rest of the Amish community will be even worse. As far as they're concerned, I turned my back on them and walked away. Abandoned them. How can they think anything else?"

Sorrow surged through Sarah, and she dug deep within, hoping to find something to say that might help her dear cousin. Katrina had been gone far too long. More than likely, her *Englischer* ways wouldn't fit in their community and would raise Miriam's ire. Was there anything she could say that would make her return easier? She quirked a brow. "Katrina?"

"Yes, Sarah. I'm here."

"You must remember this. Gott has not abandoned you. He is still here. He has not turned his back on you, and He never will. It doesn't matter what man—or woman, for that matter—thinks of you. He loves you. Try to remember that?" Her heartbeat picked up, beating in time to her own drumming hope for her cousin. It couldn't be easy, returning to a community that would surely find displeasure in one of their own who chose the world instead of her faith.

Katrina didn't answer for several long seconds, then her voice came over the line in a bare whisper. "Thank you, Sarah. I'll try. But honestly, I don't think it will do any good. God gave up on me when I walked away from Cave City and my family. And so did almost everyone else."

Chapter Four

KATHY STARED AT THE FAMILIAR LANDSCAPE around her as she got within a few miles of Cave City. She blinked as an Amish farmhouse appeared off to the right, with another one a quarter mile farther along. An Amish buggy came toward her in the other lane, and she slowed, hoping she could see and maybe identify the driver. However, the bearded man had his hat pulled over his eyes, and he kept his gaze straight ahead. Something akin to excitement stirred, but dread and a niggling fear came along with it—both emotions she'd dealt with too often in years past when she still lived at home.

She remembered the times she'd feared her parents would be disappointed in her and the guilt that came with her decision not to join the church. She'd never forgotten *Mamm's* face and the silent tears that coursed down her cheeks as she'd said goodbye.

That first year, she'd been so homesick she'd almost run home to the farm a dozen times, but the yearning for adventure and the desire to travel the globe had kept her feet planted in the *Englischer* world. It was too late to look back—too late for regrets. All she could do now was continue down the path she'd chosen and shove the guilt aside. If only Sarah could be right—if only God still approved of her and loved her. But she'd wounded Him too. Of that she was for sure and for certain, as her mother used to say.

She still missed *Mamm*, even four years after she'd passed. Miriam and their cousins were all that were left. *Mamm* and *Daed* hadn't realized the big family they'd hoped for. Two miscarriages of little boys born after her older sister Miriam had nearly broken her parents' hearts, and the final one lost had put an end to the pregnancies.

Her phone rang, and she nearly swerved off the road. She pushed the button on her steering wheel without checking to see the caller's name. Maybe she should have checked and let it go to voicemail. It didn't feel quite right to bring her other life into this old one, somehow. "Hello?"

"Hey, I want you to know I'm thinking of you and sending you positive energy out there in Amish land. I forgot. Where are you headed again? Are you there yet?" Evelyn's voice would normally cheer her up, and her comment would bring a smile, but not today.

Kathy resisted the urge to push the off button and disconnect the call. Her *mamm* and *daed* would be horrified to hear about positive energy coming her way. They believed in prayer and God's hand guiding their lives, not some nebulous energy that had no real meaning. "Thanks, Evelyn. Cave City, Kentucky. And yes, I'm on the outskirts of town right now."

"Oh, how exciting! Are there tons of people in long skirts and buggies in sight? You must take pictures and send them to me."

Kathy tried not to sigh so Evelyn could hear. "The Amish don't like their pictures taken, remember?"

"Oh, right. I was thinking you could take a few when they aren't looking. You honestly used to be Amish? That's so crazy!"

"I still kind of am. I never joined the church, so I wasn't shunned. I left after my *Rumschpringe* when I turned eighteen, almost ten years ago." Kathy pulled over, too distracted to feel safe passing buggies or cars while talking.

"Hey, I have an idea. Let's put the new *Broke Girl's*

Travel Guide on hold and have you write a book about the Amish and your roots. I'll bet that would be another best seller. Your readers would eat it up."

"No thanks, Evelyn. That's not what I want to be known for. I've chosen my direction, and I plan to stick with it."

Evelyn chuckled. "It could be worse. But hey, I get that. It probably would be too far off from what readers are used to from you, anyway. Jacques said you still have a few small reservations about the show. I don't want to push you or anything, with all you're going through."

"Thanks." A little of the tension in Kathy's spine released, and she leaned into the seat of the Lexus. She'd been sure this call would be increased pressure to make a decision. It was nice to be wrong for a change.

"So ... the thing is ... Jacques's agent keeps calling. He says he needs a decision soon. I know, I know, you need more time. I'm just not sure what to tell him." Evelyn's normally confident tone had morphed into something less than assured.

"Honestly, Evelyn, I can't think about that right now. I need a few days to grieve my father, see my sister and cousins. I can't decide my future when my past has thrown itself in my face. You understand that, don't you?" Kathy tried to keep the brittle tone out of her voice, and she ended up coming off as almost begging. Not something she ever wanted to do. "I mean, I missed my own dad's funeral." She swiped at a tear escaping from the corner of her eye. "I haven't made peace with that yet. Give me a few days to work through this, okay?"

"I know you did, darling, and I'm sorry, the timing stinks. They say not to mix business with pleasure, but you and Jacques are made for each other. This seems like a no-brainer to me. If you need help deciding, it's an easy yes from me. Of course, I'm only your agent, and it's your decision. But if my opinion carries any weight, there it is."

Kathy put on her blinker, waited for a truck to pass, and pulled out onto the road. She needed to end this conversation and get to Sarah's house where she could unwind and rest before facing Miriam. "It may be an easy yes from you, but there's nothing easy about it on my end. You say you think Jacques and I are perfect for each other, but no one is perfect."

A giggle came through the speaker. "I thought my two ex-husbands were perfect when I married them. Of course, I ended up finding out neither of them were."

"Exactly. Hey, I need to go. Let's talk later, okay?" Kathy spotted a farm stand a short distance ahead and her heartrate accelerated. That seemed familiar. She pulled into the parking lot.

"Fine, darling. Have a good rest of your day. All I ask is you don't make me and Prince Charming wait too long for your answer. Ta-ta!"

Kathy eased out of her car and stood for a moment, taking in the scenery and atmosphere as memories from the past assaulted her mind. A number of cars and at least three or four Amish buggies were parked with the horses tied to posts around the graveled lot. Would she run into anyone from her old life? If so, would they shun her or simply be coldly polite and hurry away? Neither felt like good options, and she almost turned and jumped back in her car.

She steeled herself to move forward, taking a

cleansing breath and blowing it back out in a soft whoosh. There was no time like the present to plunge in again, even if she did dread what might come. How bad could it be, anyway? She was a grown woman who had traveled the world. It shouldn't bother her to return to her hometown.

Strolling toward the open-air produce stand containing not only fruits and vegetables, but homemade jams, jellies, preserves, pies, and more, Kathy inhaled the fragrance of what must be a fresh apple pie, the cinnamon and apple combination making her mouth water. Her stomach made it clear that breakfast was a distant memory. She stopped in front of the pie display, housed behind glass, and bent to get a closer look. Sure enough, an apple pie and a cobbler. She could see what appeared to be blackberry or boysenberry, peach, and a couple of others she couldn't identify as easily.

"Is that Katrina Yoder with her nose pressed up against the pie case?" A man's voice caused Kathy to spin around. Isaac Mast stood a few feet away, holding his black, flat-brimmed hat and smiling, his beard reminding her this man was married. Or had been. She'd heard he'd been widowed a few years ago.

Kathy walked toward him and opened her arms, wanting nothing more than to hug her childhood friend. "Isaac! It's wonderful to see you."

He stiffened, then held out his hand for her to shake. "*Ya. Wunderbar*, for sure and for certain."

She dropped her arms, suddenly conscious of the glances coming from both Amish and *Englischers* alike. An Amish man would not want to be seen in public hugging a woman not his wife, and especially not an *Englischer*. "How have you been, Isaac?"

"*Gutt.* I wish you were here under happier

circumstances, however. I am so sorry about your *daed*. He was a good man and well respected. We will all miss him." He bowed his head for a moment, then he raised it and his brown eyes met hers, flooding her with warmth.

"Thank you, Isaac. I wish..."

"Who is she, Papa?" A little blonde girl, possibly six or seven, scampered over and took Isaac's hand. "She's pretty." She twisted back and forth, twirling her long blue skirt in the exact way Kathy remembered doing at the same age.

Isaac kept his warm eyes fixed on Kathy. "Sadie, this is Miss Katrina Yoder, a young lady who used to live here a very long time ago."

Kathy planted her hands on her hips. "Not *that* long ago, Isaac. And I go by Kathy now, not Katrina." She almost dropped her gaze. That intent expression brought back feelings she hadn't experienced since her teen years.

He raised his brows. "How very ... *Englisch*."

"I like *Englisch*, Papa." Sadie skipped in place and giggled, then hopped forward and handed Kathy a dandelion. "For you."

"How pretty." Kathy took the slightly wilted flower and tucked it behind her ear. "Do you like it?"

"It is *wunderbar*." Sadie gave her an impish grin and giggled.

"Cousin Katrina!" A woman hurried out from behind a counter where she'd finished helping a customer and strode toward Kathy, arms outstretched, a wide smile pulling at her cheeks.

"Cousin Hazel! I stopped here to see you as soon as I got into town. I've missed you, my friend."

Hazel enveloped Kathy in a warm hug, then drew back, holding her at arms' length. "That's because you wanted my pie. I know you, Katrina." She stepped away and looked Kathy up and down. "You are far too thin. I think we'll have to fatten you up while you're here, *ya*?" She turned and waved toward the pie case. "Pick what you want, it's my treat."

Kathy shook her head. "No. I'll pay for it."

"*Nein.* You are family. I won't take your money."

"What about me, Hazel?" Isaac picked up two pies he'd set on a counter nearby and held them up.

Hazel laughed. "For you, that will be twenty dollars."

Isaac dug in his back trouser pocket and handed over a twenty, then waited for Hazel to place the pies in a box. "*Denke*, Hazel."

She shook her head. "Boysenberry. It's always boysenberry."

"What other kind of pie is there?" He gave her a soft smile and tucked the box under his arm. "Come, Sadie. Say goodbye to Miss Yoder. We need to go home."

The little girl walked over to Kathy and tugged on her hand. "Will you come see me sometime? Please?"

Kathy leaned over. "I'm not sure how long I'll be here, Sadie, but I'd like that." She straightened and looked at Isaac. "We need to catch up and have a long talk. I want to know everything that's happened since I saw you last."

"That won't take long. Nothing much ever changes here."

"I'm serious, Isaac. We should get together." She saw his eyes widen and she rushed ahead. "Over a cup of coffee? Nothing formal, of course."

He placed his hat back on his head, then touched the brim and gave her a slight bow. "It was *gutt* to see you, Katrina. I hope you have an enjoyable stay." He held out his hand to his daughter. "Sadie. It's time to go home now." Isaac strode with firm steps away from Kathy, as the little girl turned her head and peered over her shoulder. He helped Sadie into the buggy, then settled beside her, picked up the reins, and clucked to his mare. "Let's go. We have work to do."

Kathy watched him go, and something inside twisted. She glanced at Hazel. "I hope I didn't offend him. I didn't mean anything by it when I said get together, other than catching up and talking about old times. He seemed upset."

"Actually, that's the happiest I've seen him in a long time. He smiled today, and that's a first in a while. He spends all his time cooped up in his workshop, making furniture." She plucked a broom from behind the counter and swept off the wood floor where a few leaves had blown in. "If it wasn't for Sadie, I don't know if he'd ever leave his place. She's all that kept him from sinking into depression and losing himself."

She snapped her mouth shut and turned away. "Enough gossip. Let me get your pie." Scurrying behind the counter, Hazel pulled out a box and a heavy piece of cardboard. She placed one pie inside, put the cardboard on top, then set another pie on top of the first. She carefully closed the box and handed it to Kathy. "For you."

Kathy held up her hands. "I can't eat two pies! I can't even eat one. Seriously, Hazel, keep them. Do you have one you can cut and send a piece home with me?"

"*Nein.*"

Kathy opened her purse and reached for her wallet.

Hazel narrowed her eyes. "You take that wallet out, Cousin, and you *will* offend me." She thrust the box into Kathy's hands.

Kathy took it, then leaned forward and placed a soft kiss on Hazel's cheek. "You always were my favorite cousin. Thank you."

Hazel squeezed Kathy's arm. "Welcome home, Katrina. Welcome home."

Kathy walked to her car, trying to keep the tears from spilling onto her cheeks. She felt as far from home right now as if she'd been in dense jungle on another planet. Nothing felt right, yet there seemed to be a tiny pinprick of light in the distance. Maybe she needed to believe that light would grow and lead her in the right direction. She'd believed in God as a child. She'd even prayed and given her life to Him. She wasn't sure what had happened to that little girl or if it was possible to find that light again, but maybe it would be worthwhile to try.

Isaac did his best not to look back at Hazel's fruit stand as he clucked to his mare and drove out of the graveled parking lot. Katrina Yoder was here to see her sister and cousins after losing her father. She had not returned to see him, and he'd make sure his heart remembered that.

"Papa?" A gentle tug on his sleeve from Sadie brought him back to the present. "Who was that pretty lady?"

"She's someone I used to know when I was little like you."

Her eyes brightened. "Did you play dolls with her like I do with my friend Mary?"

He chuckled and shook his head. "Boys don't often play with dolls, Sadie. We went fishing together, and I taught her how to skip rocks across the water on the pond. Sometimes we chased butterflies, and other times we played in a tree fort my *daed* built for me. We were great friends." A smile tugged at his lips as the memories tumbled over one another in their eagerness not to be forgotten. So many memories, and most of them good. All until that last day, one that he'd chosen long ago to forget.

"Why don't I have a treehouse, Papa?" Sadie's lips puckered in a pout.

"I guess I never thought about building one. Maybe I'll see about making you a dollhouse instead, when I have time. It's safer than a treehouse. Would you like that?" He was glad she'd so quickly forgotten about her interest in Katrina Yoder.

"*Ya*, that would be very nice. And maybe Miss Yoder can come to our house and play dollies with me, since she never did with you." She nodded, looking every bit the wise little woman. "After you get it built, you can help me write an invitation to send her, all right, Papa?"

He slapped his reins against his mare's flank. "Get up there, girl. No more lazing along. It's time to get home." The last thing he wanted was for Katrina to come visit at his house. He was already haunted after one glance into her warm, hazel-green eyes. Another venture down that road could be his undoing. "She's not going to be here long enough for me to get a dollhouse built and send her an invitation, Sadie, I'm sorry. You can invite your friend Mary over to play once it's done. How would that be?"

He didn't have time to take away from his custom furniture business to build a dollhouse, but he hadn't spent enough time with Sadie since Ruth's death. A dollhouse was a small price to pay if it helped keep his daughter happy—and helped keep her mind off a certain *Englischer* he could never have.

Chapter Five

SARAH HURRIED TO THE DOOR, a bright smile lighting her face at the sound of the knock. She hadn't expected Katrina quite so soon, and she hadn't heard her car arrive, but she'd been busy in the kitchen preparing a meal and must have missed it. She swung open the door and froze.

Bishop Swarey stood there, his hat firmly on his head and his blue eyes staring at her with fierce determination. "Sarah. I have come to see if you've made a decision yet. We talked when that *Englischer*, Annie, lived here. She has been gone for months now, and you still have not closed this inn or taken a husband. I have been patient, but you must make a decision. Are you going to allow my Jeremiah to court you, or close your inn?"

Sarah squared her shoulders and lifted her chin. Her bishop had intimidated her in the past and almost forced her to close her business. A business her husband Ezra had spoken his blessing on, before he'd died. Then Annie came along and helped Sarah understand her worth. She respected this man of *Gott*, but she wouldn't allow him to force her into a decision she wasn't ready to make. "No, sir. I have not made that decision yet. Jeremiah is a good man, and I care for him as a friend. However, friendship is not enough to make the decision to marry—or even to court. I loved my Ezra, and I will not settle for less than love a second time. I will continue to run my inn for now, but I will do as we agreed, and only take *Englischers* if they have no other place to stay. I am no longer running advertisements, and I mostly care for our own people who are passing through on their way to see family in other districts."

He gave a curt nod. "So be it. Will you allow Jeremiah to call on you?"

She held back a sigh. "Jeremiah may come visit any time he wishes. But I do not want him to feel he's obligated to court me or come calling. That must be his decision—and mine. We are not young children beginning our *Rumschpringe*, Bishop. We are adults. While I am not happy I was widowed, I am waiting on *Gott* for my future. I will not rush that." She couldn't believe she'd said all that to her bishop. Never had she been able to stand up to the man before. Partly from fear of his strong personality, but also partly from respect for what he stood for in their community.

Their bishop was a stern man, yes, but a fair one. He'd never been unjust with those who'd needed discipline, and he'd been patient with her for a year now, waiting on her decision. Somehow, she'd found the strength to find her own way. She would value his counsel, but the decision must be between her and *Gott*.

His face darkened. As he opened his mouth to speak, a car pulled off the road and drew up to the gate. He pivoted and stared, then swung back around to look at Sarah. "What is she doing here?" A storm brewed in his eyes that didn't bode well for Katrina.

Sarah clenched her hands into fists by her side. "She is my second cousin. As you know, her *daed* passed away. Katrina has come to pay her respects and, I assume, see her family."

"Is it not a bit late for respects, after her *daed* is dead and buried? If she truly had respect, she would not have left our community and joined the world—and broken her *mamm*'s heart." The bishop shook his head.

"You would do well not to keep entertaining *Englischers* in your home, Sarah. I bid you a good day." He turned and went carefully down the stairs, staring straight ahead.

Katrina shut her car door, her suitcase in hand, and reached the gate at the same time the bishop did. She swung it open and extended her hand. "Bishop Swarey. It's good to see you."

The bishop gave a slight jerk of his head and moved past her. He untied his horse from the hitching rail, then climbed up into the seat. Without another word to Sarah or Katrina, he slapped the reins against the horse's back and headed for the road.

Kathy gazed at the buggy as the horse trotted up the road, pulling it at a brisk pace. She turned to watch Sarah walk toward her down the front path, wearing a troubled expression. Kathy remembered her own encounters with the firm leader of their community ten years ago, and the memory didn't do anything to bring a smile to her own face. "I'm so sorry, Sarah. I obviously came at a very bad time. I hope I didn't make trouble for you coming here? I'm sure I can get a hotel somewhere, it's no trouble."

"*Nein.* You will not go anywhere else. You are family, and you will stay here tonight, as we agreed." She reached for Kathy's bag. "*Kumm.* I have your room ready. Are you sure you will be able to adjust to not having all the fine things you have grown accustomed to in your new, fancy life?" She gave Kathy a gentle smile.

"You might not believe this, but simple sounds heavenly at the moment." She took the bag out of

Sarah's hand and placed it on the ground. "I could use a hug, my friend. I've missed you." She gathered Sarah into the first real hug she'd had in a long time. Of course, Hazel had given her a brief one. But Sarah was different. Sarah had never judged Kathy for leaving their community. She'd always thought that somehow Sarah understood.

"*Ya.* Simple can be heavenly." Sarah straightened her *Kapp* and giggled. "When you aren't doing laundry or working in the garden or cooking or cleaning." She took the suitcase again and waved toward the house. "Let's get you settled, then you can tell me about the fancy life you've been living and all your travels and the interesting places you've seen. Then I can tell you all about my plain life and the work I do here. Maybe you will decide you'd like to trade for a few days?" She giggled again. "I have iced tea waiting and oatmeal chocolate chips cookies warm out of the oven."

Kathy's mouth began to water. "With coconut to keep them soft?"

"*Ya.*" Sarah's eyes sparkled. "With walnuts and a lot of chocolate chips, since I remembered you always liked them that way."

"Oh. That reminds me. Just a sec." Kathy dashed for the car and reached in for the pie box. "One of Hazel's boysenberry pies. Actually, two of them." She smirked. "Here I thought I'd have to eat it all alone. Now I don't have to feel so guilty." She moved up beside Sarah and slipped her hand through her cousin's arm as they walked toward the house together.

Later that night, as Sarah and Kathy curled up under a handmade quilt on the couch next to a crackling fire,

Kathy felt a sense of contentment she hadn't experienced in years. She pushed that to the back of her mind, not wanting to examine the why at the moment. Experiencing it was enough for now. "Sarah?"

"Hmm?" Sarah turned dreamy eyes her way, a soft smile lighting her sweet face.

"What was the bishop upset about when I came today? Besides my arrival, of course. You don't have to answer if you'd rather not, but I want you to know I care."

"*Denke*, I know you do. It would be nice to have someone to talk to about what's been happening. My friend Annie is out of town right now, and I've missed my discussions with her. You came at a time when I could use a little counsel."

Kathy sat up straight. "I don't know how much counsel I can give, but I'm happy to listen, if that helps."

"*Ya*, it does." Sarah smiled again. "Our bishop thinks I should marry and give up the inn. He has a son, Jeremiah, who wishes to court me. I have gotten past the death of my husband, and while it still saddens me, I am ready to move on with my life. I am not sure if I want to marry again. I have been happy running my inn and have done well making a life for myself."

Kathy leaned forward and tightened her grip on the coffee cup. "Jeremiah, huh? Do you care for him? What's he like?"

"He is a kind and gentle man. He told me I wouldn't have to stop running my inn if we married. I was grateful, but I'm not sure and certain yet."

"You feel like the bishop is rushing you?"

"Yes, and no. I understand that time is passing, and Jeremiah and I are not getting younger. I have no *bopplies* yet, but I do not want a marriage of convenience, even if he is a kind man. I loved my first husband. Is it too much to hope for another marriage like that one?"

Kathy reached out and took Sarah's hand. "I don't think it's too much to ask for at all. I'd like a marriage like that someday, myself."

"Ah, yes." Sarah beamed at her. "Let us pray that happens for both of us, *ya*?"

Kathy smiled back. "*Ya.*"

The image of Isaac as he'd looked at her with such sad eyes right before he'd reached for his daughter's hand trickled into her memory. Suddenly, the light and happiness she'd felt moments ago dimmed. Maybe she'd made the wrong choice in coming back. Maybe she should call Evelyn and Jacques and accept that show after all. She'd made Isaac unhappy and stirred up trouble for Sarah with the bishop. Nothing had changed in all the years since she'd left—she was still hurting the people she cared about, and that needed to stop.

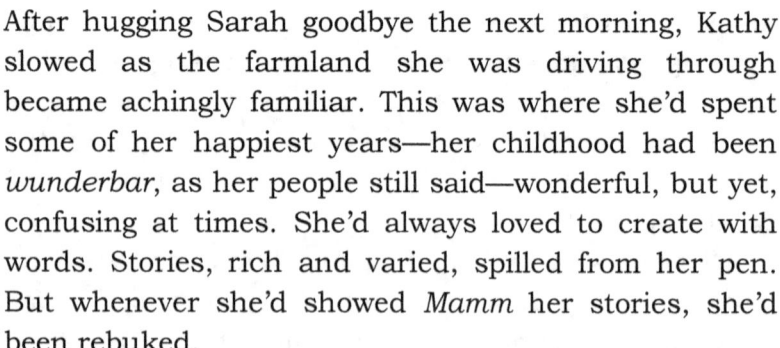

After hugging Sarah goodbye the next morning, Kathy slowed as the farmland she was driving through became achingly familiar. This was where she'd spent some of her happiest years—her childhood had been *wunderbar*, as her people still said—wonderful, but yet, confusing at times. She'd always loved to create with words. Stories, rich and varied, spilled from her pen. But whenever she'd showed *Mamm* her stories, she'd been rebuked.

The Amish did not make up stories. Their feet were firmly rooted in the present world, and she needed to stay planted there, not off in a fantasy land. Maybe that's why she never went back to her first love of stories and started writing travel journals for women on a budget. Doing so didn't quite feel like she was betraying her people and their beliefs. Should she have stayed in this life and not followed her dreams?

She pulled into a graveled driveway and continued down the long lane, the farmhouse in sight in the distance. She'd never understood why her grandfather had put the house so far away from the main road. It made for ever so much more work when it snowed, trying to keep the lane plowed, but he'd insisted he didn't want the noise from cars passing to distract him from his work or time with his family.

Kathy had to admit, the peace residing in this area couldn't be beat. She'd traveled the world and never found any place where her heart had been more content. At least, not until her teen years when she'd begun to question so much, and discontent had crept in.

She braked only a few yards from the house, next to a black buggy, and swung her legs out of the car, pausing for a moment to look around. The medium-sized, single-story house she'd grown up in lay in front of her, as neat and tidy as she remembered it being as a child. The large barn was off to the side and toward the back of the house, and on the other side, the cabin where her grandparents had lived until their death. She reached back inside and grabbed her backpack, slinging it over her shoulder.

Finally, she plucked the second boxed pie Hazel had given her off the seat and walked the hard-packed path to the front door. She rapped, her heart feeling as though it would pound its way through her chest wall. She wiped her damp palms on her jeans, suddenly wondering what her sister and her family would think, seeing her wearing *Englisch* clothes. She shrugged. It wasn't like they didn't know where she lived and what she did. She wasn't going to wear a skirt and pretend to be someone she wasn't to make her sister happy. Besides, she doubted that wearing a skirt would do much to appease her sister's ire.

She waited another minute and rapped again, listening for footsteps on the other side. The door didn't swing open. Where could everyone be? If she remembered correctly, her sister Miriam and her husband Amos had three children, two boys and a girl. It saddened her that she'd never met them, but that was on her, not on Miriam. Kathy let out a long sigh. Why had she waited so long to come home? Sure, she'd been busy writing and traveling to research and promote her books, but that was no excuse. Family mattered, and she needed to make this up to Miriam, now that their father was gone.

Kathy walked to the edge of the porch and shielded her eyes with her hand against the glare of the bright Kentucky sun. The rolling farmland stretched, covering over a hundred acres planted in corn and other crops. A large red barn stood to one side, with two milk cows grazing on the lush grass in the nearby pasture. In the distance, a car blasted by, and not far behind came a black buggy, pulled by a chestnut moving at a fast clip. Kathy shook her head at the sight of the two worlds nearly colliding. When would *Englischers* learn to slow down on roads within the Amish community? Everyone who lived around here knew to drive carefully. Good thing the horse didn't appear to be a spooky creature, or that could have been bad.

She stepped off the porch and strode around the

side of the house. Maybe Miriam and the children were in the *Daadi Haus* where her grandparents had lived after her father and mother married and moved into the main house to raise their *bopplies* ... er ... babies. Kathy grinned, amazed that her mind was reverting to her childhood language so easily. She'd better watch herself, though, or she'd say something that might reveal her background to the public and bring the press down on her community. She couldn't allow that to happen.

A rose bush was in full bloom next to the path, and Kathy leaned close to sniff the wonderful fragrance. Why didn't they have things like this growing wild in cities? She smirked, trying to envision lilac bushes on every corner in L.A. Not likely. She rounded another slight bend and came within site of the *Daadi Haus*. A light shone in the window. Miriam must be there cleaning. Maybe she was preparing the house for her? Kathy doubted it, but she'd try to keep a positive outlook until she learned differently.

She raised her hand and tapped lightly against the wooden door with her knuckles, holding her breath, wondering who would open it. After a full thirty seconds, she let her breath out in a whoosh. Apparently, someone had left a light burning inside but had stepped out and left it lit. She tried the knob, which she'd never known to be locked, and it turned easily under her hand. She pushed the door open and slipped inside, leaving it standing open to let in a little sunshine.

Kathy stood in the opening, letting her gaze rest on the homey, familiar surroundings. The two-room cabin was sparsely but pleasantly furnished. Her eyes swept the large room that served as a living room, kitchen, and dining area, with a fireplace set into the far wall. A few crumbs were on the table, as though someone didn't have the heart to clean up the remains of *Daed's* last meal in this house. The house was tidy, with a pair of trousers neatly folded on the back of the couch, and a doll-sized quilt draped over the back of a rocking chair.

Drawing close, Kathy set the pie down on a nearby table, then picked up the quilt and stroked an unfinished edge as moisture gathered in her eyes. She carefully folded the diminutive quilt, then swung her backpack off her shoulder and tucked the tiny quilt inside.

"Can I help you with something?"

Kathy swung around, clutching her backpack to her chest.

Kathy's sister stood in the open doorway to the bedroom, her hands planted firmly on her hips. "What are you doing here? I didn't hear anyone knock."

Miriam's face had aged since Kathy had last seen her, but she was still an attractive woman in her mid-twenties, only two years Kathy's senior. However, no smile lit her face, and the frown that tugged at her lips didn't bode well for a happy reunion.

"Miriam, it's me. Kathy." She took a step toward her sister and held out her arms.

Miriam pointedly folded her arms across her chest. "I know who you are, Katrina. What I don't know is, why are you here? The meeting with our Amish arbitrator is not until tomorrow. It is no longer at his home, but here at our farm. Please be here at nine o'clock sharp. We will have work to do when we finish, and we don't care to be late."

Kathy stopped moving and lowered her arms. Why

was she surprised? It wasn't like she'd expected a warm welcome from her older sister. She bit her lip and studied Miriam. Fine lines surrounded her mouth, which seemed to be locked in a permanent scowl. When had Miriam become so angry? "I know, but I wanted to see you and your family before the meeting. I'm staying with our cousin Sarah Stoltzfus tonight, but her inn is full from tomorrow on. I hoped I might stay with you."

Miriam's eyes narrowed. "You did not make it home for our father's funeral, so there was no need for you to come now. Our house is full."

Kathy held up her phone. "I was in a place where I didn't have my phone for three days, so I didn't get your call until Monday. I'm sorry."

Miriam walked past her without a word. She stepped through the door and held onto the knob. "Then Amos and I will see you tomorrow. Please, take your *Englisch* car and your fancy clothes and go now. There is no place for you here anymore."

A fierce pain waged with a smidgen of anger in Kathy's heart. Sure, she didn't make it to the funeral, and she was sorry for that, but did that give Miriam the right to practically throw her off their father's land? She opened her mouth to protest, then thought better of it. She knew from past experience that when her sister got that steely gleam in her eyes, there was nothing more she could say or do to change her mind until she calmed down. If she calmed down.

She walked through the door and turned back, only to see Miriam pull it shut hard enough that it almost slammed. So much for making peace with her sister.

Kathy pressed her phone's on button and held it for a second, then lifted the phone to her mouth and activated the voice search. "Find the closest hotel."

"The closest hotel is twenty-six miles from your present location."

"Great." Kathy kicked at a rock on the path and trudged toward her car. "Siri, find the closest inn or bed and breakfast."

"Two locations found." The search gave her the name and address of Sarah's inn and another that was only a few miles away. She'd go back to Sarah's to say goodbye and see if Sarah could direct her to this other inn. As soon as she finished with the reading of the will with the arbitrator tomorrow, she'd be on the road to the airport and a flight back to L.A. She wasn't wanted here, and she could barely remember why she'd bothered to come.

Chapter Six

KATHY WALKED UP THE STEPS TO Sarah's inn and hesitated, wondering if she should knock. A horse hitched to an Amish buggy was tied to the rail in front of the house, and while it didn't appear to be the same one the bishop drove, she couldn't be certain. Even though guests always walked in and out without knocking, she decided to err on the side of caution and gave a brisk rap.

"*Kumm* in." Sarah's soft voice barely penetrated the heavy oak door.

Kathy turned the knob and pushed open the door, peeking around the edge into the foyer. A tall Amish man who didn't yet sport a beard stood with his hat in his hands, staring at Sarah with a warm, caring gaze. If she didn't know better, she'd say with love in his eyes. "I'm sorry for intruding, Sarah. I won't stay long."

Sarah hurried over from where she'd been standing a few feet from the man and slipped her hand through the crook of Kathy's arm. "*Nein.* There is no rush." She waved at the man. "Jeremiah was just telling me *gutt-bye*. He invited me for a drive, but I have a guest coming in soon, so I cannot leave this afternoon." She smiled and nodded at Jeremiah. "This is my cousin Katrina Yoder, here for a visit with her sister. I don't know if you have met Katrina?"

Jeremiah tipped his head but didn't offer his hand, yet his eyes remained warm and his smile genuine. "Miss Yoder. It is nice to meet you. I believe I remember you from when you were a girl in pigtails, but I was a few years older, so I doubt you would remember me."

She gazed at him then shook her head. "I'm sorry, I

don't believe I do. Please don't rush off on my account. I wanted to let Sarah know where I'd be staying tonight, if the other inn has room. If not, I'll be driving to a hotel. When I finish at Miriam's home, I'll catch a flight home."

"*Ach, nein*, Katrina. If the other inn is full, you must come here. I can make a place for you, for sure. I will not have you driving so far away and trying to come back for an early morning meeting." She shook her head, setting the loose ties from her *Kapp* dancing. "What is the address and name of the other inn? I am thinking it must be Isaac Mast's, as his is the only other one that I know of in this area."

Kathy gave a soft gasp. "Isaac Mast? He's running an inn? I had no idea."

Sarah gave a brisk nod. "*Ya*. After his wife died, he moved out of the big house and into a small cabin on his property. He works all day in his workshop making furniture, and he rents out the rooms in the house to anyone who needs a place to stay." She swept a hand around the foyer. "It is not like this house. It's smaller, and only has three bedrooms. He often rents the entire house to a family for a week or two, but he doesn't advertise or try to keep it full. I am not sure he cares if it is rented or not." She shook her head and tsk'd. "Poor man. Sometimes I think he has been lost in a fog since his Ruth died. It is *gutt* that he has Sadie to make him keep living, or he might drift away."

Kathy shivered and rubbed her hands on her arms. Should she even go over and bother Isaac? Would he welcome her or wish she'd never come? "Do you know if it's rented now? Maybe I should just head to a hotel and come back tomorrow for the appointment. It's not that long of a drive."

"The roads are narrow and twisting, and I can tell

you are still tired. I spoke to Isaac a couple of days ago, and he mentioned business had been slow. From what he said, I do not believe he has rented it recently, so you should be fine." She patted Kathy's arm. "It would do him and Sadie both good to have a friendly face around the place, even for one day. But you should consider staying a few nights, Katrina. Rest a bit before you rush back to the busy life in the big city, *ya*? Besides, I would love to have another chat before you leave, and maybe a cup of tea?" She shot a quick peek out the corner of her eye toward Jeremiah, who was silently listening to the conversation.

She turned to the man as though she'd made a sudden decision, a warm smile creasing her face. "Jeremiah, would it be possible to visit sometime in the next few days? I think I would like that, if you have time."

A huge grin broke out and he nodded. "*Ya.* I would like that too, Sarah. I'll call on you after dinner around seven one evening soon, if that works for you?"

"That works fine. *Denke.*" She stepped to the door and opened it, giving him another sweet smile as he headed toward his buggy.

Kathy waited until the door closed behind him, then pivoted to face Sarah. "Did you decide to allow him to court you? What's changed? He seems like a very nice man."

Sarah shook her head. "Not yet. But I decided I am not being fair if I do not at least give him a chance. How can I know if I want to be courted if I don't spend a little time with him?" She tipped her head to one side. "As I remember, Isaac used to court you before you left."

Warmth flooded Kathy's cheeks and she bit her lip. "Court might be too strong of a word. We were friends since we were children. We loved to go fishing together, and we talked for hours at a time." Sweet memories flooded her, and she smiled. "He was my best friend, besides you and Hazel, but we didn't get to the serious courting stage. At least, I didn't think so."

Sarah raised her brows. "But he did?"

"Maybe. It might not be the best idea to go over, huh?"

"I would think it is fine, Katrina. He ended up marrying Ruth, and they had a child. I doubt he is still harboring feelings for you after all these years. But since you were close friends, it may do his heart *gutt* to spend time with an old friend again. I think you should go. Maybe this is the reason *Gott* brought you back to our town, *ya*?"

Kathy couldn't imagine her friendship years ago with Isaac had anything to do with her return. That was only due to her father's death, and from the way Miriam had acted, she might as well have stayed in L.A.

Thirty minutes later, Kathy had said goodbye to Sarah after agreeing to meet her for tea and cookies later tomorrow and jotting down the directions to Isaac's land. She still wasn't convinced this was a good idea, but she wasn't in the mood to try to find the hotel. If it didn't work out at Isaac's for more than one night, or the appointment tomorrow cleared up all her business in town, she could find a nice hotel on the way to the airport tomorrow evening, camp out there, and catch a flight the next day. For now, though, she'd try to enjoy seeing Isaac and Sadie again, and not worry about what might come tomorrow.

She stepped out of her car and shut the door, wondering if she should go to the main house, the cabin a short distance away that might be a *Daadi Haus* meant for one of the parents, or if Isaac might be in his workshop. Why hadn't she thought to call ahead? Even if he didn't have a cell phone, most Amish were allowed a business phone in their home or in an outbuilding.

"Isaac?" She stood, slowly turning in a circle, wondering where to begin. What if he wasn't even home? He could be delivering a piece of furniture to a store that carried his work for sale. She headed to what appeared to be a barn of sorts that must contain his work area.

A large door slid open on a well-oiled track, as it didn't so much as squeak in protest. Isaac stepped out, wiping his hands on a rag. His eyes widened when he saw her. "Katrina? What are you doing here?" He must have realized it sounded rude, as he turned, tossed the rag back inside, then strode toward her, his hands outstretched.

She rushed to meet him, her heart soaring at the calm but happy expression he wore. "Isaac." She took his outstretched hands and squeezed them, then let go, remembering her attempt at a hug the last time she'd seen him and the way he'd kept his distance. This time she wouldn't overstep her bounds. "Sarah told me you sometimes rent out a room in your home to people traveling through who are in need." She smiled and waved toward the car. "I'm traveling, and I'm in need. Would you happen to have a small room you could let me rent for the night? I promise I won't be any trouble."

He lifted his chin and chuckled. "You? No trouble? That is not what I remember of you, Katrina. I seem to recall many times you got me in trouble, *ya*?" He ran his hand over his neatly trimmed beard.

She giggled at one such memory of her pushing him

into a pond when he didn't know she'd snuck up behind him. "I remember the time you had to go home soaking wet and try to explain to your *daed* why your brand-new trousers were wet and muddy."

He shook his finger at her. "I did not have dessert for an entire week after that happened. However, I seem to remember I got even with you for that one." He pressed his lips together but didn't quite keep a smirk from showing. "Do you recall the frog in your lunch pail a few days later?"

She shuddered. "I've never liked frogs since then, thanks to you." She looked around. "Is Sadie home?"

"*Ya.* She is getting ready for bed. Let me show you to your room before she spots you, or you will never have a moment of peace. My daughter likes to talk just like her mother did." The grin he'd been wearing faded, and he turned away.

Kathy stepped forward and touched his arm. "I'm so sorry about your wife, Isaac. Truly. I can't imagine how hard that must have been."

"*Ya. Denke.* But we are doing fine." He strode to her car. "Do you have luggage you would like me to bring?"

"I have a backpack and one suitcase. I'll pop the trunk so you can grab the case, and I'll get my backpack out of the backseat." She reached inside, popped the trunk, then grabbed her pack and slipped one strap over her shoulder. "You know, I can stay in the cabin. There's no reason for you and Sadie not to stay in your own home. I don't need a big house or anything ... fancy." She smiled over her shoulder at him, but his face remained solemn.

"*Nein.* We like our cabin. The house is only for visitors now. Nothing more. I hope you will be comfortable." He pushed open the front door and set her suitcase inside. "I will not *kumm* in with you.

Please, make yourself at home."

"You need to show me which bedroom is mine. Sarah said you have three. Won't you come in and let me put on a pot of coffee or tea?"

"*Denke*, but no. I must return to my work then check on Sadie. You may take your pick of bedrooms. You are my only guest right now. Normally, I only allow one guest at a time, and they have the use of the full house. And unlike Hazel, I do take checks or cash." He gave her a soft, somewhat impish smile. "For you, my rates will be very fair. We can settle up tomorrow. I keep the refrigerator stocked with basic supplies since I have renters very often. Eggs, milk, bread, butter, jam, and there are cans of soup along with other items in the cupboards. I'm not a true bed and breakfast like Sarah runs. People who stay here are expected to take care of themselves, although I will supply clean linens when you need them. Now, have a good evening and sleep well, Katrina."

He didn't wait for her to reply but turned and walked down the steps and across the short distance to his shop, slipping into the door and pulling it shut behind him.

Kathy stood there, gazing after him, wondering if she should stay in the house or go after Isaac. His sadness was palpable, although only a few minutes before he'd been laughing and reminding her of their childhood pranks. Something told her he needed to be alone right now, and she would respect that.

Isaac pushed into his cabin, glad that Sadie was already in bed. The last person he'd expected to have show up on his doorstep was Katrina Yoder. He had assumed she'd be staying with Miriam's family or her cousin Sarah, since she had a bed and breakfast in her home.

Why did it bother him so much that she'd appeared and was staying in his home? The home he'd shared with his wife before her death? Ruth had been a sweet, solid woman whom he'd come to care for, but when he'd designed that house in his head, she wasn't the woman he'd thought he'd be sharing it with. *Nein.* That woman was inside the four walls right now.

Why had he rejected her offer to have a cup of coffee with her? He could have checked on Sadie and been safe spending a few minutes with his old friend. But his heart had rebelled at the thought of being inside with her. Guilt hit him hard at the memory of dreaming of her in that house, even when he'd started building it for him and Ruth. That wasn't right.

Ya, it was an arranged marriage between their families, but he'd agreed without complaint or argument. Ruth was a good woman, and he knew she would make a fine wife and mother. Somehow, he had put the thought of Katrina behind him, until the house building had begun.

In the years since, he'd buried the memories of Katrina deep within himself, and even when Ruth died, he hadn't allowed them to be resurrected. Now here she was, sleeping in the house he'd built with her in mind, with him living one hundred feet away in a cabin with his daughter. His entire life had been upended, and he didn't have any idea at all on how to put it to rights.

She swung her backpack onto a nearby chair and headed toward the kitchen when her cell phone buzzed.

Pulling it out of her back pocket, she glanced at the screen. A text from Jacques. *How's everything going?* With all that had been happening, she'd completely forgotten to call him or Evelyn. What must they be thinking by now? She slid her finger across the screen to reply, but her phone showed a red bar and went dead. "Blast it."

Kathy grabbed her backpack and rummaged through it until she found her charger. "Now to find a plug-in." She searched the base of the nearby wall. Nothing. She moved to the next room and checked all four walls. Still nothing.

Finally, she slapped her forehead. What was she thinking? This was an Amish house, built for an Amish family. There would be no outlets. She'd have to wait and charge it in her car while on the way to meet with the arbitrator at Miriam's farm. Maybe she could let her car run for a bit in the morning before she left to allow the phone to get more of a charge before she got to the appointment. Jacques could wait a few more hours, and she'd be sure to call him first thing tomorrow. Right now, she wanted to explore this house and make a cup of tea.

A few minutes later, cup in hand, she headed to the living room then on to the bedrooms. She stepped into one with a queen-sized bed and an adjoining small bathroom. A rocker sat in one corner, and a handmade quilt with a sunburst pattern covered the bed. There were no pictures on the wall, but crocheted doilies graced the top of the dresser and nightstand, and decorative kerosene lanterns were on each side of the bed, complete with a small matchbook. This looked perfect, and the view of the quaint cabin in the distance brought a rush of longing. If only Isaac would come over to visit.

She shook herself. What was she doing thinking of Isaac when Jacques had declared his intention to become her future? Well, tonight neither one was here, so she'd take this evening to put her feet up and relax and not worry about who was vying for her attention or the constant demands on her time. She didn't even want to think about the TV show Evelyn and Jacques were pushing her to accept. A good book and this cup of tea were far more enticing at the moment.

Wandering back to the living room where she'd spotted a bookcase on the way through, she stopped to peruse the selection. Her mouth nearly dropped open. Shakespeare. Keats. Longfellow. Her fingers ran along the spines of the books until she stopped at Dickenson. Emily. Kathy smiled and slid the book out reverently, then hugged it to her chest.

She found a quilt on the back of the couch and covered her lap, then snuggled up in the corner of the couch with her book. An hour later, she yawned but focused on the book, determined to finish this passage. It had been too long since she'd indulged herself like this.

> The cricket sang,
> And set the sun,
> And workmen finished, one by one,
> Their seam the day upon.
>
> The low grass loaded with the dew,
> The twilight stood as strangers do
> With hat in hand, polite and new,
> To stay as if, or go.
>
> A vastness, as a neighbor, came.
> A wisdom without face or name,

A peace, as hemispheres at home,
And so the night became.

She peered out the window once more, toward the cabin not far away, wondering if Isaac was reading to his little girl, or sitting in the waning light, pondering his loss and the years ahead.

Setting the book aside, she pushed to her feet. Time to quit thinking. Time to sleep and hope she didn't dream. Time to forget the past and try to discover her future.

Chapter Seven

SOMEHOW, THE AMAZING PEACE OF THE house lulled Kathy to sleep, and she didn't wake up in time to charge her phone before she hit the road. She rushed around making coffee and toast, glancing across the way at the cabin. Would Isaac come check on her or go straight to work in the barn? Not that it was any of her business. At least she'd had time to slip into a nice pair of slacks and a light-blue filmy blouse with a lace scallop-edged tank underneath. Maybe Miriam would feel more kindly toward her today if she wasn't wearing jeans for a business meeting—although anything short of Amish clothing would probably still get a frown.

She glanced at her watch, thankful she still wore one and didn't totally depend on her phone. *Yikes!* She had twenty minutes to get to the farm. She raced to the bathroom and applied a touch of lip gloss and mascara, knowing Miriam would comment, or at the very least, frown, if she wore anything more. Although Miriam probably wore a perpetual frown nowadays where Kathy was concerned.

She rushed to her car, still wishing she could at least tell Isaac goodbye. Maybe she wouldn't be in such a hurry to head back to L.A. when she finished the meeting this morning. After all, she hadn't packed her bag or made her bed. She started the car and drove down the lane. She'd need to pick up her room when she returned, if only out of courtesy to her host.

Kathy pulled into the lane leading to her *daed's* house at ten o'clock on the dot and parked next to a very nice buggy that must belong to the arbitrator.

Hopefully, since she wasn't really late, Miriam wouldn't scold. Walking at a brisk pace, she leapt the last few feet and landed on the low porch. Should she walk right in or knock first? Better be safe and not cause more stress. She rapped lightly on the door and waited.

Seconds passed while Kathy's dread rose, and her heart sank. Finally, she heard light steps approaching the door and it swung open. Miriam stood there, her posture stiff and unyielding, and her expression no different from the one she'd worn the day before. "Katrina. I see you decided to *kumm*. I thought you might leave town."

"Good morning to you, Miriam. Of course I came. I told you I'd be here."

Miriam grudgingly stepped aside, then waited for Kathy to enter and shut the door with a slight thud. "Please. Sit." She waved toward the small dining area situated between the kitchen and living area.

Kathy's eyes flooded with tears at the familiar surroundings. Regret tore at her soul—she should have come home and spent time with *Daed*. They'd lost *Mamm* years ago, but somehow, she'd always thought *Daed* would live forever. Foolish. Stupid, even. No one lived forever. But he'd been a fixture in her life for what felt like forever, and it didn't seem possible he could be gone. Miriam preceded her to the table, giving Kathy a chance to wipe the moisture from her eyes.

An older, rather portly gentleman with a bushy beard pushed to his feet as Miriam approached the table. He waited for her to be seated, then nodded at Kathy. "Miss Yoder? I am Timothy Russo." He extended his hand.

Kathy took it and endured the vigorous handshake, peeking out the corner of her eye at Miriam, who sat next to her husband, Amos. The man had always possessed somewhat of a poker face, even if the description wasn't appropriate for someone of the Amish faith. She had never quite been able to read him, and of course, Miriam and he had married after Kathy had left her parents' home. She'd only returned twice. Once, when her mother had died, and later, on a trip through Kentucky on a book tour. Neither time had given her a chance to get to know Miriam's husband. Right now, he wore a stern, somber expression that almost perfectly matched her sister's.

Mr. Russo gestured to a chair next to his and across from Amos and Miriam. He turned to Kathy as she drew her seat closer to the table. "It is nice to meet you." He nodded at Amos. "You know Miriam's husband of course? Amos."

Kathy nodded. "We met a few years ago, but only briefly. It's good to see you, Amos." She stood and reached across the table, but he only grunted and folded his arms across his chest.

Mr. Russo raised his brows. "Let us get started, shall we?" He picked up a stack of papers and shuffled through them for a moment, then reached into his coat breast pocket and pulled out a pair of glasses. "As you all no doubt are aware, Mr. Yoder"—he looked up at Miriam, then turned to Kathy—"was not a wealthy man. However, he did own this farm with no debt. He made his wishes known to me, and he was very clear. He chose to leave the farm to ..." He took off his glasses and breathed on them, then pulled a handkerchief from his pocket and polished them.

Miriam reached for Amos's hand, gripping it hard as it lay on top of the table. "Please, Mr. Russo. Would you continue?"

"Yes, yes. So sorry." He slid the glasses back onto his nose and peered at the document as though trying to find his place. "It states, 'I, Caleb Yoder, being of sound mind, do hereby bequeath all my land, home, and belongings, to both of my daughters, Miriam and Katrina, to be divided equally between them.'"

"Both?" Miriam gasped and placed a hand over her mouth.

Kathy gaped at her sister, then turned to Mr. Russo. "Both?"

Amos was silent, but his eyes bored accusatory holes into Kathy.

"That cannot be so. For sure and for certain, it cannot be so." Miriam's voice rose in pitch with each word.

Mr. Russo separated the papers and pushed one over to Miriam and one next to Kathy. "You may read it for yourselves. It is quite clear." He pointed to the correct line on each document. "Take a moment and read this section."

Miriam finally met Kathy's eyes. "But she has not been here to stay or help for ten years. She left home—she practically ran away—and she has never cared enough about this farm or our father to *kumm* back. I poured my life and strength into this farm, staying to help my father, while she ran off to become an *Englischer*."

Amos patted her hand that was clenched into a fist on the tabletop. "Miriam. You must calm yourself."

She turned and glared.

He pressed his lips together, then gave a short nod toward Mr. Russo. "It is her business, not mine. I will stay silent."

Kathy's stomach churned, and she was thankful

she hadn't taken time to do more than nibble a piece of toast. She didn't think she could have kept more down. She'd seen her sister angry before, but this went beyond anger. Betrayal, grief, and torment seemed to race each other across her features. Kathy took a few slow breaths to calm her racing heart. "You're right, Miriam. It should be yours. I have no plans to move back, and this is still your home. You belong here. I don't. I'll give it to you."

Miriam's mouth snapped closed and she leaned back in her chair, the red that had stained her cheeks draining away. "You will ... what? Give it to me? Why would you do that?"

"Because you're my sister. I love you, Miriam. The land should be yours. I'll give you my half."

"You will? Truly?"

"Truly." Kathy turned to Mr. Russo. "I can do that, can't I?" At her question, she saw the hope fade from Miriam's eyes.

Mr. Russo shuffled the papers again, looking them over with quiet deliberation. "You can, but not for thirty days. I don't know if your father anticipated you offering this or not. But he stipulated you must stay in the area for that amount of time. You must either live here for that thirty days, stay with a relative, or live with another Amish family. You may not stay in a hotel or with other *Englischers*. If you try to sell the farm or leave the area before the thirty days is up, the entire farm is to be sold and the proceeds split between you."

A small cry escaped Miriam's lips. Her face twisted and she whispered, "I cannot lose this farm. It is where my *bopplies* were born. Where I was married. Where I grew up and our parents are buried. It would kill me to lose this farm."

Mr. Russo held up his hand. "There is one other thing you need to be aware of, Miriam and Amos. Even if Katrina decides to stay the thirty days and give you her half, there will be high property taxes that come with it. It is a valuable piece of land, and the taxes are due in three months. If you split the property, only half of the tax will be your responsibility."

Kathy waved her hand. "I can pay all the property tax for the year, so that's not an issue."

Miriam straightened and raised her chin. "No. If you choose to stay for the thirty days so we don't lose our home, I will be"—she closed her eyes for a moment—"grateful. But *we* will pay the taxes."

"I make a very good income, Miriam. It's not a problem for me to take care of them."

Amos met her eyes and gave a hard shake of his head. "*Nein.* We will pay. No more will be said."

Kathy raised her hands. "Fine. Got it."

Miriam stared at Kathy. "You said you were returning to your *Englisch* life after we met with Mr. Russo today." She gripped her hands together on the table so tightly Kathy could see the knuckles turn white. "But now ... I do not even want to ask this ... will you reconsider? If you leave, we will lose our home."

Kathy turned to Mr. Russo. "Do I have any time to think about this? I have obligations at home. A trip I was supposed to take for my next book. The flight has already been purchased. I need to call my agent." She took in Miriam's white face then saw Amos drop his head, his beard touching his chest. "Could I have a day or two, please? I know this should be an easy decision, but I need a little time."

Mr. Russo nodded. "I can give you three days to talk to your agent and come back with a decision. Will that be sufficient time? Where are you staying now, Miss Yoder?" He glanced out the window at her car. "I take it you are not staying here with your family?"

She shook her head. "I was at our cousin Sarah's inn the first night, but it's full for a few days, so I stayed at Isaac Mast's inn last night."

"Ah. Yes. I see. Will three days be enough time to make a decision? I can get the figures for the taxes for Amos and Miriam and have the papers ready to sign should you decide to accept your *daed's* wishes. If not, there is another set of papers you will both have to sign to put the place on the market."

"I guess I could stay at Isaac's inn for another two or three nights. But you said if I stay, I'd need to move in with a relative or stay with an Amish family?"

"Yes. I don't suppose you could move in here?" He looked from Miriam's stormy face to Kathy's and shook his head. "If not, then maybe back to your cousin Sarah's inn?"

Miriam folded her arms. "If she does not have room, we will see what we can do. But with the three children and the *bopplie* on the way ..." She touched her stomach and her voice trailed off.

Kathy's eyes widened. "You didn't tell me. I'm so happy for you, Miriam!"

Miriam waved away her comment. "It does not matter now. Saving the farm is what matters. If you must stay here, so be it. But you will be without all your fancy gadgets, and you may not influence the children in any way. I must have that understood."

"Thank you, Miriam. But I think I'll check with Sarah and see if she'll have room first." She pushed to her feet. "I find I'm suddenly a bit tired, and I need time to think." She turned to the arbitrator. "Mr. Russo, is there a way I can call you with my decision?"

He reached into his pocket and pulled out a paper and pen, jotted a number down, then handed it to her. "My farm is not far away, but we do have a phone in an outbuilding."

She took it, nodded at Miriam, and turned to walk out the door.

Chapter Eight

KATHY SHOOK AS SHE STARTED her car and drove down the long lane to the highway. Overwhelmed didn't begin to encompass what she felt right now. Besides the fact that *Daed* had left her half of the farm, she was shocked at the level of dislike Miriam had shown. She understood that leaving the farm instead of joining the church must have upset Miriam, but why would she take it so personally? Why, ten years later, did it still poison her attitude toward her only sibling?

She steered around a corner, slowed for a buggy traveling at a steady clip ahead of her, then made a wide arc around it as soon as it was safe to do so. "Breathe, Kathy. Just breathe." She followed her own advice, allowing the peace of her surroundings to seep into her soul. How long had it been since she'd prayed and asked the Lord for peace? She'd found a very conservative church to attend after she'd left home, and she'd learned even more about the Lord than she had as a child. She'd come to a realization that He was truly alive and cared about her.

Why had she allowed that knowledge—and the relationship she'd developed with Him—to slip these past three or four years? It had been months since she'd picked up her Bible and read it or spent time in true communion with God. Maybe that was why He'd brought her back home—to make her aware of what she'd ignored for too long. To let her see her own personal need. "Help me, Lord?" He understood that she had many areas where she needed help. Wisdom. A renewal of her faith. Peace. And so much more.

She turned into the lane that led to Sarah's inn—

having another woman to talk to right now was extremely attractive. Hopefully, she was home and free for that cup of tea they'd talked about the day before. She parked in the empty parking area reserved for guests.

She strode up the path and tapped on the door, then slipped inside. "Sarah? Are you home?"

"*Ya. Gutt* to see you, Katrina." Sarah stepped out of the kitchen into the hall leading to the foyer, wiping her hands on a dishtowel. "Is it already time for tea? Did everything go well with your family?"

Kathy blew out a hard breath, making her cheeks puff out, as some of the tension from the morning tried to sneak back in. "I'm a lot earlier for tea than I'd planned. We talked about getting together this afternoon. If this is a bad time?" She clenched her hands to keep from wringing them, but her distress must have come through in her voice or her expression.

Sarah tossed the towel into the kitchen and rushed forward. She pulled Kathy into a long hug and held her in a firm grip until Kathy began to relax, then Sarah stepped back, keeping her hands on Kathy's shoulders. "What happened, Katrina? Something hurt you, *ya*? I can tell you are upset. Was Miriam unkind?"

Kathy gave a hollow laugh that sounded mocking even to her own ears. "Unkind? I suppose you could call it that, but apparently, I don't merit courteous treatment. Both times I've seen her now, she's been very cold and ... unkind. Yes." She reached out and gave Sarah another quick hug then stepped away. "Thank you. I needed that hug. Now I could use a cup of tea."

"I agree. My guests are out for the day, so we won't be interrupted. I've made fresh strawberry scones. Are you hungry?"

Kathy's stomach rumbled and she grinned. "I didn't realize it, but I guess I am. I only had a piece of toast for breakfast, so a strawberry scone sounds lovely." She followed Sarah down the short hall to the kitchen. "Can I help?"

"*Nein.* The tea kettle is always hot, and the scones only need to be put onto a plate and we're ready to go. Sit." Sarah waved at the table for four tucked into a corner of the kitchen.

"Thank you." Kathy sank down with a soft sigh. "I'm so glad you're home and have time to talk. I guess I could use a friend right now."

Sarah placed a steaming cup of fragrant tea and a warm-from-the-oven scone in front of her, making Kathy's mouth water, then placed tea and a scone across the table and slipped into her chair. "Now. Eat first, then tell me all about it. Or, tell me as much as you'd like to. I do not want to pry."

"You aren't prying at all. I'd love to have another woman to talk to, and there's no one I can think of that I trust more than you." She lifted the teacup and took a sip, then sampled the scone and closed her eyes. "Yum. That's wonderful! Your guests will be in heaven when they try these."

"*Denke.*" Sarah bobbed her head and smiled. "Eat, then we can talk."

The next few minutes, Kathy savored her treat and the quiet companionship. Finally, she sat back and smiled. "*Denke,* Sarah."

Sarah's brows rose and her expression grew comical. "Katrina." She suddenly giggled. "Did you do that on purpose or to tease me?"

Kathy laughed along with her cousin. "A little of both, I guess. But not to tease. More to feel that I'm home, if even for a few minutes."

Sarah sobered and reached her hand across the table to cover Kathy's. "Why only for a few minutes? If your heart is here, why do you not *kumm* home?"

"It's not that simple. Besides, I honestly don't know where my heart is right now. When I'm in L.A., it's there. When I'm on a road trip investigating a new country, I feel at home there as well, although I must admit that traveling is getting old." She shook her head. "I can't trust my heart to lead me, Sarah. But I did pray today, for the first time in a long time, and asked God to give me wisdom and help."

Sarah patted Kathy's hand then leaned back. "*Gutt.* That is for the best. Now, tell me about your day. What, besides Miriam's treatment of you since you arrived, has you so troubled?"

Kathy took another sip of tea, considering where to start. Maybe it would be best to get it over with in one simple statement. "*Daed* left half of the farm to me and half to Miriam." She waited for Sarah's shock to register, but her cousin's placid expression didn't change.

"*Ya*? That is bad, why?" Sarah's brows wrinkled. "You were both his daughters. Why would he do anything less?"

Kathy blinked a few times as she took in the question. "I guess … I expected he'd leave it all to Miriam and maybe leave a few household items that had meaning to me. After all, I left the farm and my family. I didn't come back. Miriam stayed by his side. She's the one who helped care for him in his final years and helped work the farm. I did nothing. I didn't earn half of the farm."

"Did you earn your salvation, Kathy?" Sarah tipped her head to one side and studied her closely.

"Excuse me?" Kathy frowned at her cousin. "Of

course not. I mean, you can't do anything to earn salvation. That was a free gift, paid for by Jesus."

"And why did He do that, do you think?"

"Because He loved us. And because God loves us, even when we did not deserve it."

"Ah. I see." Sarah got up and plucked the tea kettle off the stove, then turned and refilled both of their cups.

Kathy allowed the comment to settle in as she took a sip of the hot tea. "Right. I understand your point. *Daed* still loved me as his daughter, even though I didn't choose the Amish life. That's what you're saying?"

"*Ya.* He did not love one of you more than the other. I am sure he appreciated Miriam's sacrifice on his behalf, but that did not change the depth of his love for you. Nor did the fact that you chose to leave. That probably saddened him, and he would have changed it if he could, but maybe he hoped leaving you half of the farm would entice you to return to your roots." She hunched one shoulder. "Of course, that is only a guess with nothing to back it up, so do not put too much weight on what I am saying." She waved her hand in dismissal.

"You may be more accurate than you realize, Sarah." Kathy pressed her lips together for a few seconds, thinking about the events of the morning. "*Daed* put in his will that I must stay for thirty days—either at the farm or with a family member or another Amish family—or the entire farm must be sold, and the money divided between the two of us."

Sarah let out a soft gasp and placed her fingers over her lips.

Kathy nodded. "Yes. That was my reaction, and believe me, Miriam's was much stronger. I had already told her I'd give her my half of the farm, and she had agreed, when the arbitrator told us the terms of the will."

"You said you would give her your half? Why, Katrina? It is your birthright as well as Miriam's."

Kathy tipped her head back, trying to assess the reasons behind her earlier decision. "I guess it was spontaneous and given somewhat out of guilt. I'm the sister who abandoned the family. She's the one who stayed and spent years caring for the farm and for *Daed*. She's earned that half. I did not. Kind of like I didn't earn my salvation." She gave a soft groan. "Was I wrong to give up my half, Sarah?"

"Wrong? *Nein*. Such a generous action is not wrong. Foolish? Probably not, if you don't choose to stay and make your life on the farm. Will you regret it in the future? I cannot say. I hope not. I assume you do not need the money that the sale of the farm could bring?"

"No. My books have done well, and there are other things in play right now that could make me even more in the future. I'm not hurting for money. I even offered to pay the property taxes for the next year, but I'm afraid that offended both Miriam and Amos."

"I can see why that might hurt their pride. It is one thing to give up your half to your sister because you won't be living there, but offering to pay for the taxes might imply they cannot afford it. That would cause most men to bristle, even if it came from someone…" She shook her head. "I am sorry, Katrina. It was not kind to say that."

"From someone they dearly loved and could accept such a gift from. Yeah, I get that, and it wasn't unkind, it was true. I wanted to talk to you because I knew you'd speak truth in love. I appreciate that."

"So." Sarah took a sip of her tea, then placed the

cup on the saucer with a decisive clink. "You must stay with someone who is Amish for thirty days. I assume Miriam did not open her arms or home to you with any degree of graciousness?"

"No. She did not." Kathy gave a rueful smile. "I'm still trying to think through that whole thirty-day thing. I don't want the farm to be sold, but this puts me in a very difficult position. There are things happening right now—a trip I was supposed to take, a TV show ..."

Sarah blinked wide eyes at Kathy. "You are going to be on the television? Your own show?"

"Oops." Kathy put her hand over her lips. "It's not for sure. It wouldn't be my own show, it would be with Jacques—my ... friend. And I haven't said yes. I guess if I stay, I'll need to say no. Maybe that would be for the best. I haven't had peace about moving forward with the program. It feels like it's going a different direction than my heart is leading."

"Your heart can be treacherous, but it can also lead you onto the right path. I would counsel you to think and pray about this decision. How soon do you have to make a decision?"

"Mr. Russo gave me three days. I can stay at Isaac's inn for those three days and maybe longer. If I decide to stay and agree to the terms of the will, then I should probably move. I honestly can't see myself living at the farm. Maybe Hazel would have room. I should ask her."

Sarah shook her head. "*Nein.* That will not be necessary. One of my guests is leaving next week, and that room is not booked again for some time. I will hold it for you." She held up her hand when Kathy opened her mouth to argue. "You may pay me if you insist, but I will give you the family discount. It is not as though I had the room reserved, so it would not have made me money, anyway. Besides, it would be lovely to have you close for three weeks. We can stay up and talk half the night, like we did when we were children."

"Thank you, Sarah. I'll take you up on your offer. I didn't realize how much I'd missed you until I came home. I want to come back soon and have you fill me in on Jeremiah."

A soft blush rose in Sarah's cheeks. "There is nothing to fill you in on, Katrina."

"Uh-huh. I can tell." Kathy laughed. "Now spill it, dear friend. What is holding you back from allowing Jeremiah to court you?"

Little worry lines appeared between Sarah's brows. "That is a *gutt* question. I have been giving it a lot of thought the past few days. I think ... I think it is a memory from my past that is holding me back." Rosy color suffused her cheeks.

"That sounds interesting. Care to share?" Kathy kept her voice light, as she could tell this might be something close to her cousin's heart.

"*Ya.* I think so. Years ago, before I met and married Ezra, do you remember a young man I took buggy rides with, named Gabriel?"

"Hmm." Kathy thought for a moment. "Gabe Hostetler? Very handsome Amish boy who didn't join the church and went off to join the Army when he left school?"

"*Ya.* That is him. At the time, I thought ... well, I thought we might marry. After Ezra died, I guess I kind of hoped he might *kumm* home. It was foolish, I know. He only wrote to me a few times, then I never heard from him again. His last letter said to forget him. That he had made choices where I could not follow, and he would never *kumm* home again. I prayed and decided I must let it go. Not long after, Ezra moved to our community, and we fell in love. I have not regretted my years of marriage, but I also haven't quite been able to forget Gabe."

"Wow." Kathy sat back hard in her chair. "I had no idea. That's amazing. Do you think you can come to care for Jeremiah in the same way, or are you wanting to guard your heart after losing two men you cared for in the past?"

Sarah gave a firm nod. "I think that is it—I have been worried about losing another man I am beginning to care for—and that scares me. Do I ignore that and pretend it does not matter and allow Jeremiah to court me?"

"I wish I could answer that question. I can't even figure out my own love life." Kathy twisted her mouth into what was supposed to be a smile but felt like a grimace.

"Your love life? Are you seeing someone and did not tell me, Katrina?"

"Yes and no. I've been seeing a man back home. He's an actor. Jacques. A decent, kind man who has strong feelings for me. Kind of like Jeremiah seems to have for you. But I haven't been able to return those feelings ... at least, not yet. Then, there's Isaac."

Sarah's eyes widened. "Isaac Mast? Our Isaac?" She drummed her fingers on the table. "*Ya.* The two of you spent much time together while growing up. I know there was talk about you courting and possibly marrying, but I always assumed that must not be the case after you left. That if you had loved him, you would have stayed."

"You would think so, right?" Kathy took a sip of her now cold tea and set it on the table, then waved Sarah back into her seat when she started to rise. "I'm good. I cared for Isaac, a lot. But I was so young and so sure I wanted to learn more about living in the *Englisch* world.

Courting seemed exciting, but I wasn't ready to make a commitment to marriage, and that's where courting would have led. I tried to explain that to Isaac, and I think he understood. After all, we weren't promised to each other. But still, it was hard to let go."

Sarah's solemn face shone with understanding. "I understand. We shall pray for each other to make wise choices, *ya?*"

"*Ya.*" Kathy pushed to her feet and walked around the table to give Sarah another hug. "Thank you for allowing me to come back in a few days, but I'd better go for now. I need to return a call and texts soon, although I'm kind of glad my phone has been dead, so I don't have to answer awkward questions from ... anyone."

Chapter Nine

KATHY DROVE AROUND FOR ANOTHER THIRTY minutes, reacquainting herself with the area while allowing her phone to charge. As much as she didn't want to face the questions she knew would come, she'd better return Jacques's text, or he'd call, or worse yet, show up without being invited.

That thought jerked her up short and caused her to dig deep. Not to try to figure out why she wouldn't want him to call, but why it would be worse if he appeared. She cared for this man, didn't she? She'd thought before coming here that they were on the road to a solid relationship that could lead to marriage. He'd hinted at that fact more than once. But that was before she'd seen Isaac again.

She almost laughed out loud at the foolish direction her thoughts had taken her. Isaac had done nothing to make her believe he still had any feelings for her left over from the past. He'd married, moved on with his life, had a daughter he loved, and gone an entirely different direction than he would have with her. So why assume he still cared? She should take the bird in the hand and quit worrying about the one who might fly out of the bush and disappear at any moment—exactly like *she* had done ten years ago.

Why did everything have to be so difficult? Couldn't life be easy and smooth, even for a few days? She coasted up to Isaac's house and powered her phone on. Might as well get this over with. Who knew, it might go better than she hoped, and she'd be glad she connected again. Maybe she'd go into the house and get comfortable first ... and let her phone charge a little longer. She plugged it back into the cord, left the car running and the doors open, and went in to change. Dress clothing for a meeting with the arbitrator was fine, but right now she longed to be in a pair of loose, comfy jeans and a t-shirt.

A few minutes later, a tapping sounded at the front door, and Isaac stuck his head in. "Katrina? Are you home? Your car is running out front and wasting gas. Did you forget to shut it off?"

Kathy trotted through the living room, tucking her t-shirt into her jeans. "I'll be right out."

Isaac stepped to the side of the open door and waited for her to exit. "I don't know too much about automobiles, or I would shut it off for you. I wouldn't want to accidently bump something and cause it to drive or wreck." He gave her a sheepish smile, and her heart jerked a little at the dimple she'd forgotten about at the corner of his mouth.

This was the first time she'd seen a true smile—no, it might even be called a grin—since she'd bumped into him at Hazel's farm stand. Hazel. She must get over to Hazel's house and visit soon. "It's fine, Isaac. I left it running to get my phone fully charged, since you don't have any electrical outlets. Maybe tomorrow I'll run into town and find an internet café. It appears I'll be here for a few days, if that's all right with you?"

"I can hook up a generator. I do that for guests who don't want to live plain while they're here. Some prefer it, as they want to see what it's like to completely get away from all technology for a few days. A few find it refreshing, but most of them end up going crazy and asking for the generator."

She reached into the car and unplugged her phone,

then turned off the ignition and shut the door. "You do remember I grew up Amish, right? Although I will admit I'm thankful for your propane refrigerator and stove, as well as running water. I guess not having electricity isn't too high of a price to pay for a few days." She flicked her fingers at the house. "I like it the way it is. Don't hook up the generator. The lanterns in the evening are perfect, and I can light a fire in the fireplace if I get chilled. You have plenty of kindling and firewood cut." She fanned herself. "But as warm as it's been this summer, I don't know that I'll need to worry about that."

Isaac bent over and plucked a wicker basket off the floor of the porch. "I brought you fresh eggs from our hens and milk from our cow." He nodded at the little blonde girl skipping across the lawn toward them. "Sadie collected the eggs while I milked the cow."

Sadie stopped beside her father and reached up to take his hand. "One of the hens tried to peck at me when I reached under her for the egg, but I shooed her away and got it anyway."

She gazed up at Kathy. "Did you ever see a chicken before? I can show you mine. I have eleven chickens and today we got eight eggs." She frowned. "Three of my chickens didn't want to lay eggs today." The little girl shook her head as though it was a complete tragedy, then heaved a huge sigh. "I have talks with them every day about being good hens and laying eggs like they're 'sposed to, but they do not always listen."

Kathy bit her lip to keep from laughing at the delightful little girl. "I know what you mean, Sadie. My chickens were the same way. I used to have talks with them too."

Sadie's eyes grew wide. "You did? I thought you

lived in a big city. That's what Papa told me." She looked up at Isaac. "How can she have chickens in a big city? Won't they get run over by all the cars and trucks?"

This time, Kathy allowed a little giggle to slip out. "I do live in a city, Sadie, but I don't have chickens there. I meant that I used to have them when I was a little girl, like you. I even remember a few of their names."

Sadie bounced up and down. "What? Tell me, tell me!"

Kathy laughed as pure delight over this precious child flooded her. "Let's see. Billina was my favorite. I named her after a hen in *Ozma of Oz*, one of the *Oz* books, but I didn't get to read that book until I was older. We had a rooster we named Little Jerry, because he was so big, and I thought it was funny to call him little. Then there was Henrietta, because she was a hen."

"Oh, I like all those names. Maybe I'll call one of my hens Henrietta. Is that all right, Miss Yoder?"

"Of course." Kathy reached out and tugged at one of the little girl's braids. "I'd be very happy to know one of your hens has the same name mine did." She turned to Isaac, who had been watching the exchange with a very solemn expression. "I stopped at a grocery store and bought a few things. With the eggs and milk, I can probably scare up a decent meal. Would you like to join me?"

He took a half-step back, pulling Sadie with him. "*Nein, denke.* You are very kind, but we have food waiting in the house, and we must go." He shushed Sadie as she protested and drew her toward his little cabin, not once glancing back over his shoulder.

Kathy stared after them. Had she upset him by

mentioning *Ozma of Oz*? She'd discovered that book as a teen and had smuggled it into her home and read it at night by lantern light after hanging a blanket over her window so the light wouldn't escape and alert her parents to what she was doing. Disappointment hit her harder than she'd expected. She hadn't realized how much she'd hoped Isaac and Sadie might join her for lunch.

Isaac ushered Sadie into the house with a firm hand and directed her to the table. "Sadie, stop pouting. You are a big girl and you can't pout every time you do not get your way."

She folded her tiny arms over her chest and her bottom lip stuck out. "But Miss Yoder asked us to come to dinner. Why can't we? She's staying at our house, so it wouldn't be wrong to eat with her. She's a nice lady, and she had chickens like me!"

"Go wash your hands. We both forgot. *Kumm.* Get clean then we will make sandwiches and heat up the soup."

"I'm tired of soup. I want whatever Miss Yoder was going to fix us." She flounced over to the sink and washed, all the while keeping a frown on her face.

Frustration and a sense of despair hit Isaac so hard he wanted to sit down and bury his face in his hands, but he couldn't allow his little one to see how he felt. He'd wanted nothing more than to spend time with Katrina, even though he knew it was foolish to do so. She would do what she had done before—leave and break his heart.

He could handle that. His heart had been broken

twice in his lifetime, so once more probably couldn't do too much damage, but he had to think of Sadie. He couldn't allow her to get attached to someone who would be leaving in a few days. She already asked why she couldn't have another mother and why he didn't find a new wife, so she could be like the other girls. The last thing he needed was for her to decide Katrina would fill that role nicely.

If only she hadn't gotten it into her head ten years ago that she needed more than what their simple life could give her. In some ways, he understood. He harbored a secret of his own that would be frowned on by his people should they find out, but he'd never taken it to the point Katrina had. She had always been braver than he was, though. She was the one who took the risks when they were children. He could dare her to jump a wide creek, and she'd do it without a second thought, while he hung back, worried about how much trouble he'd be in if he came home with muddy shoes.

Maybe that was why she decided to leave after he opened his heart and told her he cared. She must have wanted to try out her wings and fly, but she knew that his fear of taking a risk, of trying something new, would keep him tied at home. He was happy in his life now. He had been then, as well, but he'd come to the place of true contentment. His life here with Ruth and Sadie had brought as much contentment as he'd ever expected to have, even with the small bumps they'd hit along the way in their marriage. Ruth wasn't always an easy woman to please, but he'd made a commitment when he took his marriage vows. He would have remained faithful until he died, if she hadn't gone first. Now he had Sadie, the best gift Ruth could have left him. It was up to him to watch over her little heart and make sure she didn't have to endure the same pain she'd felt when she lost her mother, or that he'd felt when Katrina went away. Keeping himself and his daughter away from Katrina Yoder was important—even more important now than it was ten years ago, and somehow, he'd figure out how to keep his heart from breaking again.

A knock sounded at Sarah's door. Most people knew it was an inn and walked into the entry and waited at the front desk. She hurried to answer it and swung open the heavy wood door. "Jeremiah. I was not expecting you. Would you like to *kumm* in?"

He gave her a shy glance and bobbed his head once. "*Guder daag*, Sarah. *Nein*. I was hoping you might want to go for a buggy ride with me. It is a lovely evening. I know life has been busy for you with Katrina arriving and the guests that stay here, but I wondered if you might have an hour for me?"

Sarah didn't hesitate but a second. "A ride sounds *wunderbar. Denke*. It's warm enough I shouldn't need shawl." She smoothed her apron. "Oh, a moment, please?" Dashing to her kitchen she shut off the gas flame under the tea pot right as it began to whistle. Her tea could wait. She was not going to make Jeremiah wait again. Hurrying back through the house, she touched her *Kapp* to be sure it was on straight and her hair tucked in with no wayward strands peaking out. Pride in one's appearance was a sin, but she did not want to embarrass Jeremiah by appearing untidy, either.

He still waited in the open doorway, his broad-brimmed straw hat clutched in his hands, his knuckles almost white from his tight grip. Could he be nervous about taking her on a ride? She slowed and gave him an encouraging smile. "I am ready now, *denke* for giving me an extra moment."

He nodded and his shoulders seemed to relax. "Ya. Of course." He held out his arm and waited for her to slip her hand into the crook of his elbow. "And *denke* for being willing to *kumm* with me." He walked beside her then helped her up onto the buggy seat.

As Sarah settled in, her heartbeat increased. If only she could decide if she cared for this man. If only Gabriel wasn't still lurking in the back of her memory from so many years ago. Why was it so hard to let go and allow her heart to grow attached to another?

Jeremiah picked up the reins and clucked to his horse. Early crickets chirped as they clopped out of Sarah's yard, and the sound brought comfort and a sense of peace to her heart. She would enjoy this time with Jeremiah and not try to think too far into the future. This time together was enough for now.

After turning onto a country lane that branched off from her driveway, he gave her a quiet smile. "How have you been, Sarah? Is all well with your life?"

"*Ya.* All is well. It has been so *gutt* to spend time with my cousin Katrina again. The inn is doing well, and my garden is flourishing." She almost blurted out that there was nothing more she could ask for, but she didn't want to hurt him when she knew he wanted to court her. "And you?"

He kept his focus ahead of the horse but gave a short nod. "I am beginning to feel that the months are speeding past and I find myself still alone." He gave her a quick glance. "*Daed* has been pushing me hard to marry, as he has been pushing you to give up your inn and take a husband."

Sarah stiffened. Surely Jeremiah wasn't going to make the same demands.

He reached over and touched her hand for a moment, then returned his to the reins again. "That is something I would like to talk to you about, if I may?"

She gave a silent nod, almost wishing she hadn't agreed to drive with him this evening. "*Ya.* I suppose you may."

"Please do not worry, Sarah. I am not my father. He and I do not think alike on many things. I told you months ago that I didn't care if you kept the inn, even if we were to eventually marry. I meant what I said. I can tell how much it means to you, and I would never take that away from you, or ask you to change." He shifted in the seat next to her and reined the horse over to a wide spot off the road then turned to face her. "Do you believe me?"

Sarah blinked back the moisture gathering in her eyes then swiped at one lone tear that managed to slip out and roll down her cheek. "*Ya.* I do believe you. I wasn't sure when we spoke about it in the past. I know how the bishop feels, and I thought he would have made you change by this time. *Denke* for telling me this. It means a lot to me."

"You are welcome, Sarah. I would never do anything to hurt you. I hope you know I care for you, but I am not going to force you to make a decision. I want you to be for sure and for certain before I court you."

"*Denke*, Jeremiah. You are a very kind man."

Kathy powered on her phone as she entered the house and shut the door behind her. She kicked off her shoes then walked to the couch and sank into it, still confused over the rejection from Isaac minutes ago. She couldn't allow it to matter. After all, she had a full life waiting for her back in L.A. Connecting with Jacques would solidify the reality of that life and remind her that anything here was only a fantasy that could never come true.

She hit speed dial for his number and waited as it rang six times. Her thumb was hovering over the off button when his breathless voice answered.

"Kathy! How are you? I was working out in my home gym and didn't hear the phone. Sorry about that. I sent you several texts. Why didn't you answer?"

Kathy rolled her eyes, wondering which question he wanted her to answer first. "The gym sounds fun. Get in some exercise for me too while you're at it."

"So ... how are you and why didn't you text me when you got there?"

"I'm fine. I meant to get in touch after I arrived, but I forgot to plug my phone into my car when I was driving here, and I haven't had a chance to charge it since."

"You haven't had a chance to charge it? What's with that? You practically live with your phone. I can't imagine you forgetting to keep it charged." His tone was somewhere between annoyance and amusement.

Kathy stretched out on the couch and tucked a throw pillow under her head. "Right. But remember, I'm in Amish country. No electricity at the inn."

"What? You mean they don't cater to other people? Normal people? They can live a rustic life if they want to, but why would they make you do that?"

"Because I'm staying at an Amish inn, not a hotel."

His voice rose a notch. "Why in the world would you choose to do that? Were all the hotels full?"

"It's a small town, Jacques. There isn't an abundance of five-star hotels to choose from. Besides, my cousin runs a lovely B&B, and I wanted to spend time with her."

"Oh, well, I guess that's different. Did she give you the nicest room in the place?"

Kathy crossed her leg over her knee and bounced her foot. "Actually, I was only able to stay the first night with her, since she didn't have advance notice. Now I'm at the other inn, but I'm going back to Sarah's next week when she has a room open."

"That's a royal pain. I can't believe you can exist without electricity, a TV, and everything else you're used to having when you travel."

"Don't forget, I was raised Amish. I lived this way for eighteen years, so this isn't new to me."

"Yes, but you've been spoiled for the past few years." He snorted a laugh. "A Himalayan base camp has more luxuries."

"Not hardly. Look at all the trips I've taken to prove a girl can travel cheap. As I recall, you spent the night in a yurt on a mountainside with a group of Mongolian goat herders one time. I'm guessing they didn't have electricity or a TV." Kathy felt a sense of satisfaction well up at reminding him of that fact. She didn't feel a bit deprived—in fact, it was kind of nice to return to her roots. As far as being spoiled, maybe she had been, a little bit. She wasn't so sure being spoiled was all it was cracked up to be, either. It could leave a person feeling less than honorable.

"I guess I even fooled you on that one." Jacques

laughed. "That was all for the cameras. As soon as they stopped rolling, I headed straight for a Four Seasons hotel and basked in luxury the next twenty-four hours, until I got the smell of goat herder out of my nostrils and off my body."

Something about the way he said that made Kathy cringe. They'd joked around in the past about roughing it on their trips, and how they felt about some of their experiences, but this felt different. It felt like he was belittling the simple way of life those goat herders experienced—and even belittling her Amish roots—and she didn't like it one bit.

This was probably a good time to break the news to him that she might be staying for another thirty days and couldn't make a commitment to the new show. Family needed to come first for once. She'd neglected personal obligations for too long. She opened her mouth to explain. "Jacques."

"Yeah. Hey, babe. I need to run. I've got something I have to take care of. I know you're dealing with a lot right now, but don't forget me, and don't forget about the great opportunity we're being offered, all right? You'll think about it and let me know soon?"

She bit her lip for a second. "Yes. Yes, I'll think about it and let you know soon. Good talking to you."

"Yeah, you too. Later." The phone went dead.

Kathy pulled it away from her ear and stared at it. That was strange. Normally, she was the one trying to get off the line first. Oh well, at least she hadn't needed to go into a long explanation about saving the farm for her family and staying thirty days.

A sudden thought hit her. He hadn't once asked about her family or how she was dealing with the loss of her father. Same old Jacques.

Chapter Ten

THE NEXT MORNING, KATHY SAT AT the kitchen table with a copy of Shakespeare and a cup of hot tea, reveling in the need to do absolutely nothing. Her life back home was always so ... scheduled. Structured. The constant flurry of activity and meetings left her wanting nothing more than an hour to herself without interruption. This farm house was a tiny bit of heaven on earth.

Someone rapped on the front door, and Kathy jumped. Had Isaac decided to check on her? Sadie should be in school, and besides, it was too heavy of a knock for a small child.

"Coming." She hurried to the door and swung it open, hoping Isaac had decided to stop in for a chat. "Hazel! What a pleasant surprise. Come in." She swung the door wide so Hazel could step in with her armful of pie boxes. "What in the world are you doing? Are you trying to feed the entire neighborhood?"

Hazel's brown eyes sparkled under the fringe of hair that peeked out from under the side of her *Kapp*. "If I know you, there is no pie left from what you took the other day. You probably found some needy person and gave it away." She stepped into the kitchen and placed four stacked boxes on the table. "I thought it would be fun to catch up, and I have a girl at the farm stand filling in for me for two hours."

"Works for me. And no, I didn't give all the pie away. I ate my share. Since I only had coffee so far this morning, I think I could manage a slice or two." She lifted the lid and inhaled. "Cherry. Yum. Still warm from the oven too. That couldn't be more perfect. You are the best, cousin."

"I know." Hazel smirked. "I'll even let you wait on me, since I baked the pies." She perched on a kitchen chair, her long, straight skirt almost touching the floor over her very sensible shoes.

Kathy held up the tea pot. "Is tea all right? I don't have any fresh-brewed coffee." At Hazel's nod, she poured a fresh cup for herself and a cup for her cousin, then lifted two earthenware plates from a plain shelf and retrieved forks from a drawer. "It's been way too long since I've seen you." Kathy slid into the chair across the table. "Catch me up on your life while I dive into this delicious pie." She placed a slice each onto two plates and pushed one toward Hazel.

"There isn't that much to tell. I've been running the farm stand for nearly ten years, and it's doing well. Lots of *Englischers* want to see an Amish woman up close, so they stop." She shrugged. "I suppose I am a bit of a tourist attraction. But it brings in business, and they always buy several items, so I cannot complain. Thankfully, my three children are all in school now, so I no longer have to bring a *bopplie* to work with me. Of course, being my own boss, it didn't much matter, but it *is* easier to get things done without children underfoot."

"How old are they now? I met John and Mary the last time I stopped by, but Mary was in diapers and John wasn't quite in school yet."

Hazel laughed and almost snorted her tea. "That shows how longs it's been since you've visited your family, Katrina. My two are six, nine, and eleven years old. Miriam's son John is a strapping boy of twelve now, Mary is eight, and little Deborah is six. I didn't know yet that I was expecting the last time you were here. My Paul is farming the land his *daed* left him. We live in the main house, and his *mamm* lives in the *Daadi*

Haus." She forked a piece of pie into her mouth and chewed for a moment. "Hmm." She waved her fork at Kathy. "It's your turn now. First, how did things go with Miriam and Amos?"

Kathy almost choked on her last bite of pie at the abrupt change of subject—and not one she found to be pleasant. She placed a napkin over her lips. "Sorry." Taking a sip of tea to wash the pie down, she swallowed then set the teacup down with a soft clink. "I got a rather chilly reception, and it only got worse when Mr. Russo read *Daed's* will."

Hazel leaned forward. "Gossip often moves fast through the Amish community, but I haven't heard anything about the will or Miriam being upset about what was left."

"Let me tell you, I'm not sure who was more shocked, Miriam or me. *Daed* split the ownership of the farm between the two of us." She shook her head. "I thought Miriam was going to fall over when Mr. Russo told us."

Hazel gave a slow nod. "I'm guessing she felt she's the one who should have inherited, since you left, and she stayed? Kind of like the parable of the prodigal son returning and being given a banquet and gifts, and the son who'd stayed and worked resenting his brother, *ya*?"

Now it was Kathy's turn to consider and nod. "I would imagine you could be right. All I know is she was very angry. I offered to pay all the property tax for this year when Mr. Russo explained it would be a large amount, but she and Amos were both offended. I know I hurt their pride. But she didn't object when I told Mr. Russo I'd sign over my half of the farm to her."

"You did what?" Hazel leaned back into her chair, hard. "If your father wanted to you have it, you should not give it away, Katrina."

Kathy hadn't considered it from that perspective. Would *Daed* be unhappy with her that she'd so easily give her inheritance away, or would he be proud of her that she cared about her sister and wanted to make her happy? "I'm not so sure, Hazel. I think if *Daed* had considered it carefully, he would have realized I wouldn't move back to the farm, and that splitting it would cause Miriam much grief. Maybe I'll regret my decision someday, but right now it feels like it's the right thing to do."

"You have a very generous heart." Hazel reached across the table and patted Kathy's arm. "So, how are your accommodations here? You are comfortable, *ya*? When do you go back to Los Angeles? Soon, I would imagine."

"Well, that's the other thing *Daed* put in his will." She proceeded to explain the terms he'd imposed.

"What will you do? Have you decided? I imagine you are chomping at the bit to return to your life, *ya*? This simple life must seem very slow and ponderous to you now."

Kathy thought of last night, curled up with a book in the lantern light, and this morning with her cup of tea and peaceful atmosphere. No taxis or cars honking outside her apartment window, no emergency service vehicles with sirens blaring, no rushing to get to the next appointment or answer yet another call. Just silence. Peace. Suddenly she knew what she needed to do. "I'm staying. I think Mr. Russo will allow the thirty days to begin when I first arrived and stayed at Sarah's, since she's family, and since she didn't have room there for a few days. I'll move back in with her as soon as her visitor leaves. I'm not going to allow the farm to be sold out from under Miriam."

Hazel's eyes twinkled as she peered out the window over Kathy's shoulder. "Would Isaac Mast have anything to do with that decision, Cousin?"

Kathy turned to look out the window in time to see Isaac standing outside his workshop, dusting off his hands, then heading to the water pump nearby. She felt heat rise in her cheeks and turned away. "Of course not. He's still grieving his wife. I don't think he's willing to come in here unless he has to. Besides, I have a boyfriend back home, remember?"

Hazel tipped her head to the side and met Kathy's eyes. "What I remember is that you haven't mentioned this other man's name one time since you arrived. You certainly do not act like a woman who is pining for a distant love." She took a final sip of her tea. "But you are right. It's heartbreaking that Isaac chose to live in the cabin and not this beautiful home he built for his Ruth."

"I know. It seems wrong for me to be in this big house while he and Sadie are living in that tiny cabin."

Hazel pushed to her feet. "I must quit gossiping and get back to work. I told my helper I wouldn't be gone long." She reached over and gave Kathy a hug. "Do not be a stranger, Katrina. Come see me since you aren't leaving soon." She gave a sly glance out the window again. "And don't be in too big a rush to head back to Sarah's to stay."

Kathy stretched and yawned, then picked up her phone and checked the time. She couldn't believe she'd fallen asleep. Hazel had left almost two hours ago. Jumping to her feet from the couch, she ran her fingers through her hair, wishing she could use her curling iron. Maybe her

Amish roots didn't run as deep as she'd implied to Isaac. She did appreciate electricity.

She wandered into the kitchen and her gaze landed on the pie boxes. How could Hazel possibly think she could finish off four pies? The two of them had only eaten a slice apiece. She could give Isaac one, but he only had Sadie to help him eat it. She'd keep one, but that still left two. Miriam? A smile lit her face. Maybe a pie would help smooth troubled waters.

After running a brush through her hair and avoiding the temptation of lipstick, she placed the two boxes into the passenger seat of the car and climbed in behind the wheel. No one could resist Hazel's pies, not even her sister.

A few minutes later, she slowed the car a couple of miles before the turnoff, wondering if she'd made a hasty decision. From what she remembered, Miriam was an accomplished baker, and it was doubtful she needed extra pastries. However, she had a hardworking husband and three growing children, not to mention a little one on the way. Miriam might not have the time or energy to bake. Surely, her sister couldn't fault her for being courteous and bringing a pie?

She parked a few yards from the main house, wondering if she should go to the door or wait and see if someone came out. After a few seconds, she pushed open her door, then reached across and grabbed the boxes. Better to beard the dragon in her lair than to allow her to come out and blast her before she even stepped out of the car. She grinned, then shot up a small prayer for forgiveness for her uncharitable thought—although truly, the last two times she'd seen Miriam, it wasn't a far cry from how she acted. Kathy sobered then forced herself to wear a pleasant smile. No sense of going to the door with combat on her mind, or

Miriam would sense it and respond in kind.

Kathy walked across the porch and glanced in a window to the side of the front door, which she knew looked into the dining area. Her heart sank. It hadn't occurred to her she might be coming at lunch time. Maybe heading back to Isaac's might be a good idea. She swiveled to leave, then hesitated. It might be the perfect time, with the children present and Amos in from the fields. Miriam might be on her best behavior in front of her family. At least, she could hope.

Shifting the two boxes to one arm, she raised the other hand and rapped on the door. "Hello! Anyone home?"

Footsteps sounded inside, too light to be Amos but too heavy to be one of the children. Miriam's voice drifted out before the door opened. "John. Get back in your seat. I will take care of whoever is here. It is not your business."

"Uh-oh." Kathy sighed. *Not a good start.* She pasted on a big smile as the door swung open. "Hey, there!" She thrust the boxes into Miriam's arms, and she fumbled to catch them before they slipped out of her grasp.

Miriam blinked, seemingly frozen in shock. She looked at Kathy, then at the boxes, then back at Kathy again.

Kathy rushed forward, determined to fill the silence before Miriam could shoo her away. "I got these from Hazel. I can't believe she's running the farm stand instead of her mother now. She's an amazing baker. I think her pies are even better than her *mamm's*, from what I remember."

John and Mary appeared behind their mother, with Amos coming hard on their heels, a toddler in his arms. "You children get back to the table." He waved his arm.

"Pie!" Mary danced on her tiptoes, squealing and clapping. "*Mamm*, you haven't baked a pie in forevermore. May we have a piece, please?"

John took a step closer. "Who are you? You are *Englisch*."

Kathy nodded. "Yes. I'm your aunt Kathy. I haven't seen you for several years, so you might not remember me."

His brows drew together, and he turned to his mother. "Do we have an Aunt Kathy?"

Kathy felt as though someone had stabbed her. Miriam and Amos hadn't even told their children about her? "I know. You don't recognize my name? I'm Katrina Yoder, but I go by Kathy now. I'm your *mamm's* sister."

Mary pulled on her mother's sleeve. "Is she our aunt?"

John nodded. "I remember Granddaddy talking about her when I was younger."

"I like your clothes. You are very pretty." Mary stared at her with wide eyes.

"You only like her clothes because they're *Englisch*." John turned on her with a scowl.

"Children. You need to come back to the table. Now." Amos shifted the toddler to one hip as the child began to cry. "Let your *mamm* talk to the visitor."

The visitor. Kathy barely kept her lip from curling. The visitor who was gifting them half of the farm. Wasn't that nice.

Amos caught Mary's hand and drew her away from the door, but she called over her shoulder. "Is that your car? Can I have a ride? Will you stay for dinner?"

Kathy almost giggled this time, charmed at this little girl. "It's a rental, but it's mine for as long as I'm in town. It would be up to your mother if she wants me to come in. I can't invite myself to dinner."

Miriam seemed to snap out of her shock. "You children get back to the table like your *daed* told you to, or you will go do your chores without eating. Mind your father. Now." The sharp tone broke through the children's fascination with their aunt, and they scampered back to the table.

Miriam swung back to Kathy. "How dare you come and disrupt our meal—and our lives? You and your fancy clothes and car. What would you do? Lure my daughter away to the world as well? Or my son? Do you have no respect for our beliefs or our lives, that you would come here and try to fill their heads with worldliness?"

Kathy straightened and stood stiff in front of her sister. "I hardly think bringing you pies is trying to influence or lure your children away, Miriam. If you don't want the pies, fine. But the children don't even know me. It sounds like they didn't even know I existed until now. Why didn't you tell them about me? Is that the Christian thing to do to your own family?"

"I did not want them getting any silly ideas about following in their aunt's footsteps and running off to the world. They are Amish. I want them to remain so."

Kathy had heard about all she could handle. She'd come out with the best of intentions, and she was getting her kindness shoved back in her face. "It will be their choice to stay Amish or leave when they turn eighteen, won't it, Miriam?"

Miriam shoved the two boxes into Kathy's arms, her face ablaze with fury that Kathy could barely comprehend. "You do not belong here. I am not sure you ever did. You abandoned your family. You turned your back on us, the church, and our community. No amount of money, pies, or even half of the farm can ever change that fact. Take these and go, Katrina." She took a step back and gave the door a firm shove. It clicked shut only inches from Kathy's face.

"I didn't abandon anyone." Kathy said the words loud enough she hoped her sister would hear her, then she dropped her voice to a whisper as she backed away from the door. "I only wanted to find my own way. My own life. Was that such a terrible thing?"

Chapter Eleven

KATHY PULLED OUT HER PHONE AND got ready to speed dial Evelyn as she drove down the farm lane to the main road. She'd been so hurt by Miriam's accusations, she'd almost rescinded her offer to give her half the farm. It wasn't like she'd signed the papers yet. Evelyn would demand an answer about the new show opportunity. If she backed out on her offer to Miriam, she could go home and jump right into preparations for the show, not to mention the Kenya trip Evelyn had lined up.

She drummed her fingers on the steering wheel, hating the feeling of being trapped between two different choices, neither of which made her happy. Was her happiness the most important in this situation? If not, why not? She scowled, not even caring about the beautiful landscape that often drew her attention. Why did she have to be the kind sister? Why couldn't Miriam put out an effort to reconcile and ... just be nice?

She reviewed what Miriam had said right before shutting the door in her face. Her sister believed she'd abandoned the family and their Amish community. How could she feel that way when Kathy hadn't chosen to join the church? It wasn't as if she'd done anything immoral—she simply chose a different path for her life, a path that made her happy at the time. She clutched the steering wheel. *At the time?* She was still happy with her choice, wasn't she?

All she knew was she must make a decision about the farm and the TV show, and that must happen soon. She tucked her phone back into her bag and took the fork in the road that would lead her to Sarah's inn.

Right now, she needed someone to talk to, and she couldn't think of anyone better than her thoughtful, sweet cousin to ask for advice.

A few minutes later she pulled to a stop, then climbed from her car. Holding one pie box, she headed up the walk to Sarah's. She pushed open the white picket gate, inhaling the fragrance of the roses lining the walk. Sarah definitely had a green thumb. Remembering Sarah's admonition to enter without knocking, Kathy stepped into the foyer and took in the feeling of peace that always settled around her when entering this home. It must be the close walk Sarah had developed with God. She envied that walk, and somehow, she needed to get back to that place herself.

"Sarah? Are you home?" She walked toward the kitchen, then stopped at the total silence that seemed to encompass the house. She hadn't thought to check to see if Sarah's buggy was here. She should have called Sarah's business phone first to see if she'd be home. She spun and headed for the front door.

"Katrina?" Footsteps padded down the stairs from the second floor and seconds later, Sarah appeared. "I was changing the linens on the beds and didn't hear your car. I am glad you came in. I wouldn't have heard you knock." She rushed forward and pulled Kathy into a hug that caused Kathy to finally relax. "It is so *gutt* to see you! *Kumm*. I have the tea kettle on."

Kathy reached for the pie where she'd set it on an entry table when she'd walked through the door. "Hazel dropped these at the house this morning. I thought you might like one. I can't eat all this pie, or I'll be a blimp in no time." She grinned as she pushed the box into Sarah's hands. "I already had a piece this morning, so it's all yours."

"That is the second pie you have brought me. Is

Hazel trying to put herself out of business, or are you baking in your spare time?" Sarah gave her an impish smile.

Kathy held up her hands. "Not me. You know I'd rather quilt than bake. Hey, let me show you something." She reached for her backpack she'd set on the floor and unzipped it, remembering the small quilt for the first time. "I picked this up at the *Daadi Haus* the first time I was there."

Sarah stared at her with wide eyes.

"I didn't steal it, Sarah. It's mine. I can't believe it was still there. I started this before I left home. I had such big plans for this quilt. I hoped it would be my wedding quilt, but I never finished it, and I didn't imagine I'd have a place to work on it in my new life, so I left it behind. I guess *Mamm* didn't want to work on it, either."

Sarah stroked the fabric containing blues, greens, and gold tones in a ring pattern. "The wedding ring quilt. It is gorgeous. But then, I am looking at the work of the best junior quilter in the county three years running."

"Stop." Kathy gathered the quilt to her chest.

"It is true. You were the envy of many of the girls our age and older. Quite an honor, if you ask me. I always thought you might open your own quilt shop one day." She shrugged.

"I haven't held a quilting needle in ten years." She shrugged. "I guess it wasn't as important to me as I once thought."

"That is a shame for all your talent to go to waste. But you loved it at one time."

"Yeah, I suppose I did. I saw it and didn't want it collecting dust in *Daed*'s house. Or worse yet, to have Miriam decide to use it for a dust rag." She shuddered.

"Things were good when I was growing up, until I decided to leave and broke everyone's heart."

Sarah narrowed her eyes. "Who are you talking about? Isaac?"

"No." Kathy waved her hand. "I went to see Miriam today. I thought maybe a little peace offering—you know, a couple of pies—might help mend fences, and she'd at least sit down and talk to me for once."

"I assume it did not work as you had hoped? But then, if giving her half the land didn't soften her heart, I am not sure a pie would do more." She flicked a finger toward the pie box. "Not that Hazel's pies would not turn many a heart, but still …"

"She's so angry. She blames me for leaving the family, the church, our community. I guess I understand, but I don't understand why she's held a grudge for so long—why she has to slam the door in my face every time I come see her and try to talk and make things right."

"Give her time, Katrina. That is all you can do. And forgive her."

"Forgive *her*?" Shock rippled through Kathy. "She thinks I'm the one who needs forgiveness."

"*Ya*, that too. But it sounds like Miriam is holding onto a lot of hurt and unforgiveness, which can fester and poison a person if they don't give it over to *Gott* and ask for His help. I have not seen her when she's smiling or laughing for far too long."

"You think that's my fault?" Kathy whispered the words and wrapped her arms around herself.

Sarah leaned forward and squeezed Kathy's shoulder. "*Nein.* I am not putting her anger on you. That is her own decision. Her choice. As it was your choice to leave, it was her choice how she would respond to your decision. She could have wished you well and gone on with her life, remaining happy and at peace. Instead, she chose to foster unhappiness and maybe a bit of jealousy."

"Ha! That can't be true. Miriam would never be jealous of someone who chose the *Englisch* life. She is very proud to be Amish and never lets an opportunity go by to let me know how much she despises my life."

Sarah shrugged. "Perhaps so. We cannot know the heart of another. Maybe you should pray for her, *ya?*"

Kathy felt as though all the air whooshed out of her lungs. It had never occurred to her to pray for her sister, much less to try to understand what drove the deep emotions she constantly expressed. "You might be right. Thank you for giving me so much to think about, Sarah." She leaned forward, placing her arms on the kitchen table. "Now tell me what's been happening with you. Have you gone for that drive with Jeremiah yet?"

Sarah's face paled and she shook her head. "*Nein.*"

"What's wrong?" Kathy sat upright as fear jolted her heart. "Has something bad happened?"

"I do not know what to think." Sarah's voice had dropped to a whisper.

"Is it something you can tell me?" Kathy wanted to pull the words out of her dear friend, but she must respect her privacy and allow her to share if that's what she desired.

"I ... think so. *Ya.*" Sarah nodded then looked away for a second. "Gabriel has returned to Cave City. He came to see me yesterday to tell me he was sorry for not staying in touch—for leaving when we were starting to court." She gave a sad smile. "He is only here to wrap up family business—like you—but my heart wasn't expecting to see him after so many years. Now, I am confused. I thought I was beginning to care for Jeremiah, until I saw Gabriel again."

"Could you tell if Gabe feels anything for you? Did he say anything that would ... give you hope?" Kathy didn't know what to think. Her heart hurt for Sarah.

"I do not think he does anymore. That was one thing that was hard. I always thought, if I saw him again, I would be in love all over again. But I do not know what I feel now, other than confusion. Jeremiah came as Gabe was leaving yesterday, and he acted like he had seen a ghost."

"He knows Gabe? Does he know the two of you were close once?"

"*Ya.* Gabe's and Jeremiah's mothers are second cousins, remember?"

Kathy shook her head. "I'd completely forgotten they were related. It all seems so long ago." She squeezed Sarah's hand. "I'm sorry. This must be hard for you. What did Jeremiah say?"

"Nothing. He stood on the porch as Gabe left, then he turned and got into his buggy without a word." Sarah clenched her hands together on the table. "Maybe I will stay a widow for the rest of my life. I will give up the inn if the bishop demands it and see if I can find a family member to live with. If I sell the inn, I won't need to be a burden to anyone who takes me in. I am a *gutt* cook, so I can be a help to any family." She snapped her lips closed. "I am rambling. I'm sorry."

"Sarah, I'll pray for you too. God will surely show you what to do. I've never met anyone in the Amish community with your faith and prayer life."

"We all must bear our share of trials and burdens, Katrina. Losing Gabe and driving a wedge between myself and Jeremiah may be mine. Besides, now that

I've seen Gabe again, I'm not even sure if I could be happy with Jeremiah."

Kathy got up and pulled her cousin to her feet. "I think we could both use a hug."

Sarah nodded, and Kathy felt moisture soak through her blouse as sobs shook Sarah's frame.

Chapter Twelve

ON THE WAY BACK TO ISAAC'S, Kathy made the call she'd been dreading and put it on speaker. "Evelyn? How are you?" She infused as much cheerfulness into her voice as she could muster.

"Hello, darling. I thought you'd fallen off the face of the earth—or maybe decided to become Amish again and we'd never see you." She gave a loud cackle. "Seriously, it's good to hear your voice. Jacques told me you can't charge your phone very often. Why in the world aren't you staying at a hotel instead of some little Amish inn with no electricity or even a jacuzzi? I'm sure the beds must be like rocks, and the meals..." She gave what sounded like a shudder mixed with a groan. "Don't get me started. Fill me in on when you're coming home and what you decided about the show. Jacques's agent has nearly hounded the life out of me the last forty-eight hours."

"I'm sorry. I shouldn't have waited so long to call you. I appreciate you giving me a bit of space to deal with things and not pressuring me to make a decision, but I also realize it's put you in a difficult position."

"Thank you. It has, but I accept your apology. That is, as long as you have the answer I'm looking for and you're coming home soon. We have a lot to do to get you ready for everything that's looming."

"Well, that's the thing..." Kathy suddenly had no idea how to break the news to her agent.

"Don't tell me you really have decided to go back to your Amish life? If that's the case, I'm flying out there first thing tomorrow to talk sense into you and drag you back home."

"No. No, I haven't. It's complicated, though. I mean, there are family issues involved, and it's not just about me. I have my sister and her family to think of too."

"In what way?" The cold steel that had crept into Evelyn's voice let Kathy know exactly what she was thinking, and it wasn't good. "If you aren't going to become Amish again, what does your family have to do with anything? I mean, I know you lost your father, and I'm truly sorry for your loss, Kath. I think once you come home and get back into your old life, you'll deal with it better than staying there and wallowing in the emotions."

"Like I said, it's not that simple." She sucked in a harsh breath. "I have to stay for another four weeks or my sister and her husband lose the family farm."

Dead silence greeted her statement.

"Evelyn? Are you still there?" Kathy put on her blinker, then turned onto the road that led to Isaac's farm.

"I'm still here, but I don't think I heard you correctly. You didn't just say you are staying another four weeks, did you? That's not possible. Your career can't take that kind of hit. You must return in the next few days to sign the papers for this new series with Jacques. At the most, I might be able to hold the producer off for a week, but that's it. Not a month."

Kathy bit her lip, not sure what to say. She still felt torn between the two lives, but she knew now with absolute certainty what her decision must be. "I'm sorry, Evelyn. I know this is putting you in a tight place with everyone, but I'm not coming back in the next few days or the next week. I have to stay the full four weeks. Like I said, my father put it in his will that if I don't stay here, the farm is to be sold. Miriam, Amos, and their children will have to leave the only home she has ever known."

"Change can be good, you know." Evelyn's voice sounded as though she was choking out the words. "Your sister must be very selfish to expect you to place your career in danger so she can keep her farm." Sarcasm dripped from the last few words.

Kathy gripped the steering wheel hard. "She didn't demand that I stay. I offered. Actually, I haven't told her I would for sure yet. I'm going to see the arbitrator tomorrow to sign my half over to her so the farm stays in the family."

"Deed your half over? Are you crazy?" Evelyn's voice rose several notches. "Sell it, give her a little extra money so she can start over somewhere else, and hit the road, girl. This is ridiculous. You're staying for four weeks because your dead father demanded it in his will, and you're giving your half to your sister after you make that kind of sacrifice? I can't believe this!"

"Evelyn, we'll talk another time." Kathy glanced at the clock on her dashboard. "I'm sorry I've upset you, but this is the way it's going to be, and it won't change. I will make sure my sister and her family retain our family's farm, even if that means I say no to the TV series. I wasn't sure I wanted to do it anyway. All I ever wanted to do was write, and even that has turned into so much more than I ever bargained for."

"You're turning the series down? I can't believe this! Kathy, promise me you'll take a few more days to think this through. I'll see if I can buy you a little more time. Jacques's agent knows your father died, so she'll have at least a degree of empathy. Don't give me a no yet, please?"

Kathy sighed. "Fine. I won't say no yet. But I don't want to give you false hope, either."

"Right. I get that. I'm sorry for pushing so hard.

You're probably tired and distraught over everything that's happened. This will all seem better in a few days, I promise. I'll call you then, all right? Until then, please try to rest and relax. Look at this as the vacation that you've needed. When you return, you'll be ready to jump back into work. I'll be thinking of you, darling. Ta-ta!"

The line went dead. She was glad she hadn't driven too big of a wedge between herself and Evelyn. She really did care about her agent. The woman had done so much to help and train her when she was young and green, and she wouldn't forget that. But neither would she allow her or anyone else to bully her into a decision she wasn't ready to make.

Isaac sat at his workbench, sanding the top of a side table with long, careful strokes. Varnish would come next, but he must get the surface of the wood as smooth as possible for it to meet the standards people had come to expect of his furniture. He took pride in his work, even if he couldn't take much pride in the home he'd built. Maybe he should be honest with Katrina and let her know his heart still yearned for her. But *nein*. That would be so foolish.

The tires of a car rolled over the gravel outside, and the engine stilled only seconds later. His heart leapt. Could Katrina finally be home? He scowled. This was not her home and never would be, and he must stop thinking that way. He must keep her at arm's length, or his heart would get broken all over again. He dusted his hands off, trying to decide if he would stay here and keep working or be the courteous host and say hello to Katrina. Courtesy. Yes. That was the Amish way. He must not be rude.

He rose from his hard stool and stretched his back. Maybe it was time for a break, anyway. Ambling from the barn, he did his best to keep a calm, neutral expression on his face. It would not do for Katrina to see his feelings.

He slid the big barn door open, happy that the squeak had stopped once he'd oiled the wheels. "Katrina? Do you need help bringing anything into the house?" He took another step out into the sunshine, just in time to see Katrina's face before she disappeared into the house and pulled the door firmly behind her.

Were those tears and red splotches he saw on her cheeks? What could have happened? Should he go to the door and try to comfort her or leave her in peace to work out her problems alone? Maybe the real question should be, did he have the right to comfort her and help her work through her problems?

He stood there, staring at the closed door of his house where the woman he'd once thought he loved stood inside. *Nein.* It was not his place to comfort this woman he no longer knew. The woman who had chosen the *Englisch* way over a life with him.

He spun around and marched back into the barn, then stopped and pulled the door shut, suddenly wishing it would give the loudest squeal possible. The sound would echo his heart. Only silence descended—a silence that made him grind his teeth with frustration. No indeed. He would not go to the house this day to speak to Katrina. Whatever was wrong, it was not his place to interfere.

Kathy had heard Isaac call her name, but she hadn't

had the courage to turn and face him, not with her cheeks all blotchy from crying on the way home after hanging up with Evelyn. Why did life have to be so complicated? Why couldn't it be like it was when she was a child? Everything was simple then. Her only complaint had been not being able to read the novels she'd longed to investigate, although she'd done so as she grew older. She'd learned to sneak them into the house and read by candlelight at night in her bedroom.

Sometimes she wondered if her *daed* had suspected what she was doing, but he'd never asked her to hand over her books or confess her sin, so she'd kept on. Then one day, the longing and the guilt combined until it was too much, and she knew it was time to leave.

If her parents had been more lenient, if her church community hadn't banned all novels, would her life have been different? Might she have stayed and become Isaac's wife?

She shook her head. It didn't matter now. All that mattered was getting through the next few weeks and returning to her old life. Right now, a nap sounded awfully good. She grabbed a comforter and curled up on the couch, determined to put this day and its challenges out of her mind, even if only for an hour or two.

A few minutes later, she sat up. Naps in the middle of the day weren't her thing and never had been—she always seemed to wake up less rested than when she laid down. Pushing to her feet, she looked around. Nothing sounded good at the moment. Her gaze rested on the bookcase, and she stepped closer, then plucked a volume of Keats' poetry off the shelf. Isaac had unusual taste for a man. Interesting. She hadn't known this side of him as a teenager.

She flipped through the pages and something fell

out, hitting the floor with a soft thump. Bending over, she retrieved a small booklet that appeared to only have a couple dozen pages or so. She set the volume of Keats on the couch and sank down next to it, her attention drawn to the slender notebook. Opening it, she perused the neat, small handwriting. It appeared to be a selection of handwritten poems. Had someone left it here after their visit? If so, she should give it to Isaac so he could try to find the owner.

Bending closer to study the first poem, she blinked. This wasn't a copy of any of Keats' works, or anyone else's that she was familiar with, and she was fairly widely read when it came to poetry. Interesting. This one was quite good. Passion and longing were woven into the lines. Subtle, but still there if one had eyes and a heart to see it.

She tucked the volume of Keats beside her, then lay back on the couch, spreading a light throw over her legs and pulling it up to her chest. Better not get used to this life of leisure, as it wouldn't last long, but she planned to enjoy this next hour regardless. She read another three poems, enjoying each one more than the last, until her body relaxed and her eyes grew heavy. The light coming through the window dimmed as the sun lowered in the sky, no longer casting a golden glow through the panes.

She snuggled deeper under the throw and sighed, then laid the small booklet on her chest and allowed her eyes to close for just a minute or two. Then she'd make herself get up and find something productive to do.

Chapter Thirteen

THE WANING LIGHT WAS MAKING IT more difficult for Isaac to do the quality work on this armoire that he demanded of himself. He'd enjoyed being outside in the sun for the past hour, and he'd secretly hoped he might get a glimpse of Katrina. Maybe chopping a little wood for Katrina's fireplace would be a *gutt* idea. Then he could take it to the door and let her know he could start a fire for her this evening, if the house became chilled.

He already had a stack of wood beside his cabin, but the exercise sounded inviting. He grabbed his heavy splitting maul and set a short piece of wood on the chopping block, bringing the maul down on the end of it. A sense of satisfaction filled him at the perfectly placed strike as the wood broke apart. He repositioned the split half and broke it and then the other half into more pieces. Finally, he took one piece with straight grain and split off a dozen or so pieces of kindling. That would be perfect. The wood was dry and should make a warm fire for Katrina.

The side door opened, and she stepped out, yawning and gazing his direction. "Isaac? What are you doing? I heard banging out here and wasn't sure what was going on."

"Earlier, I was working on a new armoire, then I decided to chop wood for your fire, in case it grows cold tonight." He bent over and gathered the kindling. "I will bring it in for you and lay the fire, if you would like." He narrowed his eyes and looked at her more closely. "Did I wake you?"

She stepped down off the porch and walked over, gazing at the equipment just inside his open workshop door and holding a covered bowl in one hand. "Is that a power tool?"

"It is." He smiled at what appeared to be confusion clouding her face.

"But we ... you aren't allowed to use electricity."

"*Ya.* I do not use electricity. The ones I use are powered by air, driven by a diesel motor. Many of our people are using these now, although many still do much the old way. I have areas of my furniture making that I will only do by hand. The dovetails, for example. They are a sign of a good craftsman." He waved his hand in the air. "You did not come out here to talk shop. You were sleeping? I hope you are well?"

"A short rest, that's all. You are quite the modern Amishman, aren't you?" She walked through the large sliding door into the barn he used as a workshop. "You made all these pieces?" Her eyes grew wide as she walked from one of his projects to another. She touched a small, delicate desk he was working on for a woman client who had given him very exacting instructions. "Desks, armoires, end tables ... these are all stunning. The wood, the finish, the eye to detail. These are works of art, not furniture. I had no idea you were so talented, Isaac." Her hand stroked the top of the desk as she turned admiring eyes his way.

He shrugged. "I don't see it that way. I do my best to make my customers happy and to make a living for Sadie and me. My *daed* taught me that if I was going to do a job, I should do it with my whole heart and as unto the Lord, so that is what I do."

"You made all of these? You don't have anyone who helps?" She turned in a circle, taking in the projects he had sitting in various places, all at different levels of completion.

He laughed. "You don't see anyone else here, do

you? No. I don't have help. I do each piece from start to finish. Sadie plagues me from time to time to allow her to help. I make small things for her to sand or varnish, so she feels included. Other than that, it is only me." He touched the armoire close by. "Do not fall in love."

She swung to face him, her eyes wide. "What?"

Realizing how that must have sounded, he struggled to get the explanation out and almost tripped over his words. "Do not fall in love with any of these pieces. They are all spoken for, and each one has a deposit that has been paid on it."

"Oh. That makes sense. Although I would love to have that desk ..." She touched the surface with a gentle hand. "How did you start? Where did you find your customers? Do you have a store in town?"

"*Nein.* One of my regulars who rents the house for two weeks each year is a well-known interior designer from New York. He saw a couple of my pieces in the house and asked who made them. When I told him I did, he put in an order and has been ordering ever since. I assume word spread due to his purchases, as I now have a waiting list. I am beginning to worry I won't be able to fill all the orders on time, as they seem to keep coming in. But that is a *gutt* thing, *ya*? Too much work instead of too little? I am thankful for the orders, but it is hard work." He smiled at her, hoping she wouldn't think he was bragging or complaining.

"Yeah, I get that. Hey, I was experimenting with a bit of cooking, and made a dish I thought you might like to try." She walked over and handed him the small covered bowl.

He raised the bowl and sniffed. "What is it?"

"It's a Moroccan dish. I learned how to make it when I was there for one of my books. I used your eggs and a few other ingredients I picked up at the market."

He raised one brow. "It sounds a bit ... worldly to me. I am used to simple Amish dishes. Nothing fancy. But *denke* for thinking of me."

"It isn't fancy. In fact, it was very simple to make."

"I suppose I have little interest in foreign foods."

"How do you know when you've never tried any? Don't you ever have a desire to travel? To see things beyond your limited experience here?" Her arm swept out, and curiosity brimmed in her eyes.

"I am very happy here. Besides, you know that traveling the world is not our way. Everything I need is here in Cave City or on my property. I have my work, my home, my daughter, my church, my friends. What more is there?" He eyed Katrina when she didn't respond, wondering if he'd wounded her by his blunt answer. He pried the lid off the bowl and sniffed it, then took a pinch of the food and placed it in his mouth. He kept his face as neutral as he could, but his tongue was on fire. "It is a little..."

"Spicy?" She bit her lip as though trying not to giggle. "That's how it's supposed to taste, silly."

"If you say so."

She reached out and took the bowl from his hand, then lifted a piece out and put it in her mouth. Almost immediately, she spit it out. "Yikes!"

He grinned. "Too spicy?"

"Uh, yeah. I guess the pinch they suggested was supposed to only be a real pinch, not a teaspoon." She wrinkled her nose.

This time he laughed. "I have not eaten yet. I got too busy. How does bacon and eggs sound? I will cook. I know it is not breakfast time, but ..."

"Perfect. It sounds perfect. Especially if you're cooking." She stepped over and slipped her hand through his arm. "Your place or mine?" She gazed up into his eyes and grinned. Somehow, he felt transported back at least ten years in time, and all the pain and frustration of the past few years fell away. He blinked. Hard. This was no time to lose his head. He'd like nothing more than to lean over and kiss this woman, but it would not be right. She was an *Englischer* now. Their worlds could not cross.

He turned away and pointed toward his cabin. "Would you mind coming to my cabin? I told Sadie to get in bed, but I don't want to leave her alone any longer. She had dinner a couple of hours ago, but I got so busy working, I didn't bother to eat. I am afraid I am not always the best father."

"Oh. Sure. No problem. Why don't you go check on her, and I'll be right over. I want to grab something in the house first."

He nodded. "Sounds *gutt*. I will get the bacon going."

A few minutes later, Kathy tiptoed into Isaac's cabin, not knowing if Sadie was asleep and hating to wake the child. It was the first time she'd been inside, and she allowed her eyes to adjust to the light from three separate lanterns casting their soft glow over the small kitchen.

The house appeared to be very basic—a living area with a kitchen in one corner and a small wooden table with four chairs between the two areas. A closed door was set in a far wall, and a set of steps led up to what appeared to be a loft. The glow of a lantern shone from over the edge. Kathy nodded toward the upstairs area but kept her voice low. "Is Sadie sleeping up there?"

"Yes, and *denke* for talking softly, but it is not really

necessary." Isaac spoke in a normal tone while he lifted the bacon out of the pan and laid it on folded paper towels. "Sadie is such a sound sleeper, I have to almost shake her awake in the morning to get up for school. I could drop a tin bucket next to her bed, and she wouldn't stir."

"Oh, good. I'm glad. I would have enjoyed seeing her before she went to sleep, but I'm thankful my presence won't wake her."

"It will be our secret that you had dinner with me tonight. She would not forgive me if she knew you were here and I didn't wake her so she could join us." He leaned back in his chair and grinned. "She may only be a small child, but she is a grown tyrant at times in her heart. When she wants something, she is very determined to find a way to attain it."

"That sounds like someone else I used to know." She shot him her sassiest grin. "I remember when you wanted to go fishing one morning, and your *daed* said you had to do your chores before we could go. I never heard a boy make so many good arguments why he should be allowed to fish and help supply meat to the family table as you did that day."

Isaac chucked as he cracked eggs into a stoneware bowl and began to whip them. "Ah, but that was a true statement. As I recall, when we finally were allowed to go—"

"After you got your chores done with me helping—"

"As I was saying. When we were allowed to go, I brought back a very nice string of trout, and we ate several of them for supper that night."

Kathy planted her hands on her hips, amused indignation rising in her throat and bubbling out in a laugh. "And who was it that caught most of those trout, I'd like to know?"

He had the grace to appear sheepish. "I suppose you contributed a few."

She grabbed a dishtowel from a nearby rack and flipped it at him, catching his arm with the tail of the towel. "The truth, Mr. Mast, or I'll have to smack you again."

"All right, I surrender!" He held up his hands and grinned. "You caught most of them, and you were so nice, you did not even tell my *daed* that."

"I may be some things, but I'm not stupid. If he thought you caught most of them, he was more apt to let you go again." Kathy hadn't felt this good—this right—in years. Maybe it was the memories this conversation evoked. Maybe it was being here with Isaac—she couldn't be sure. Whatever it was, she didn't want it to stop.

She lowered herself into the chair across from him and bowed her head a second after he did to offer silent thanksgiving for their meal. Picking up her fork, she dug into the eggs, then picked up a crisp piece of bacon and took a bite. "Yum. You always were a better cook than me. This is perfection." She waved the remaining piece of bacon in the air. "I'm glad I didn't try to force that spicy dish on you, and you offered to cook this instead. It's ever so much better than mine."

"It is not that hard to cook bacon and scrambled eggs." He took a bite of eggs, then sipped his coffee. They sat in peaceful silence for a few minutes as they finished their meal. "Yours was not so bad. I imagine if you had not put in quite so much spice, it might have been … *gutt*." He pressed his lips together as though suppressing a grin. "In all seriousness, I would be happy to try your dish again when you get the recipe right."

"No worries. I have no desire to try that one again.

I'm pretty content with good old-fashioned Amish food at the moment."

This time he did grin, and it lit up his face. "I would guess that *Englischers* eat this food as well, *ya*? I do not think bacon and eggs can be called Amish food."

She pointed her fork at him. "Right now, it's Amish food because an Amish gentleman cooked it for this *Englisch* lady. *Denke* for that, by the way."

His face sobered. "You are welcome, Katrina. Always."

She cleared her throat and looked away, not sure where to put her gaze. His eyes seemed to speak to her—if only she could understand exactly what they were saying. There was a mixture of ... what? Longing? Compassion? Something else? And what did all that mean, and most of all, what, if anything, should she do about it?

She shook her head and put her hand in her pocket, then pulled out the small booklet of poems. "I found this in the house. Have you seen it before?"

He leaned back in his chair and crossed his arms over his chest. "What is it?"

"I was restless and needed something to do, so I was poking through your bookcase. This fell out of a volume of Keats."

"My renters have left a variety of things behind over the years." His expressionless face told Kathy nothing.

"I don't think a renter left this, unless you've rented the house to Amish as well as *Englischers*. Most of them are about Amish life, or the dreams of someone who sounds Amish. I was up late reading this before I fell asleep."

"That bad, huh? It put you to sleep?"

Kathy narrowed her eyes. Was he hiding something? Could he possibly know who this belonged to and wanted to protect their identity for some reason? "On the contrary. It was like stumbling on the forgotten works of a master poet. I've never seen the Amish experience expressed with such simple, beautiful language. I'm dying to know who wrote them."

He rose from the table and started clearing the dishes. She began to rise, but he held up his hand before turning back to the sink. "Sit. This is an easy job, and there is no room for both of us at the sink. This farm was in my wife's family for generations. After we built the house, we found many things in the *Daadi Haus* and moved them here. This cover seems worn from old age or much handling. Perhaps it belonged to one of Ruth's ancestors."

"I honestly can't imagine any older Amish person writing poetry. I can't really imagine any of the Amish in our community writing it either. But I'd love to meet whoever did so. The poems are lovely and should be published."

He kept his back to her, but his words came clearly over his shoulder. "That is foolish. No one would want to read the words of an Amish poet, if such a thing even exists."

Kathy wasn't sure what had happened, but Isaac had withdrawn after their conversation about the booklet. She had put it back in her pocket, sipped at her coffee in the silence, then said her goodbyes and headed back to the house. Now, she sat in the lamplight staring at nothing. She felt so unsettled. So unsure of herself. It had been years—her teen years, in fact—since she'd experienced this type of confusion.

There must be something she could do besides

read. As much as she loved it, she couldn't see herself sitting with her feet up and a book in her hands for the next four weeks. She stood and paced the area downstairs until her gaze landed on the small quilt she'd brought back from the *Daadi Haus*. She plucked it from the back of the rocker where she'd placed it and held it against her chest. An idea began to percolate, but she'd need supplies. Maybe...

Chapter Fourteen

EARLY THE NEXT AFTERNOON, KATHY UNLOADED a box from her car and jogged up the path to the house, eager to get started. She unpacked it, laying different pieces of fabric, needles and thread, scissors, and other quilting supplies on the kitchen table. She'd need a quilting frame at some point, but by then she'd be back at Sarah's and could use hers, if she had one.

It had been years, but it should be like riding a bike, right? Once you learned to quilt, you didn't forget. She carefully cut a variety of squares, laid them out in a pattern, then stood back to survey her handiwork. "Not bad. Now to see if my fingers aren't all thumbs and I can do the tiny, neat stitches I used to do."

It took her a couple of tries and one or two poked fingers, but the remembered skills returned in short order. She hummed a song, making the needed stitches, all the while thinking about the strange expression on Isaac's face when he'd turned his back on her to wash the dishes. She was certain of it now. He had written the poems and was trying to hide it.

"Ouch." She put her stinging finger in her mouth. Maybe she shouldn't be trying to work with a needle when her mind was on something else. She picked up the little booklet again, then thought better of it. Hurrying to the bathroom, she opened the cabinet above the sink. The last thing she wanted to do was get blood on the old book that appeared as though it could be an antique. She wrapped her finger, then headed back to the living room, settling in to read through the poems one more time.

Her eyes reached one of her favorite parts that somehow stirred a dim memory.

> We play in the shadows of giants turned to stone,
> Behind green hills, where two can be alone...

She jumped to her feet. "Wait! I know this place. I'm sure I do." She glanced at her phone. Still plenty of daylight left. She grabbed her keys with one hand while holding the booklet with the other and raced for her car.

Twenty minutes later, she pulled off to the side of the road, wondering if her memory had brought her to the right spot. She stepped out of the car, looking at the overgrown landscape, brush, rocks, and trees obscuring her view from what lay beyond the edge of the road. She walked along the edge of the road, peering through the grass and low brush. "Ah. Found you." A faint path, barely discernable unless a person was searching for it, meandered through the bushes. She pushed her way through and followed along it, certain now that she could find her way.

A brisk five-minute walk brought her out of a copse of trees and into the bright sunlight of a green meadow. Wildflowers dotted the edge of the meadow and birds trilled their song overhead. Peace permeated the place, and she stood for a moment, drinking it in. Then she walked with purpose across the meadow, heading directly for the headstones a few yards away. Some were old, leaning a bit like an old man swaying on his feet. Others were small, denoting a life that had ended too young. A few were dotted with fresh flowers, others with ones so wilted she couldn't tell for sure what variety they were.

Headstones dated back as far as the 1800s and as new as the late 1900s. It appeared this area was no longer used for burials, but it appeared to still be well tended and cared for. She traced a finger on one marker. *Dearly loved and always missed.*

The words from the poem came back.

We play in the shadows of giants turned to stone...

She glanced behind her at the rolling green hills in the distance.

Behind green hills, where two can be alone...

Kathy took a few steps, moving past the last headstone, then stopped to stare at a pond not far ahead. The afternoon sunlight sparkled and shimmered off the still surface of the water. She slipped the booklet out of her pocket and checked the next line.

Light splatters like an egg on the surface of the water...

The sunset has nothing on a farmer's daughter.

She stood for a moment, staring at the pond, then back at the book. She sank down onto a flat rock on the edge of the pond as the memories of her fourteenth year flooded her mind.

She hid behind a large, very old gravestone, her bookbag slung over her shoulder. Carefully she peeked around the marker, trying not to giggle. She heard the crunch of footsteps on fallen leaves, brittle with the now cold nights.

"Kumm on, Katrina. Where are you?" Isaac's voice

echoed through the cemetery, seeming to bounce off the headstones. "You had better kumm out. The ghosts of our great-grandfathers might rise from the graves to haunt us if we stay any longer, like the ghosts in the Englisch stories you've told me about."

Katrina shivered at the words, suddenly wondering if she should have hidden in a cemetery. She peeked again, but still no sign of Isaac. Where could he be that she could hear him so clearly but not see him? Maybe it was time to go home.

"Boo!"

Katrina jumped and screamed, then whirled toward Isaac.

He doubled over laughing, then sank onto the ground and slipped his shoes back on. "The leaves were crunching too much with these shoes, so I thought I might be able to sneak up on you if I took them off. I guess it worked." He held out his hand, all the while wearing a cocky grin.

She reached out and grasped his hand, helping him to his feet. An awareness she'd never had of Isaac before caused her to drop his hand and take a step back. What had just happened? "That was not kind, Isaac."

"No, but it was fun. You were only scared for a second or two until you saw me, so no harm was done. Kumm." He beckoned toward the pond. "Let's see who can skip rocks the farthest."

"You always win." Katrina perched on a rock, smoothed her skirts out around her, then withdrew a book from her bookbag and opened it.

Isaac peered at the cover. "Around the World in Ninety Days?" He shook his head. "They are going to catch you one of these days, then you will be in awful trouble."

"Don't be silly. This book was written one hundred years ago. There is nothing sinful in it."

"That doesn't matter, and you know it." Isaac tossed a flat rock underhand and watched it skip three times across the calm surface of the pond before it sank out of sight. "You shouldn't have gotten that library card. Who knows what you might find that is sinful?"

She hunched a shoulder and flipped a page without looking up. "Maybe I don't care if I find something. Maybe I want to see what I do find."

He turned a shocked face toward her, and Katrina's heart skipped a beat. Isaac shook his head. "What could you possibly hope to find? Everything we need is here in the place we were born."

"For you, maybe. Think of our ancestors, the founders who came here generations ago. They were explorers who came from a different place. Why is it so bad to want to explore the world beyond our Amish boundaries?" She motioned toward the cemetery. "They came all the way from Europe. I can't imagine never seeing anything beyond Cave City. Don't you want to see where our ancestors came from?"

"It's probably not so great if they decided to leave and come here." He threw another rock with more energy this time, and Katrina watched it skip four times. "We'd better get going. I don't want to miss supper or get in trouble for staying too late. It will be dark soon."

"Please wait? I want to see the sunset." Katrina glanced up at him, putting all her longing into her voice and eyes.

Isaac sank down beside her on the flat rock. "Okay, okay." He huffed a breath. "You wouldn't really leave, would you, Katrina?" He reached over and took her hand, cradling it in his.

"I don't know," she whispered in a soft voice. "I guess I'll have to see."

Kathy lifted her head from the book of poetry and gazed at the horizon, where the sun was setting in a brilliant flash of gold and crimson. "Isaac..."

The sunset had disappeared as Kathy pulled into Isaac's parking area. She switched off the ignition and reached for the little book. She wasn't going to put this off any longer—she must talk to Isaac. She swung out of the car, shutting the door quietly behind her, then walked to his cabin. Raising her hand to knock, she hesitated. Voices drifted through the open window a couple of yards from the door.

"This poem is called 'The Singing Rooster.'" Isaac's voice grew more distinct as Kathy walked closer to the window.

"Did you write it for me?" The young, sweet sound of Sadie's voice met Kathy's ears.

"Just for you, sweetheart. Here, let me tuck your covers around your shoulders. It's a little cool tonight. Close your eyes and listen."

"Okay, Papa. My eyes are shut, and I'm listening."

"The rooster sings at daybreak,
But why not sing at night?
Is he praying over supper?
Is he hiding out of sight?
Is he tucking in his chickies?
Is he raising them up right?
To learn the family song,
At dawn's first early light?"

"One more, Papa? Please?"

"I told you that was the last one. It's time to sleep now. No more talking or there will be no poems or stories tomorrow at bedtime."

"Yes, Papa. I love you."

"I love you too, Sadie. Goodnight."

Kathy smiled as she clearly heard the sound of a kiss drift through the window. It must be Sadie kissing Isaac, as it had a distinctly childlike smacking quality.

She waited a couple of minutes, then walked back to the cabin door and softly rapped, not wanting to disturb Sadie.

Isaac pulled open the door, his startled expression changing to one of humor. "Did you come to ask for the generator after all?" He glanced over at the dark house.

"No." She held up the small booklet. "I came to talk. About this. I know you wrote it."

He gave her a long, intent look, then sighed. "Let's talk outside."

Isaac glanced at Kathy in the dim light filtering through his kitchen window as they sat in wooden chairs outside, bundled up in warm coats against the evening chill. "How did you find out?" Dismay hit him hard. He'd hoped this secret would never be uncovered.

She arched her brows. "'We play in the shadows of giants turned to stone...'"

He winced. "I wrote that as an older teenager. It hasn't aged well."

"You were writing poetry when we were kids? Why didn't you tell me? I can't believe you'd keep that a secret from me."

He shifted in his seat, even more uncomfortable than he'd been minutes ago, and he wouldn't have thought that possible. "You weren't the only one sneaking library books. You loved reading so much, I figured there must be something to it. When I discovered poetry, it was like ... discovering myself. I didn't build up the courage to try my own hand at it until well after you left." He hung his head. "I think that's when all my emotions began pouring out through my pen and onto paper."

"But why didn't you tell me? I was your best friend. I wouldn't have made fun of you or told on you. Didn't you think you could trust me?"

He shrugged. "You know the Amish don't believe in self-expression. Our parish isn't nearly as conservative as some, but many in the community would not speak kindly about my writing. Or me. I didn't want to dishonor my family by doing something against the *Ordnung*."

"I can't believe you didn't think you could tell me."

"You left, Katrina." He let the words settle in the stillness around him, then wondered if he should have said something so harsh. But it was true, *ya*? "Sadie and Ruth are the only ones who have ever known about my poetry. I choose to keep it private. My poems aren't for the public, they are only for me—and for Sadie, as long as she cares to hear them. I have never intended for others to read them."

An expression of incredulity covered Katrina's face. "These are wonderful." She held up the little book and shook it almost in his face. "They should be published. You have a gift, and it should be shared with the world. I meant it when I said these should be recognized. *You* should be recognized."

He drew back in his chair, wishing he could get up and bolt away from her. Run and hide, the way she had done when they were young. Instead, he forced himself to relax and do nothing. "*Nein.* Sharing these poems would scandalize our Amish community. I could be shunned. I am content with my life, Katrina. I do not wish for change, or to live an *Englisch* life as you do. Of this I am certain."

She seemed to take time to digest his words, then nodded. "All right. I don't agree, and I can't say I even understand. But I won't push you on this." She held out the booklet to him, her hand visibly shaking.

"You keep it for now. If you want to read it again, you may. But remember, I am trusting you, Katrina."

She nodded and tucked the little book into her jacket pocket. "Goodnight, Isaac."

His heart seemed to die a little as she walked away toward his home. "Goodnight, Katrina." His voice was barely a whisper as she shut the door behind her.

Kathy lay in bed with a lantern lit beside her. She read the last few lines of the final poem in the booklet for the third time, then set it on the nightstand with a sigh. "So good. Amazing, actually."

She bit her lip, wondering, thinking ... would it be so wrong? She hadn't promised to never show anyone, only that she wouldn't push him to publish them. Powering on her phone, she went to her camera app and snapped pictures of four pages, containing three poems. She hesitated again, then tapped on her text app.

Top secret. Do NOT share these with anyone. Tell me what you think?

She attached the photos, entered Evelyn's name, then waited again. Her finger hovered over the send button, not sure this was the right thing to do.

But she'd told her it was a secret and not to share it, so what was the harm in letting Evelyn read them? It wasn't like she was asking her agent to represent Isaac. These were so special—there was so much emotion attached to this work—they needed to be read by someone besides herself and Sadie, even if no one else ever saw them. Her hand hovered over the screen for a moment, then she hit send.

Chapter Fifteen

KATHY WOKE THE NEXT MORNING TO the clatter of hooves, voices in the distance, and the clang of machinery. She rubbed her eyes. Was it even daylight yet? She sat up and swung her legs over the edge of the bed, noting the early morning sun streaming in the window. Was Isaac hosting a party of some kind, this early in the morning? If she didn't know he already had a barn, she'd think a large group of Amish had come for a barn raising.

She walked to the window and peered through the curtains at the bustling scene outside. Several buggies were parked around the barn while men, women, and children talked, worked, or ran and played in the field to the side of the barn. The women were toting bags and boxes out of the buggies while a couple of men set up tables near the cabin.

In the distance she could see Amos driving a horse-drawn baler as bales of hay tumbled out one side. Isaac and several other men followed behind, hoisting the bales onto a flatbed wagon pulled by a team of four horses.

The sound of pans rattling downstairs reminded Kathy she was in her nightgown and she might need to change. Warmth at the sight of the community working together filled her as she hurried to brush her hair and teeth and ready herself for the day.

A few minutes later, dressed in a pair of jeans and eager to dive in and help wherever she was needed, she headed for her bedroom door. A trilling noise from her nightstand startled her. She'd put her phone in the drawer last night so she wouldn't be awakened.

Rushing over, she opened the drawer and pulled

out the phone, swiping it on at the same time she saw the name. "Good morning, Jacques. Isn't it awfully early for you to be up and working? It's only six a.m. here in Kentucky, so that makes it ... what? Four a.m. in L.A.? It's hard to believe you're up. And what's more, why would you think I'd be up?"

"Yeah, yeah. Good morning to you too. Actually, I'm not up early. I'm up late. We've been editing the *Jacques's Voyages* finale and just finished. The editors didn't find a single camera angle that makes me look good. I figured since you're living the Amish lifestyle now, you'd be up with the birds. Since I rarely get to talk to you anymore, this seemed as good a time as any to call. Did I wake you?"

She laughed. "That's a lot to throw at me first thing in the morning. Sorry to hear you aren't happy with your appearance in the finale, but I think I've heard that before, and your fans are always adoring no matter what. You'll be fine, Jacques."

"Okay, so, moving on. How's home sweet home? Find any good sushi bars around there or a good massage therapist? I can't imagine what you're finding to keep you occupied." His voice was light and teasing, but still held a slightly petulant note.

She rolled her eyes, suddenly realizing there wasn't a lot about L.A. that she missed at the moment. "Very funny. I'm doing well, thanks for asking. And no sushi bars or massages." She glanced at the quilt folded neatly on the top of her bureau. "In fact, I've taken up quilting again in my spare time."

His tone sobered. "I had no idea you were a quilter. It appears there's a lot I still don't know about you, Kath."

She walked over and stroked the small quilt. "My mother was an expert, and I was on my way to being good as a teen, but I'm afraid I'm out of practice."

"Well, you're not going to have time to practice once you're back in L.A. I'll keep you too busy for that. Evelyn says you still haven't given her an answer about the series?" He hesitated for a few seconds, then plunged ahead. "I miss you. A lot. I know you might have to stay a bit longer, from what Evelyn told me, but hey ... how about you catch a weekend flight home? We could get some sun on the beach, drive to Carmel—see a show. Talk. We need to talk, Kath. About a lot of things—not just the show, but about us."

"I know I owe you answers, and I'm sorry I haven't been able to concentrate on much since I've been here. That's not kind or fair to you. I need a little more time." She sank into the rocking chair by the window and stared out at the people intent on doing a variety of jobs. Laughter rang out, voices chattered, and children shouted.

"Yeah, that's what you've said before. How much time? It's already been longer than I expected. I'm getting impatient, Kathy. I need answers."

"I'm not sure how to explain. Since I've been here, away from the noise and craziness of L.A., I've been able to think. Really think. I've even prayed, Jacques. I know you don't do the whole church scene, but you believe in God, right? I mean, this is the first time in years I've felt a deep sense of peace. It's hard to explain, but I'm not ready to let go of this until I figure out what I really want for my life. My family needs to come first right now. You can understand that, can't you?"

"Kathy, I love you..."

"Kathy? Are you up there?" Hazel's voice echoed up the stairs. "Sarah and I are coming up, so you'd better be decent."

"Jacques, I'm sorry to run, but I have to go."

"Wait—darling—I need an answer..."

"I'll call you when it's a better time. 'Bye!" Guilt niggled at the edge of her mind as she hit the end button to cancel the call before he could say anything more. He'd told her he loved her in the past, but she'd never said it to him. Somehow, this time felt different. More intense. More insistent. It couldn't be helped. She was in no position to make a commitment to anyone right now.

"Ka-trin-a!" Hazel's voice was followed by a sharp rap. "Are you decent?"

"Yes, come in." Kathy swung the door wide to see her cousins standing side by side in the hall. "What's going on outside? I know Isaac doesn't need a barn, and I see they're cutting and baling hay, but why? He's a woodworker. I mean, he makes stunning furniture, so why is he bothering with hay?"

Sarah shook her head and laughed. "Because he owns a farm, even if he does make furniture. Every year, he invites the men over to help him cut and bale the fields. He tells everyone to bring a wagon and take hay home, and he keeps what's left for his own livestock. If it were left up to him, it would rot in the field. They cut it a week ago, then he turned the hay a couple of times so it would cure, and now they're baling it."

Kathy smiled. "I'd almost forgotten what a caring community we live in." She ducked her head. "I mean, you all live in."

Sarah tossed a knowing glance at Hazel. "The women are using Isaac's cabin to prepare lunch for later, but the kitchen is very tiny. Would you mind terribly if a few of us take over your kitchen as well?"

Hazel snickered. "Actually, only two or three will stay at Isaac's and the rest will need to move over here."

She pursed her lips. "I should tell you that Miriam is here."

Kathy nodded. "I saw Amos in the field helping, so I figured she and the children would be here as well."

"Would you like to help us prepare the meal?" Sarah reached out and touched Kathy's arm as though to reassure her of her welcome.

"I'm guessing Miriam won't like that." Kathy shot a glance at the stairwell where a door opened and shut, and the sound of women's voices increased.

Hazel sniffed. "You might seem like an *Englischer*, but you're still one of us, whether you like it or not, Katrina. It is not like you joined the church then left and were shunned."

"I don't know, Hazel. I'd hate to upset her again. She's already angry at me."

Sarah shook her head. "I don't think she'll say much in front of the other women. It might be a chance to get on her good side."

Kathy snorted a laugh. "Or not."

Hazel nodded. "Or not. But you won't know if you don't try. However…" She looked Kathy up and down.

"What?" Kathy crossed her arms over her chest.

"Your wardrobe. It might go over better with everyone if you were a bit more modestly dressed?"

Kathy glanced down at her t-shirt and jeans. "I think I brought a dress or a skirt. Let me check my closet." She headed for the other side of the room.

"Wait." Hazel held up her hand. "I may have brought something with me that might fit you." Her lips quirked to the side. "Before I left my house, I was thinking about the fact that you might make a better impression if I brought you something a bit more appropriate. Wait right here. I'll hurry."

Kathy looked at Sarah, who shrugged. "She didn't

tell me what she brought. I guess we both will find out at the same time."

"While we wait, is Jeremiah here? And how about Gabe? Is he still in town?"

"*Nein.* Gabe left the same day he came to see me." She bowed her head for a moment, then raised her chin. "I haven't seen Jeremiah since that day when he walked off my porch without coming in. But *ya*, he will be here later today. I heard the bishop say so to one of the men."

Kathy brightened. "Maybe we can make it so the two of you happen to sit next to each other at dinner." She rubbed her hands. "I used to be somewhat of a matchmaker."

"*Nein.*" Sarah took a step away and the color left her cheeks. "No matchmaking. If *Gott* is not in this, or if Jeremiah has no desire to court me any longer because he saw Gabe visit me, then so be it. I will not pursue him."

"I'm sorry, Sarah. I didn't mean to push. I won't say another word about it." She stepped close and put an arm around Sarah's shoulders and gave her a squeeze, then stepped back when she heard Hazel's steps thumping up the stairs.

Hazel burst into the room and laid a long bag on the bed. "We will go downstairs. Change and *kumm* down as soon as you finish. I will tell the women you are going to help, so it will prepare Miriam—and others—for your arrival."

"That bad, huh?" Kathy let out a little groan. "Maybe I'd better stay in my room for the day and work on my next book."

"*Nein.* You will not huddle up here in your room and allow Miriam to keep you away from old friends and neighbors." She nodded toward the bed. "We'll go now. You change. Do not dilly-dally, Katrina."

Kathy wanted to giggle and snap a salute, but she only nodded and waited for the door to shut behind her.

Thirty minutes later, Kathy walked slowly down the staircase, wanting nothing more than to run back to her room and hide. She was a charlatan. A sham. Wearing this beautiful lavender Amish dress with the crisp white apron and *Kapp*. What was Hazel thinking to bring this and expect her to wear it? She and Sarah had probably given up on her ever coming down, but it had taken her fifteen minutes to decide whether or not to don the outfit, then ten minutes to get into it all and pin up her hair to fit under the *Kapp*, and another five minutes to wonder who she'd become. Was she Katrina Yoder, the girl who had loved the Amish life when she was a youngster, or Kathy Yoder, world traveler and successful writer?

Someone must have heard her coming down the stairs, as Sarah poked her head into the foyer and then hurried to meet Kathy at the bottom of the stairs. "You are lovely. Hazel is a sneaky one, *ya*?"

"*Ya*, I would say so." Kathy wasn't sure if she wanted to giggle or throw up from nerves.

"*Kumm*. I will stay beside you when we go into the kitchen." She walked right next to Kathy, and when they arrived at the kitchen door, she cleared her throat. The room fell silent, and Sarah beamed at the women doing a variety of tasks at the table, countertops, and stove. "Ladies. I would like to reintroduce you to my cousin and Hazel's, Katrina Yoder. She moved away from the area a few years ago, but she is home now to help settle her father's affairs and see her family."

Several pairs of eyes turned to glance at Miriam, who seemed to make a point of looking away. Kathy noted a few brows raised and more than one brow raised at Miriam. Kathy reached up and fiddled with the strings from her *Kapp*. "Hello, everyone. I recognize many of your faces. It's *gutt* to see you again." She was shocked at how easily she fell back into the cadence and dialect she'd known as a child.

A few of the women stiffened and turned away, but a couple nodded a greeting. One older woman Kathy remembered working at a quilt shop in town came over and gave her a hug. "*Gutt* to see you again, Katrina. Maybe you will stay home where you belong this time, *ya*?" Her smile was kind as she patted Kathy's hand, but the comment hit Kathy and stung.

"Thank you, Mrs. Steinman. I will be here for a few weeks, at least." How could she explain that her father's will was forcing her to stay, or that her heart longed to be accepted by these people again, while another part of her wanted to flee as fast as possible back to L.A., where life suddenly seemed so much less complicated?

Miriam turned, looked Kathy straight in the eyes, sniffed, and went back to her work next to the sink.

Hazel huffed a sigh. "Miriam, I thought Katrina might help you with the potato dumplings, *ya*?"

Miriam pressed her lips together in a hard line and stared at Hazel. "That will not be necessary. I am very aware of Katrina's skills in an Amish kitchen. I can handle the dumplings fine on my own." She flicked a glance at Kathy then back to Hazel. "But thank you for offering, Hazel." She turned back to her work.

Hazel didn't budge from where she stood. "Miriam. Anyone can peel a potato."

Miriam swung back around, a cup of flour in one hand as she stood over a large mixing bowl. "You would think so, *ya?*"

Hazel huffed, her expression darkening. "Miriam, you need to be reasonable."

Kathy looked around at the other women. Most were watching with interest, although a few had tucked their heads and were pretending not to pay attention, but they all had ears, and all were tuned their direction. "It's fine. I'll see if there's somewhere else I can help. I don't need to stay in the kitchen." She shot Hazel a look, giving a small shake of her head.

"Fine. There are more potatoes in my buggy. If Katrina wants to fetch them, we can put her to work. She can clean them, then we will have her peel potatoes that are ready to mash." Miriam didn't turn away from her work, but her voice carried clearly in the still room.

Kathy smiled at Hazel, who winked at her. A few minutes later, Kathy stood at the sink scrubbing dirty potatoes, then she grabbed a peeler and began work on them.

Miriam swung around. "What are you doing?"

"Peeling the potatoes. Like you said." She pointed at the peel dangling from the potato in her hand.

"The boiled potatoes. We cook them with the skins on to save time. They skin easily after they are cooked and cooled." She pointed at a pot set off to the side. "That pot has cool water in it and should be ready to peel. I did not imagine I would need to walk you through every step of a dish we helped our mother fix hundreds of times." Miriam made a *tsk*ing noise and turned away.

A flood of humiliation swept through Kathy. Right now she wanted to go crawl into her bed and pull the covers over her head for the rest of the day. What was wrong with her sister? Why was she being so harsh all the time? Had it really personally impacted her so much when she left? They had gotten along as sisters growing up, although they'd had their fair share of sisterly spats, but nothing like the Miriam of today.

Kathy lifted the pot of cooling potatoes and set them on the table where she could sit and skin them easily. Maybe if she offered an olive branch, Miriam would calm down and treat her better. "I never had your skill with cooking. You know that. I enjoyed quilting and outdoor activities more than cooking or baking."

Miriam swung on her and dropped her voice to a low whisper. "Cooking does not require skill. It requires patience and the ability to follow the rules. Both are virtues we do not have in common."

Kathy sat stunned at the quiet outburst. "That's not fair. You don't know anything about my life."

Miriam turned away. "I know enough. Once you peel the potatoes, grate them into the bowl, then—"

"I know what to do next. Add them to the dough, and mix them with bread, parsley, onion, eggs. Salt and pepper to taste. Roll them into balls and boil them covered for fifteen minutes before serving." Kathy kept a close eye on her sister, expecting another sarcastic remark at any moment. Instead, she thought she saw something like begrudging respect mirrored in her eyes.

Miriam narrowed her eyes. "If you know the recipe so well, why did you peel the wrong potatoes?"

"Because I made a mistake, Miriam. I'm human. People make mistakes."

Miriam pulled chunks of bread from a pan of cold water and squeezed them until no more water dripped into the pan. "You forgot one thing, however."

"No. I didn't," Kathy said, then she dropped her voice to a whisper. "I didn't say it because I didn't care to share a family secret with the entire kitchen full of women." She glanced around. "You know how some Amish like to gossip."

Miriam glanced at the other women who appeared to be studiously doing their own work. A few chatted quietly, but no one looked their way. She pulled a shaker filled with a red substance out of a nearby drawer. "Mother only added paprika. I blend it with cinnamon and cloves. Amos goes mad for it and the children love it as well."

Kathy smiled. "I have a feeling I will too." She watched Miriam as she sprinkled it over the concoction in the pan and could have sworn she saw a slight smile trying to peek out.

Miriam slipped the container back into the drawer. "I don't know why I even told you. I'm sure you'll never make it on your own. It won't be long, and you'll be back to microwave dinners and eating out. Have you decided what you are going to do?"

"Yes. I'm staying for the full term of *Daed's* will so you don't lose the farm."

Miriam reached out and gripped the edge of the countertop as though to steady herself. "*Denke*. But even so, three weeks or so isn't that long before you return home. Not after ten years of being gone."

Kathy dropped the cold potato back into the water and turned to face her sister. "What if I come back to visit more often?"

Miriam shook her head. "It would not make much difference, Katrina. Your life is not here. It never was." This time, her face registered sadness instead of anger.

Kathy felt a surge of hope. "Maybe so, but—" The shrill ring of her phone laying on a nearby table cut off her words.

Miriam's expression hardened, and she turned away.

Kathy pulled the phone out and swiped it on, irritated at the interruption. "Can I call you back? This isn't a good time."

"Sure," Evelyn said. "Don't forget. 'Bye for now." The phone went dead.

Kathy bit her lip. "Sorry. That was my agent. Miriam..."

"You need to finish the peeling so we can get these into the oven." Miriam didn't so much as glance her way.

Chapter Sixteen

Isaac washed his hands under the outdoor spigot as children chased one another across the yard and the women set the food on the table. He hadn't seen Katrina all day, but then, he'd been out in the fields helping bring in the hay since before she would have risen this morning. He scratched his head. Would she even come out and join them for the meal? The women milled around, putting the finishing touches on the table, but he hadn't seen a single woman in the group wearing jeans or any type of *Englisch* clothes.

Peering past the line of buggies, he tried to see if her car was missing. No. The hood of the car showed in the distance, so she must still be inside. Should he go to the house and invite her to dinner? He hated the idea of her sitting in her room all alone, but she might be worried about how she'd be received by the Amish community.

Someone tapped him on the shoulder, and he turned. Sarah stood there, smiling her usual sweet smile. "Are you looking for Katrina?"

Heat flared in his cheeks as he realized how obvious he must have appeared. "I'd hate to see her go hungry. Do you think I should go to the house and invite her to join us? Have you or Hazel spoken to her today?" He tipped his head toward where Miriam herded her three children to one end of the table. "I see her sister is here."

"*Ya*. She is here. And so is Katrina." She covered her mouth with her fingers, but a giggle escaped. "I think you have a surprise coming, Isaac."

"What are you talking about?" He gazed at her as she walked off, still chuckling. Women. They were no help at all.

Their bishop stood at the head of the table, waiting for people to take their places and settle down. The women took their places at the second table, and the children joined them. Mothers with toddlers not old enough to feed themselves sat with their *bopplies* on their laps. Everyone quieted and the bishop bowed his head. Isaac and the men and older boys around him did the same. Several minutes passed while each offered their own silent prayer, then the bishop cleared his throat and people began passing food around the table.

Isaac ate in silence, still wondering what Sarah had meant about the surprise that was coming. So far, he'd seen nothing that wasn't as it always had been. Dinner was eaten quickly and, for the most part, in silence, other than a small child occasionally speaking to their mother or someone asking for a dish to be passed.

At one point, a teenage boy said something too loudly and his friend responded, laughing as he did so. The bishop stared at the two. "Every time a sheep bleats, it loses a mouthful." The two boys bowed their heads and studied their plates until the bishop returned to his meal.

As usual, each plate was cleaned thoroughly and no one rose to leave until all were finished, then the bishop offered another shorter silent prayer to end the gathering. What would Katrina have thought of all this if she'd chosen to come out to join their meal? Would it seem strange to her, or would it bring back good memories of her growing up years?

Isaac stepped over the bench he'd been sitting on

as both tables emptied and the women and older girls began clearing the plates. He turned and nearly collided with a slender Amish woman wearing a lavender dress and white apron. His eyes widened as he took in... "Katrina? Is that you? Why? What?" He almost sputtered in his confusion. This must be the surprise Sarah had been giggling about. *Ya.* He was surprised. Very. But a *gutt* surprise if he did say so. He had never thought he'd ever see Katrina Yoder dressed in Amish clothing again in this lifetime.

She smiled and dipped her head, acting like a proper unmarried Amish woman. Not too forward, but polite. "Hello, Isaac. It was a very *gutt* meal, *ya*?" Her eyes were dancing, and a smile touched her lips.

"You are teasing me." That should bother him, but somehow, it didn't. "Where did you get your clothing? Is this something you had made by an *Englisch* fashion designer before you came?"

"No. Hazel brought it for me. She thought I might be more comfortable..." She peered over her shoulder toward Miriam, then she lowered her voice. "Actually, I think she believed it would make others more comfortable if I didn't stand out in my jeans and t-shirt. I have to agree, it was a good idea." She smoothed her hand down the apron. "It feels strange, yet somehow, not so strange. Does that make sense?" She cocked her head to the side and smiled.

"Of course. After all, you were Amish for eighteen years until you left. I was thinking of that earlier when we were eating. What you might have thought of the meal if you were here." He smiled. "And all this time, you were sitting at the other table, probably wondering why I hadn't spoken to you."

Miriam walked by and glanced at Katrina but kept

going. Isaac leaned closer to Katrina. "How are things going with your sister? Have you made any progress?"

"I helped her make the dumplings, although I didn't do much besides peel the boiled potatoes."

"Your sister is famous for her dumplings. She uses some kind of special spices that make it different from what the other women make." He waggled his eyebrows at her. "Maybe you could learn something about spices for your fancy foreign dishes from her."

She gave him a coy smile. "Maybe I already did learn something."

His eyes widened. "What is her secret? What spices does she add? I've always thought I detected a hint of cinnamon."

"Isaac Mast! I do not tell family secrets, and you shouldn't ask me to, either."

He grinned. "I was only testing your loyalty."

"Right."

A group of women walked by, glancing at them and whispering. Katrina bobbed her head at them and took a half-step away from him. She must remember how easily gossip could start about an unmarried man and woman, even if he was a widower. She waited until there was no one standing close, then spoke in a low tone. "I read your booklet from beginning to end again. I'd love to discuss a few of the poems, if you have time?"

He took a step back, his jaw muscles tightening. "I must get back to the fields and help the men finish. It was *gutt* to see you, Katrina."

Kathy walked over to where Sarah stood off to the side of the gathering, shielding her eyes against the early afternoon sun. She'd done it again—said something to upset Isaac right when they were starting to fall back into their old camaraderie. Maybe she should forget about that booklet of poems. It wasn't her business, after all.

She reached her cousin's side and touched her shoulder. Sarah startled so hard she jumped. "I'm sorry, Sarah. Is something bothering you?"

"*Nein.*" Sarah turned toward Kathy and closed her eyes for a couple of seconds. "*Ya.* I guess it is so. Jeremiah hasn't arrived yet. I thought he would be here for the noon meal. I do not want to ask the bishop if he knows more, you understand?"

"Totally." After seeing the bishop's displeasure that day at Sarah's inn, she wouldn't want to bring anything more down on her head if she were her cousin, either. "Maybe he had something he needed to take care of, something that took longer than he expected. I wouldn't worry yet."

"I know. It's silly to worry over something I cannot control." She tapped her chest with her fingertips. "Something in here doesn't feel right. I will pray, *ya*? *Gott* will take care of Jeremiah, I am sure."

"That's a good idea, and something I need to think about doing more of myself." Kathy squeezed Sarah's arm to offer comfort, but she could see a layer of anxiety under Sarah's normally calm demeanor. If nothing else, this might help Sarah come to the realization that she did care for this man. Would it be enough for her to allow Jeremiah to court her and for her to possibly marry him? No way of telling on that. But the concern was there for anyone to see.

The sound of galloping hooves swung Kathy and Sarah around at the same time. They were coming too fast to be a horse working in the field. Kathy shaded her eyes and looked up the lane. She nudged Sarah. "Do you know who that is? I think it's an Amish man riding a horse bareback and coming fast."

Sarah gave a little gasp. "That is Jeremiah's cousin, Benjamin." Her entire body began to shake. "What if something has happened to Jeremiah?"

Chapter Seventeen

Kathy wrapped her arm around Sarah's shoulders, wishing she could comfort her more, even though she had no solid proof there was a need for comfort. However, from Sarah's reaction, she thought it was more than possible.

The young man riding the lathered gelding pulled back on the reins, gravel scattering from under the horse's hooves as it slid a few feet before coming to a trembling halt. "Is the bishop here?" The man had lost his hat somewhere along the way, but he didn't seem to notice or care. He slid off the gelding and tossed the reins to a nearby man. "I must speak with him."

Bishop Swarey hurried forward, his calm demeanor still in place. "What is wrong, Benjamin? Catch your breath a minute then explain, please."

Sarah shook her head and mumbled. "*Nein.* Hurry. Hurry."

Benjamin's hands were shaking as he reached for the bishop. "There has been a wreck. Jeremiah ..."

This time the bishop did react. He grabbed the younger man's hand. "What about Jeremiah? Is he all right? What kind of wreck?" He swung around and waved toward a small group of women clustered behind him. "Someone, bring him a glass of water."

Almost instantly a glass was shoved into his hand, which he pressed into Benjamin's. "Drink. Calm yourself, then explain. How far have you ridden? What has happened?"

Benjamin took a few swallows and clutched the glass in a hard grip. "Someone was driving too fast. Jeremiah was on his way here, driving his buggy. He said he hoped to take Sarah for a drive after the gathering today. I think he may have been daydreaming, because his horse drifted over the center of the road. The person coming the other way couldn't slow down enough. He missed the horse, but ..." He winced. "The automobile hit the buggy. Jeremiah was thrown out. The driver stopped and had a cell phone. He called 911. I happened on the accident as the ambulance was arriving. I unhitched my horse so I could arrive fast and let you know." He glanced from the bishop to Sarah, who was visibly trembling in Kathy's arms. "I think he would want you both to *kumm*, if..." He bit his lip and didn't continue, but Kathy knew what he was implying. *If Jeremiah made it.*

"How bad is it?" Sarah stepped out of Kathy's embrace. "He was still alive when they took him? Are they taking him to our local hospital?" She turned to the bishop. "May I *kumm* with you?"

Kathy locked eyes with the bishop. "Sir, it will take a lot longer in your buggy. I have my car here. Please, let me take you and Sarah, and Benjamin if he'd like to come as well? I have room in my car for all of you, and it would be so much faster."

He gave a nod. "*Ya*. We will come with you. *Denke*, Miss Yoder."

Isaac removed his hat and stepped close to Kathy. "I will bring your buggy if you would like me to, Bishop. That way, if Miss Yoder doesn't want to stay as long as you do, you will have a way home."

"*Ya*. That is *gutt*. *Denke*." The bishop turned and headed for Kathy's car.

An hour later, Isaac strode down the hospital corridors toward the waiting room he'd been directed to. Due to the large Amish community in this area, there was a smaller, family waiting area for privacy used when an Amish person was admitted. He rounded a corner and slowed, then entered the open door of the waiting area where the bishop, Benjamin, Sarah, and Katrina all sat in chairs, expressions ranging from stoicism to anxiety.

Katrina looked up and smiled, then patted the empty seat on one side of her. He glanced at Sarah, who sat on Katrina's other side and saw her lips moving in what must be prayer.

He sank into the seat indicated and nodded to the bishop, then leaned close to Katrina's ear, keeping his voice soft. "Have you heard from a doctor yet?"

"No. A nurse came in and said he has a head injury and a broken arm and collarbone. They're getting him stabilized and will let us know when we can see him."

"How is Sarah holding up?" He glanced at Sarah in time to see a tear trickle down her cheek.

"Not good. She's very shaken and frightened."

"I didn't know she cared for him so much. They haven't been officially courting, although I know it was being encouraged." Even though his voice was low, he hoped the sharp ears of the bishop hadn't picked up on his words. He wouldn't want anyone to think he was gossiping.

Katrina smiled. "I don't think she knows she cares for him that much—until today, that is. We need to pray he'll be all right."

"*Ya.* That is what I was doing the entire drive here. Praying hard for him and everyone."

Katrina's lips formed a small frown. "Where is Sadie?"

"I didn't want to bring her with me. Hazel offered to let her go home with her and play with her children, so I agreed. It is a blessing not to have to worry about her in times like this."

A man wearing blue scrubs with a stethoscope around his neck stepped into the room. "Mr. Swarey?" He walked to the bishop.

"*Ya.* That is me." The bishop rose and stood, his hat in his hand. "You have news about my Jeremiah? He is awake?"

The doctor shook his head. "I'm Doctor Stevens, and I'm in charge of the ER today. I was here when your son was brought in. He's stable now, but he's not awake yet."

"Can you tell me exactly what is wrong?" Bishop Swarey stood erect, with nothing but his eyes betraying the worry that must be consuming him. "How long will he need to stay?"

"He sustained a head injury when the car hit his buggy, as well as a couple of broken bones. The bones will heal nicely and aren't an issue, but the head injury is a different story. We're keeping him unconscious, as we're concerned about possible swelling on the brain. We'll know more tomorrow. Anyone who is family can come see him now, but he won't know you or be able to respond."

The bishop turned his gaze on Sarah for several seconds, then seemed to decide something. "There are three of us who would like to *kumm* in. Myself, my nephew, and Sarah." He nodded her direction, leaving no doubt of his resolve.

"We request that only two at a time come in when the patient is in critical condition." The doctor looked from one to the other of the three.

Benjamin stood. "I will stay here. It is more important that our bishop and Sarah go to see Jeremiah."

Sarah stood and touched Benjamin's arm. "*Denke.*" She wiped at a tear on her cheek. "I am ready, Bishop."

They turned and walked out the door after the doctor. Isaac yearned to go with them, to see Jeremiah, who had been his friend for years, but he understood the need for quiet and not many visitors. Right now, the best thing he could do to help would be to continue to pray.

He settled deeper into his chair, then turned to Katrina. "How long do you plan to stay? Now that the bishop's buggy is here, you can go back to the house if you'd like to."

She shook her head. "I think Sarah will need me when she comes back. I'll stay here as long as she does. I'm so sorry this happened! I hope Jeremiah wakes up soon and the head injury isn't serious."

"*Ya.* Me too." More than anything he wanted to take her hand and hold it, to comfort her and let her know he cared, but this wasn't the time. There might never be a proper time, no matter what his heart wanted. He shoved aside the desire, reminding himself over and over that she had walked away from him ten years ago. Nothing had changed. She was only here in their community to fulfill her father's last wishes and to help her sister keep the farm. Both noble decisions, but they didn't change who she was or the life she'd chosen. "Would you like to go to the cafeteria to get coffee or tea?"

"I'd love to, but I don't want to be gone when Sarah comes back."

Benjamin looked up from the farming magazine he'd been glancing through. "I will stay and watch for her. Maybe you could both go and bring coffee back for all of us?"

Isaac stood and held out his hand. Katrina took it and rose, but she didn't let go. Maybe she needed comfort the same as Sarah did? She didn't know

Jeremiah, as far as he knew, but Sarah was her cousin, and she must be worried for her state of mind. He tucked her hand into the crook of his arm to avoid any misunderstanding from anyone nearby. "*Denke*, Benjamin. I remember you like black coffee, *ya*?"

Benjamin nodded. "Sounds good. I didn't get to stay for dinner, so if you see a pastry, can you bring it too?"

"Certainly. Katrina, are you ready to go?"

"Yes. Let's hurry, though. I want to be here when Sarah returns. I don't know how long they'll allow visitors in Jeremiah's room."

A few minutes later, Kathy and Isaac returned to the waiting area, laden down with pastries and coffees. She handed a small bag and a cup to Benjamin, who had stood when they walked in. "Any word?"

"*Nein.*" He took the cup with a smile. "*Denke.* That smells *gutt.*"

"Katrina Yoder?" The bishop's stern voice echoed across the waiting area.

Kathy's head jerked up. "Yes, sir."

"Sarah would like you to *kumm.*"

Kathy's hand flew to cover her heart. "Is everything all right?"

"*Ya.* I told her she should stay with Jeremiah. The doctor says he will not wake up for a while yet, so I am going to take care of a few things then come back. Sarah needs someone with her, and since you are her family, they are making an exception and allowing you to *kumm* in. They are up this hall in Room 201."

"Oh, thank you, Bishop. *Denke.*" She nodded, hoping he would understand how much she appreciated his sacrifice to leave for a while. "I have been praying for Jeremiah."

He gave a short nod as weariness crept into his eyes. "*Denke*, Miss Yoder." He turned to Benjamin and Isaac. "I will return soon. Will both of you stay or do you need a ride back to your homes?"

"I would appreciate a ride, Bishop. If they aren't going to allow anyone else in to see Jeremiah, and they believe he won't regain consciousness soon, then there is little I can do by remaining." Benjamin pushed his hat down hard onto his head. "*Gutt-day* to you, Katrina. Isaac." He headed toward the door.

The bishop looked at Isaac and waited.

"I think I will stay for a while, but thank you for the offer of a ride. I might accept one later." Isaac glanced at Kathy. "Tell Sarah my prayers are with her and Jeremiah."

"I will. I'd better go." She gave Isaac a small smile, then hurried away.

Chapter Eighteen

Kathy tiptoed into the white, sterile ICU room and spotted Sarah sitting next to the bed where Jeremiah lay. Monitors beeped in the background, and a slow-drip IV pole was placed close to the bed, the tube going down to his arm.

Kathy drew close and noted Jeremiah's hand gripped by Sarah's. Tears streaked her cousin's cheeks, and she used the back of her free hand to wipe them away. "Katrina. I am so glad you were still here and willing to *kumm* sit with me. It was fine with the bishop here, but I felt so ... alone. He is silent, *ya*? I think he prayed the entire time he was in the room, as he did not say a word." She glanced at Jeremiah. "He did not even speak to his son." She swiped at another tear that had escaped.

"You know what a private man Bishop Swarey is, Sarah. I'm sure he cares for his son very deeply, but I doubt he will show it in front of anyone else." She drew a chair forward to sit beside Sarah.

"*Ya*, I think you are right. It is hard to know what to do or how to act when he's here. I sat against the wall and let the bishop sit here. As soon as he left, I came to Jeremiah's side and have been talking to him, urging him to get well." She put her fingers over her mouth and choked back a sob. "He cannot die, Katrina. I must have a chance to talk to him."

Kathy put her arm around Sarah's shoulder and pulled her close. "Shh. He's not going to die. The doctor didn't indicate that was a possibility."

"He didn't say he will be okay or that he is not in danger. He said there is swelling on his brain, and they must keep him unconscious. That sounds very bad to me." Sarah straightened and Kathy dropped her arm. "I can't lose him, Katrina."

"You've made a decision to allow him to court you if he recovers?"

Sarah touched Jeremiah's forehead very lightly, moving his hair over to the side. "Ever so much more than that. When I heard he had been injured, I realized I love him. I do not care about the inn anymore. If he wants me to close it, I would do so. He must get well." She cradled his hand in her own again, then picked it up and kissed his knuckles. "He must."

Kathy sat in silence, wanting to comfort Sarah but sensing what she needed right now was quiet support, not a chattering friend. What would it be like to suddenly discover you loved the man you had only thought of as a friend? To realize you wanted to spend your life with him, more than anything else you could wish for?

Her thoughts flitted to Isaac. What would she be feeling right now if it was Isaac lying in this bed? *Fear. Pain. Uncertainty.* But she wouldn't have been asked to come sit with him. The bishop wouldn't have chosen to give up part of his time so that an *Englischer* could sit with him. It was doubtful she'd even be able to see him. Agony gripped her heart as she considered that thought. She had no right to be with Isaac, whether he was injured or going about his life. She had given up that right ten years ago when she walked away.

A hand touched her shoulder, startling her out of her deep musings. "Katrina? I have spoken to you twice. Is all well?"

She raised her chin and met Sarah's eyes. "I'm sorry. I'm fine. What did you say?"

"Do you know when the bishop will return? I think

we have been at the hospital for a few hours now. I have boarders at my house, and I'm not sure if I should stay the night with Jeremiah or go home."

"He said he'd be back soon. I can go to the inn and check on things or spend the night there if you'd like to stay here. Maybe the hospital would bring in a more comfortable chair for you to sit in where you can rest."

Sarah shook her head. "I don't think I will be able to sleep or rest until I know he is out of danger. You would do that? Go to my house and watch over the boarders for me?"

"Of course. Then I'll come back first thing tomorrow. Would you like me to bring you something to eat and drink before I leave?"

"*Ya.* Coffee would be good. Or maybe a milkshake?" Her eyes lit and a soft smile tipped the corners of her mouth. "That sounds *wunderbar.*"

Kathy stood. "Strawberry, right?"

"*Ya. Denke.*"

"I'll be right back." She hurried out of the room and headed straight for the cafeteria, thankful for something to keep her occupied, if only for a few minutes.

She got in line and ordered, then stepped aside to wait for the shake. It had sounded so good, she'd ordered one for herself.

"Katrina?" Isaac's voice swung her around. His warm, caring eyes searched her face, then he nodded. "All is well with Sarah?"

"She asked me to get her something to drink, and since a milkshake sounded good to me as well, I bought two."

"Ah, I remember your love for ice cream quite well." His broad smile brought a much-needed moment of levity to Kathy's spirit. "I seem to remember you loved strawberry best, then chocolate, but you had very little use for vanilla."

Her eyes widened. "Wow. I can't believe you'd remember that."

"When you love vanilla, you remember when someone else disparages it." He pressed his lips together, his expression stern, then he broke into a chuckle. "It sounds *gutt*. If you'll wait a moment, I will order one as well, then walk you back to Jeremiah's room. How is he doing? Is there any change?"

"I'm afraid not. I told Sarah to try not to worry, but she's really struggling."

He nodded. "She is in love with Jeremiah. I have known this for a long time."

"What? How did you know that? She didn't even realize that herself until he got hurt." Kathy heard her name called and reached across the countertop to take the two large cups and straws.

"I could see it on her face when she thought no one was watching. Then, I saw her worry increase when he didn't arrive for the work day. Someone who doesn't care about a man doesn't act like she did."

Kathy stripped the paper off the straw and pushed it into the cup, then took a long drink. "Yum. *So* much better than vanilla." She gave him a wicked smile, then sobered. "I do see what you're saying. She's been in love with Jeremiah for some time, she just didn't know it until now. I hate that she had to figure it out this way, but I'm happy for her to finally know her own heart."

Isaac took the milkshake cup and straw handed over to him, then looked Kathy straight in the eyes. "*Ya.* It is always good to know your own heart, for sure and for certain. So much more is clear when that happens."

The next morning, Kathy left a note for the couple staying at the inn and included her phone number, in case they needed anything before leaving. She'd checked with them the night before to make sure all was well, and to double-check that they'd paid in full since they were leaving this morning.

She filled a thermos with hot coffee and wrapped several slices of coffee cake Sarah must have made the day before, then tucked them into her backpack and headed for the car.

She settled behind the steering wheel after placing the thermos and backpack on the passenger seat. As she pulled out onto the road, her phone rang, and she sent it to her Bluetooth. "Hello?"

"Kathy! It's Evelyn. What's going on? I haven't heard from you in days."

"I'm sorry. The last twenty-four hours have been difficult. My cousin's..." What did she say here? Jeremiah wasn't Sarah's fiancé or even her boyfriend, although Amish didn't use that term when courting. "A close friend of my cousin was in an accident. His buggy was hit by a car that was going too fast. I've been spending time with her at the hospital as she sits with him."

"Yikes! That sounds rather gruesome. I can't imagine anyone living through getting hit by a car while traveling in a lightweight contraption like a buggy. Don't those people know that's dangerous? It's amazing they haven't all been killed by now."

Kathy winced. "So, what's up, Evelyn? Are you calling to see how I'm doing, or is there something specific on your mind?"

"Holy smokes, darling! Those poems. They are marvelous. I mean, you only sent me a few, but what I saw ... wow! They make me want to sell my beach house and move to a cozy little house in Amish country. I'd buy an entire book of these."

"Yeah, I hear you. But..."

"Okay, I don't like that tone. What's the deal? Is there a catch?"

"Well, yeah. I mean, they aren't mine, so I can't make any agreement about them being published."

"I know that." The sarcasm dripped from Evelyn's voice. "I mean, you're a good writer, but a poet you are not. So who do they belong to?"

"His name is Isaac Mast. He's Amish, and someone I knew from my childhood. He was a good friend—I guess he still is a friend. I'm renting his farmhouse, and I found his notebook in a bookshelf. He has pages and pages like the ones I sent. I was gripped by the emotion behind the words. They're truly amazing. I wish they could be published."

"You wish they could be? Why can't they be? Easy-peasy. We have him sign a contract with me as his agent, and I'll have him a deal in no time. Just think—he'd be an instant hit as an Amish man. I could put a huge spin on that, and his books would sell out as a result."

Kathy spit out a chuckle, unable to hold it in. "No way would he do that. You didn't catch that I said he's Amish?"

"Back up. I missed that. You're telling me the poet is some hunky, handsome Amish farmer?"

Kathy rolled her eyes. "He's not a farmer. He makes custom furniture and sells it all over the country. Besides, I never said he was hunky or handsome." That part she'd keep to herself, or Evelyn would hop a jet and fly out here to check him out for herself.

"Ha. Even better. Kathy, I need to meet this guy. These pages have dollar signs written all over them. An

Amish poet with a heart of gold—that's how I'd spin it. The press will eat him up. I could represent two New York Times bestsellers. Tell me that wouldn't be amazing!"

"No way, Evelyn. It's not going to happen. The Amish frown on artistic expression, especially in the public eye. Isaac has no interest in publishing his work."

"That's because he's never met Evelyn Arnold. Do the Amish take conference calls? Can we do a three-way call so you can help me convince him?"

"No, Evelyn. I told you, I only wanted to share this with you because they were so beautiful, I knew you'd appreciate reading them. He won't be willing to sit in on a call. Like I told you, he's not interested."

"Do your best to convince him, darling. I know you can do it. You can wrap any man around your little finger. Between this and your new TV show, we could all be rolling in money."

Kathy's heart sank. Had she made a bad choice in sharing the poems with Evelyn? "Like I said, I'd love for his work to be recognized. This isn't about money."

"Yeah, yeah, that too. I'll be in touch. Ta-ta, darling!"

A few minutes later, Kathy pulled into the hospital parking lot, grabbed the thermos and her backpack, and moved at a brisk pace toward the front doors. At least she knew the way to the room so she could bypass the front desk.

She slipped down the hall, hoping she wouldn't be stopped since she wasn't family. Would the bishop even allow her to come in if both he and Sarah were there?

Stopping at the open door, she peeked inside. Sarah sat by Jeremiah's bedside with no sign of movement from him, and Bishop Swarey still hadn't returned.

Kathy stepped into the room. "Sarah? May I come in and keep you company?" She held up the thermos. "I brought coffee and a few slices of your coffee cake."

"Oh, *denke*, Katrina. That is *wunderbar*. I will admit I am a little hungry, after all. That milkshake was *gutt*, but it didn't last all night."

There were ceramic coffee mugs on the counter by the sink, and Kathy filled them both, then ripped off two paper towels and placed a slice of cake on each. She settled down next to Sarah and offered her a piece. "He hasn't woken up yet?"

"*Nein*. The doctor came by earlier when the bishop was here and said they took him off the medicine early this morning that is keeping him asleep. They believe the swelling has gone down enough now, and they want to see if he'll wake on his own. That will tell us a lot. He doesn't expect it to happen for at least a couple more hours, so Bishop Swarey left an hour ago and will return soon."

"He's a busy man. It must be hard for him not to be able to stay straight through. Has it been any easier for you being here with him?" Kathy shot a glance at the door and made sure her voice was low.

"*Ya*. He has been very kind this morning. It is almost like he's decided he can trust me with his son now." Sarah stroked Jeremiah's arm that lay outside the covers. "I would never do anything to hurt Jeremiah." Her fingers trailed down to Jeremiah's hand and she wrapped hers around it.

"Oh, my!" Sarah gave a small jump.

"What? What's wrong? Do I need to call a nurse or doctor?" Kathy stared at the steady lights flashing on the monitor. She couldn't see that anything had changed.

"I think he squeezed my fingers. I can't be sure. It was very slight." She leaned close over the bed. "Jeremiah. If you're awake and you can hear me, try to squeeze my hand again." She waited a few seconds, then her shoulders slumped. "Nothing." Her voice sounded on the verge of tears. "I had really hoped…"

"Talk to him again, Sarah. He might be able to hear you."

Sarah nodded and leaned closer to the man in the bed. "Jeremiah. It's me, Sarah. I've been here at the hospital with you since they brought you in. You've been in an accident. I thought—I thought I'd lost you. I am so very sorry I did not allow you to take me driving when you came that time. I am sorry you were hurt when you saw Gabriel at my home. I am sorry I did not give you an answer about courting me." A sob broke from her throat, and she covered her mouth. "So, so sorry. I hope someday you will be able to forgive me."

Kathy kept her eyes trained on Sarah's hand covering Jeremiah's. Suddenly, she saw the slightest tightening of his fingers. "Sarah. He can hear you. He moved his fingers. Keep talking."

"Jeremiah. You need to know this. I want you to court me. I care for you, very much. In fact…"

His fingers tightened even more, and his hoarse, rough voice answered in a barely discernible whisper. "It is about time, Sarah. But I do not want to court you."

Sarah let out a soft gasp.

Jeremiah's eyes opened and his voice remained soft and husky. "I love you, Sarah, and I want to marry you, as soon as you will have me."

Sarah laid her head on his chest and cried, then

raised her head a few inches. "Of course, I'll marry you. Just as soon as you're well. I love you, Jeremiah Swarey."

Kathy backed toward the door to give the couple more privacy and almost ran into Bishop Swarey, standing in the doorway and holding his hat, his face creased in the largest grin she'd ever seen on the man.

Chapter Nineteen

HUMMING A TUNE, KATHY WALKED TO Isaac's cabin. The happiness she'd seen in Sarah's face still left her nearly floating. What would it be like to be loved like that? To have someone know they wanted to marry you the moment they woke up from a medically induced coma? She couldn't imagine, but she was beyond happy for her cousin.

She rapped on Isaac's door, wanting to share her joy and see if he'd heard the news about Jeremiah. She waited a full minute, but there were no answering footsteps coming to the door. She turned and headed for his barn and workshop. More than likely he was making up for the time he'd lost while at the hospital and had gotten an early start on work.

"Hello? Isaac?" She slid the door open. The inside of the barn was blanketed in darkness. "Isaac? Anyone here?" Well, he certainly wouldn't be working in the dark, so she backed out and slid the door shut again.

She had to share the news with someone. It would have been more fun with Isaac, but maybe she'd run out to the farm stand and chat with Hazel. Maybe she'd even buy a pie or two and bring them home to share with Isaac and Sadie.

Ten minutes later, she walked into the stand and almost bumped into Hazel hurrying her way, her arms so full of boxes of pies she could barely see over the top.

"Oops! Sorry, Hazel." She steadied her cousin, then plucked the top two boxes off the stack and set them on a nearby table. "I wouldn't mind taking a couple of these off your hands, but not unless you allow me to pay for them this time."

Hazel grunted as she placed the remaining boxes on the table. "Sure. This time is fine. You are lucky. I've been so busy this week, I barely had time to bake this fresh batch."

"Do you have any shoofly pie or glazed apple pie?"

"*Ya.* Along with Montgomery pie, oatmeal pie, and cherry."

"I'll take one shoofly and one glazed apple. My mouth is watering already. *Mamm* used to make those, and they're my favorite." She closed her eyes and allowed the memories to fill her mind. "I haven't thought about them in years. I should have gotten her recipe and learned to make them."

"I will give it to you. Your *mamm* gave me her shoofly pie recipe. It is *wunderbar.*"

"Thank you, Hazel." Kathy pulled out her wallet and extracted cash. "I'll put it by the cash register."

Hazel nodded. "How is Jeremiah? I heard you were with Sarah yesterday. He is better, *ya*?"

"I haven't been over there today, but he woke up yesterday and surprised her, that's for sure." Kathy grinned, suddenly deciding to keep Sarah's secret and let her share when she was ready.

"What is that supposed to mean?" Hazel crossed her arms over her chest and scowled. "Surprised her how? Did he jump straight out of the bed when he woke up? Jeremiah is a strong man, but I do not think even he would do that after taking such a hard knock on the head."

Kathy almost giggled. "I'm afraid that's all I can say. I should let Sarah share any news herself." She made a motion of zipping her lips. "Sorry."

Hazel harrumphed and walked to the register, then put the money inside. "You are a tease. You come here to buy pie, then dangle a secret over my head. Now I will need to go to Sarah's inn to find out what is happening." She shook her head. "That is, if she isn't still camped out by Jeremiah's bed." She narrowed her eyes. "Hmm. Now I wonder..."

Kathy scooped up the two boxes. "I'd better get going. I want to work on my quilt today. See you!"

Hazel was still grumbling as Kathy scurried out to her car and climbed in.

Isaac reined in his horse and buggy at the hitching post in front of his barn, tired from the long, sleepless night and the early drive to a hardware store. Why had he been so foolish to spend time with Katrina at the hospital? And to say that it was good to know your own heart. Bah. He didn't even know his own heart. He knew what he'd like, but he also knew it was dangerous.

Staying away from Katrina was best. It was a *gutt* thing she would be moving back to Sarah's inn in a couple of days. That is, if Sarah wanted a guest while Jeremiah was recuperating. She might want to spend all her spare time with him.

He scowled. Why did life have to be so complicated? Why couldn't Katrina have stayed in her *Englisch* world and not shaken up his world by coming here?

Isaac unhitched the horse and was leading it to the pasture for a much-deserved rest when Katrina drove in and parked. He turned his back on the car and walked with firm steps toward the pasture, the mare trotting along beside him, seeming as anxious to leave as he was.

"Isaac." Katrina's lovely voice followed him like a specter in a haunted house—although he didn't believe in specters or haunted houses, he was sure this was how he would feel if he did.

"Isaac. I brought pie."

He glanced over his shoulder in time to see her wave and hold up a box. Giving in to temptation to eat the pie and visit with Katrina was not an option. He must stay strong. Footsteps scurried behind him, coming closer.

"Isaac. What in the world is wrong with you? Don't you want pie?"

"*Nein.* I had breakfast and I am not hungry. *Denke.*" There. He'd been polite, and that was all he could do. Maybe she would understand and leave. Opening the gate, he shooed the horse inside, then shut and latched it.

"Where have you been so early?" She stood right behind him.

He could smell her perfume. Shutting his eyes, he took shallow breaths, trying to block the heavenly fragrance. It did no good. "It is not your business where I've been. I have work to do." He didn't turn but stood like one of the wooden chests he made, not moving, just staring out over the field.

"Well, fine, grumpy. Be that way." Her footsteps retreated then stopped. "Is something wrong?"

He sighed and turned around. "I had a special varnish I needed to finish a project. I was out, so I drove to the hardware store to pick it up. The store is five miles away, and I'm tired, but I must get to work and finish this order."

Her eyes brightened. "I could go online and find it if you tell me the brand. I can set it up on an auto delivery, so it comes right to your house. That would save you a lot of time and you wouldn't have to drive so far to buy it."

"I prefer my horse and buggy. I like our old ways, Katrina. I am not an *Englischer* like you."

"So, no pie?"

"No pie. I have work to do. Have a *gutt* day." He went back to the buggy, grabbed the sack containing several cans of varnish, and headed to the barn. Sadie would be home from spending the night at a friend's last night while he was at the hospital. He'd need to steer her away from going to see Katrina, or his goose would be cooked. His little girl was already enamored with Katrina, and she'd only been around her a couple of times. Allowing her to get any closer could be his undoing.

Kathy sat down on the enclosed porch determined to work on her quilt and forget about Isaac Mast and his silly moods. What was wrong with the man, anyway? She huffed. Men. She leaned over her work, running her needle in and out of the fabric. It felt as though her long-ago skills were returning the more time she spent on this quilt.

"I like your quilt." A young voice spoke only a few feet away.

Kathy jumped and nearly pricked her thumb as the needle came through. She placed her hand over her heart and peered through the screen at Sadie. What a cutie she was, all golden curls and a sweet smile. "Thank you. It's one I started making with my *mamm* years ago. Would you like to see it?"

"*Ya.* I would like that. My *mamm* used to quilt, and she taught me a little until she got sick and went away to heaven." The little girl opened the screen door and walked in, stopping to peer at the pieces on Kathy's lap.

"Can you teach me how?"

Kathy stiffened. The last thing she wanted to do was try to take this child's mother's place. "I don't think I'd be a good teacher, Sadie. I'm sure I'm not nearly as good at quilting as your *mamm* was."

"But I want to learn. Please?" Sadie's face contorted into an adorable pleading expression.

How could she say no to that? "Of course. I'll show you what I'm doing. Step over here where you can see."

Sadie came close and looked at the material in Kathy's hands. "Right now, I am working on different blocks. When I finish each one, I will put them all together in a pattern." She held up the smaller piece that she and her mother had done. "You see? *Mamm* and I did a few blocks and put them together to make one small section of the quilt. She thought I'd win best junior quilter a fourth year running. Seeing her face that first time I won … it was one of the proudest moments of my childhood. My life, really."

"Why didn't you finish it with your *mamm*?"

"Maybe I'll tell you about that someday when you're older." She cleared her throat. "Now I need to make more blocks and add them to this section. Then I'll put a backing on it, if I can find someone with a quilting frame I can use."

"I think my *mamm* had one. Maybe my papa will let you use it."

"Please don't ask him, Sadie. He's very busy, and I don't think it would be good to bother him with something like that. Okay?"

Sadie nodded. "Where is your pretty dress?" She cocked her head to the side. "The one you wore at the work party."

"Oh, the lavender one. I borrowed that from Hazel. She brought it for me to wear."

"Do you want one for your very own?" Sadie grabbed Kathy's hand and tugged at her. "Get up. *Kumm* with me. I'll show you."

Kathy stood and trotted after the little girl, wondering what she was up to. Sadie led her through the house and stopped outside Kathy's bedroom door. She pushed it open and walked in, as though she knew exactly what she was doing.

"Sadie? Honey, this is where I stay. I don't have any dresses in here—only one skirt that I brought and it's in the closet."

Sadie ignored her and went to a cedar chest at the end of the bed. Carefully removing the long, crocheted throw that spanned the top of the chest, she opened the lid. "See?" She pointed to a neatly folded assortment of colors, then lifted a dress by the shoulders until the top half was showing. "Maybe these will fit you. I don't think *Daed* would care if you have them. They were my *mamm's*."

Kathy felt tears well in her eyes. She wondered if this little girl had any memories at all of her mother, or if the belongings left behind by the woman were all she had to hold onto and try to remember her by. She reached down and put her arm around Sadie, then gently closed the lid of the chest, thankful Isaac hadn't come in. "Come on, sweetheart, let's go have a piece of pie."

Chapter Twenty

ISAAC POKED HIS HEAD IN HIS cabin, realizing he'd left Sadie alone too long yet again and it was time for them to leave. The little one needed a mother. His mind flew to Katrina, then he batted the thought away. "Sadie? Are you getting hungry for dinner yet?"

The silent house testified to its empty condition. He sighed, sure he knew where he would find his adventurous daughter. He turned and trudged toward his house, then slowed when he neared the screened-in porch, hearing Sadie's giggle. Such a sweet and delightful sound!

"Sadie, it is time to go home. You must not bother Miss Yoder. I'm sure she is busy. *Kumm* now." He planted his fists at his waist and waited, tapping his foot. "Sadie, did you hear me?"

"*Ach*, please let me stay a little longer. Miss Katrina is teaching me to quilt. Five more minutes?"

"Miss Katrina is teaching you?" He moved closer to the porch and peered through the screen to see Sadie on Katrina's lap, running a needle through a quilt square under Katrina's watchful gaze. "She needs to do her own work, Sadie."

"Isaac, she's fine. Please, come on in and see what she's been doing." Katrina met his eyes and sent him an uncertain smile.

"*Ya*, Papa, *kumm* see. Miss Katrina was the best junior quilter in the county for three years!" Her little voice had a note of joy that he hadn't heard in too long.

He tried to stifle a chuckle as he opened the screen door and stepped onto the porch. "I must say, she is quite modest about her accomplishments too."

Katrina narrowed her eyes and stuck her tongue out at him, exactly as she'd done when they were children and she was annoyed—or teasing him.

"Show me quickly, then we need to leave." He bent over Sadie as she made a number of wide, random stitches across the face. "Very pretty."

"But I want to stay longer." Sadie's voice trembled as though on the verge of tears.

Katrina simply cocked an eyebrow at him and smiled as if to say it was fine with her.

"Well, Miss Sadie, you are welcome to stay with Miss Katrina, but I think Rebecca will be quite upset that you will miss her sleepover. I guess we'll forget about going to her house then, shall we?" He stroked a strand of hair out of her face while keeping a serious expression. If there was one thing Sadie loved, it was a sleepover with her best friend.

Sadie jumped off Katrina's lap. "I want to go to Rebecca's. *Gutt-bye*, Miss Katrina." She ran to her father's side.

"Your overnight bag is packed and in the buggy. We must leave in a few minutes."

"Can Miss Katrina go with us? Please?" She turned soulful eyes up to him, and his heart melted. It was so hard to say no to this child, but this time he must.

"To a little girl's sleepover? I don't think so. *Kumm*, we need to leave."

"Can she ride over with us in the buggy? She spent all this time helping me. Can she take a ride with us?" Sadie tugged on his sleeve.

"Oh. Well. Um…"

Sadie shot a beaming smile at Katrina. "Would you like to *kumm* with us?"

Katrina stared at him, seeming to notice his discomfort, then she smiled and looked him straight in the eyes. "Sure. I'd love to go, if it's okay with your papa."

What had he gotten himself into? He should have simply taken Sadie home, then ushered her to the buggy, even if she did protest. After all, he was the parent and she was the child. Her imploring face and Katrina's slightly triumphant one couldn't be ignored. He sighed. "*Ya*, she is welcome."

Kathy sat in the buggy next to Isaac as Sadie scrambled down over the side, then reached up for her bag. Kathy handed it down and blew Sadie a kiss. "Have fun."

Isaac gave his daughter a stern look. "You mind Hazel and play nicely with Rebecca, all right, Sadie?"

"I will. You have fun with Miss Katrina too, Papa."

Kathy glanced at Isaac in time to see a tinge of red creeping up his neck and almost giggled. If she didn't know better, she'd think Isaac was blushing.

Hazel patted Sadie's shoulder as the girl stood beside her. "Sadie is always a very obedient girl at our house. Now Rebecca on the other hand..." She acted disgruntled, but Kathy knew better.

Rebecca giggled and curtsied. "*Nien, Mamm*, I am always perfect, like Sadie." She grabbed her friend's hand and they ran into the house, shrieking with laughter.

"I see Sadie enjoyed a piece of my pie before she arrived."

Kathy gave a small shake of her head. "I'm sorry. I meant to wash her face, but she got so interested in learning to quilt that I forgot. Then Isaac came to get her, and everything else flitted from my mind."

Hazel arched a brow. "I am sure that it did." She

snickered and raised a hand in farewell. "We will keep a close eye on these young hooligans. Behave, you two." She directed a firm look at Isaac, then at Kathy, and winked.

Now it was Kathy's turn to blush. "Behave *yourself*, Hazel. I'll see you later." She waved as Isaac reined the horse around, flicked the buggy whip, and they headed down the drive.

They traveled in silence for a few minutes while Kathy gazed out over the green fields dotted with barns, farmhouses, and livestock. "I've seen Angkor Wat. The Eiffel Tower. Uluru Rock. Stonehenge. But nothing is as beautiful as a sunset in Amish country. To me, at least."

She peeked at Isaac's profile, but his body remained rigid and his lips silent.

"I can see why you wanted to stay and raise Sadie here. I also understand where you get your inspiration for your work. It's like that line you wrote about stepping in morning dew when you wake up to work before dawn..."

He flicked his reins and the horse moved into a trot. "I do not want to discuss my poetry. Please, talk about something else, or let's not talk at all."

She rolled her head trying to loosen the tight muscles in her neck and shoulders. What was wrong with this man? He'd seemed fine at the hospital, then he practically bit her head off this morning. It was apparent he hadn't wanted her to come on this ride, but she wasn't about to let him get away with this behavior. They'd been friends far too long for that. "Whatever is the matter with you? Ever since I saw you first thing this morning, you've been a grump. In fact, you acted weird at the work party too. Did I say or do something to upset you?"

"It is nothing." He didn't so much as glance at her.

"Isaac, it's me. We're friends. I'll listen to whatever you want to share."

"I have nothing to say."

She sat for a moment, then a thought hit her. It was probably ludicrous, but maybe it would break him out of this funk he'd fallen into. "Pull over."

"What?" This time he stared at her instead of between the horse's ears.

"Pull over." She pointed. "In that wide spot ahead."

Isaac drew the mare to a stop, then set the brake. "What is going on? Is something wrong?"

Katrina almost leapt from the buggy seat to the ground, her foot barely touching the step on the way down. "Come on!"

"Excuse me? What are you doing?"

She peered up at him and grinned. "We're going to play hide and seek. I'm going to hide, and you have to find me, like when we were kids." She took off at a run, breaking through a small stand of brush and disappearing from sight.

"Katrina. *Kumm* back here. We don't have time for foolishness." He sat for a few seconds and waited for her to tromp back to the buggy, embarrassed by her childish behavior. A full minute passed, and she didn't appear. "Very amusing. That's enough. It's time to leave."

Nothing. He sighed and wrapped the reins around the brake handle. What was wrong with that woman?

He pushed through the brush and tromped along the path in the grass made by Katrina's hurrying footsteps. It should be easy to find her with the blades bent over. This area seemed familiar. Ah, the cemetery. He hadn't been here for years. This hadn't been used for at least a generation, as a new cemetery had been established on the bishop's land. All of a sudden, he knew what she was doing. A grin spread over his face, and he leaned over and slipped off his shoes, leaving them on the grass.

He tiptoed forward, being careful to not make a sound. She'd be hiding behind the biggest headstone. If he moved quietly enough, he might be able to catch her. He leapt forward. "I caught you!" His heart pounded with a rush of adrenaline, but Katrina wasn't where he'd expected.

"Boo!" Katrina's voice behind him made him jump and spin. "Ha! I finally did it."

He laughed. "After how many years of trying? As I recall, this is the first time."

She arched a brow. "I try to live in the present, not the past."

"I find that hard to believe, dragging me to the cemetery and Founder's Pond."

She grabbed his hand and pulled him toward the water. "I have something to say and you have to listen."

He came to a stop and dropped her hand. "No. I do not have to listen." A sense of apprehension hit him. Why had her voice turned so solemn in such a light moment? Couldn't she have left things as they were and allowed a few moments of forgetfulness?

"Isaac. Please?"

He released a long breath. "Fine. Go ahead."

"I believe you need to allow your poems to be published. You have such an amazing gift. You could help people to see the Amish community as it really is, not as they perceive it from reality TV shows or movies. Your words paint a lovely picture of Amish life. The world should see that picture so they can understand. I know you're worried about the church and the bishop, but you could write under a pen name. Lots of people do that."

Isaac felt a stab of remorse that he had to disappoint her again. Her earnest face and voice told him how much this request meant to her, and how deeply his work had touched her, but it couldn't be helped. He would not share his work.

He cleared his throat, praying he could make the words come out right so she'd understand. "My daughter, my faith, and my community are what mean the most to me. I would hope you could see that. No amount of praise from the world or even helping others understand our ways would make up for the guilt I would feel if I betrayed my people.

"Even if they never knew it was my work, I would know what I had done, and living with that would tear me apart. I know my poems might appeal to the outside world, but part of being Amish is keeping that world at bay. We have chosen to live a simple life. A pure life, and that is all I want. As much as I admire *Englisch* poets, I have no desire to be one. I would stop writing forever if it meant losing what I have and the people I love."

Isaac took her hand and looked into her eyes, seeing tears welling and ready to spill over her lids. "I am sorry, Katrina. I did not mean to be harsh, but I must be honest with you. I can't allow you to believe I'll do something when my heart tells me not to."

She shook her head and squeezed his hand. "No. Please don't apologize. You're right about everything. I see that now. I thought I wanted to share you and your work with the world, but that's not what I want at all." She moved closer and tipped her face up to his.

Isaac hesitated, longing to do what he knew she was hoping for. Why did this have to be so hard? If only Katrina had never left their community. He took a step back, releasing her hand. "Katrina. No."

She reached out for him, but he stepped farther away. Her eyes widened. "I can't help it, Isaac. I thought I loved you when we were kids, but this is different." She touched her heart. "This is truly coming from my heart, and it's not just friendship. I care for you. Deeply. I'm not ready to say I'm in love with you, but something is growing inside, and I think it is in you too. That's why you've been so standoffish with me—so grumpy lately. Admit it." She crossed her arms over her chest and met his eyes.

"All right then. I will admit it. I do feel something for you, and I think it has gone beyond our old friendship. But it doesn't matter. I am Amish. You have chosen a different path. There is no middle ground, Katrina. Surely you can see that?"

She relaxed her stance. "Fine. But technically, I'm still Amish. I didn't join the church, so I didn't leave it."

Isaac shook his head. "*Nein.* Technicalities will not satisfy our community, and you know this to be true. There is only one way for us to be together."

"You wouldn't consider leaving the community and coming with me?" She bit her lip and watched him.

"I think you know the answer to that." Isaac wanted to grab her, kiss her, and tell her he'd do anything to keep from losing her now that he'd found her again, but that was no more possible than the thought of him giving up his life and raising Sadie in the *Englisch* world.

Katrina gave a slow nod. "Yes, I do. I wish things could be different, but I do understand."

"*Kumm.* We need to leave. It isn't good for us to be out here alone." Isaac couldn't help himself—he looked into her eyes one more time and saw a tear trickle down her cheek. Steeling himself to keep from pulling her into his arms and kissing her, he spun around and walked to the buggy, trusting that she would follow.

Chapter Twenty-One

KATHY CURLED INTO A TIGHT BALL on the couch, trying to sort through her roiling emotions. The ride home had been silent, and Isaac had headed to his cabin with barely a nod. Why had she embarrassed herself like that with Isaac, telling him she still cared and wanted more than friendship? She knew he'd never leave the Amish community, and she couldn't see herself ever going back, so where did that leave them?

She reached for her quilting project and studied the stitches. Every bit as good as, if not better than, when she'd lived at home and practiced under her mother's watchful eyes. Setting it aside, her gaze roved the room. She felt too uptight for quilting this evening, but nothing sounded remotely interesting. Her gaze landed on the small book of poetry. Reading it might soothe her sore heart and make her feel at least a little closer to Isaac.

If it wasn't for her sister losing the farm if she didn't stay, she'd head straight back to L.A. and not suffer like this. Kathy almost laughed out loud. Would the suffering be any less if she couldn't see Isaac? Maybe. Maybe it would allow her heart time to recover and return to being the person she was before.

Flipping through the pages of the booklet and reading one of her favorite poems over again, she stopped to reflect on that last thought. The person she was before—a woman who loved to travel, who had a kind and adoring boyfriend, who'd never wanted anything as much as she wanted to write. That pretty much encapsulated her life, didn't it? The life she'd dreamed of as a young Amish girl. Had that changed in recent days? No. It couldn't have. Life didn't flip on its head in a matter of days. That wasn't possible.

A thought struck her, and she jumped from the couch and almost raced to her bedroom. She plucked the lavender dress off the hook where she'd left it after the work day. Maybe if she stayed in the bedroom and read for a bit? Would it be so wrong to wear this again if no one saw her?

She walked to the mirror installed for guests and held the dress in front of herself. In only a few minutes, she'd slipped into the gown and placed the *Kapp* on her head. The only thing left was to tie on the apron. This felt ... right somehow. The work party had been the start of it all. Wearing this clothing and helping in the kitchen resurrected memories and feelings from her youth that were pleasant and homey—all except for Miriam. Kathy wrinkled her nose. Her sister would probably never change, but maybe pretending to be Amish for one evening might get it out of her system and allow her to go back to her *Englisch* life in peace.

She twirled around in front of the mirror, liking what she saw and how it made her feel. After all, she'd lived longer in clothing like this than in the jeans and t-shirts she typically wore in her current life. Would Isaac be upset if he saw her or like what he saw? There was little chance of that happening, based on the mood he was in.

She padded back to the living room and plucked another book off the shelf, barely caring what she grabbed this time. Maybe resting on the bed and reading for an hour would help soothe her nerves.

Kathy rolled over to grab her phone from the nightstand

as it buzzed, waking her from a deep sleep. What time was it? She grabbed it—eight thirty in the morning? She shot off the bed. The sun shone through the barely cracked blinds. How had she slept all night hardly moving—and while still in Amish clothing?

The phone continued to buzz. Evelyn. She sent it to voicemail and huffed. She'd better get changed and back into her own world. Hazel had mentioned stopping by sometime this morning to see the progress she'd made on her quilt.

A knock sounded at the door. Her dear cousin had always been an early bird, so that didn't surprise her too much. There was even pie left in the kitchen, so they could put a pot of coffee on and enjoy a chat to start the morning right.

Kathy rushed to the door and flung it open. Hazel would be tickled to see her wearing an Amish dress for the second time since she'd arrived. "Perfect timing. I haven't had breakfast yet."

She stopped and stared, her mouth hanging open. Evelyn stood on her porch, tapping something out on her iPhone.

Evelyn finished, slid her phone in her pocket, and flashed Kathy a huge smile. "Hello, darling." She swept Kathy into an embrace, then stepped back, still holding onto her shoulders. "It's so lovely to see you."

"What ... what are you doing here? You didn't call or let me know you were coming. I'm happy to see you, but surprised."

"Obviously." Evelyn looked her up and down. "I miss you. It feels like you've been out in this backwater forever. If I was stuck in the middle of nowhere, I'd want fresh air from the coast to blow in, so I decided to visit." She gestured at Kathy. "What's with the dress and little bonnet?"

Kathy touched her mussed hair, hoping she hadn't hurt the *Kapp* by sleeping in it. It was amazing it was even still on her head, but that must have been a testament to how deeply she'd slept. "I ... was just trying it on." No point in trying to explain how she still needed to sort through her turbulent emotions.

Evelyn tipped her head to the side. "Well, you'd better go get changed." She flicked a hand toward the car that Kathy hadn't noticed before. "Look who I ran into at the Cincinnati airport."

Kathy had to gulp down a gasp. "You brought Jacques?"

He slammed the trunk shut, then grabbed a suitcase with each hand. "I brought myself." He arched his brows. "You are ... interesting in that get-up, Kath."

"Right. I'll get changed. Come on in, both of you."

Jacques strode through the door, dumped the suitcases on the floor. "I'm sorry for not letting you know I was coming, but being in love with you makes me do crazy things. I felt like something was going on, but I didn't know what, and I was about to go out of my mind." He leaned over and kissed her, gently at first, then with increasing passion.

Kathy pulled back. It had never bothered her in the past when Jacques kissed her, but right now it made her uncomfortable. "It's always good to see you, Jacques, but I wish you'd called. I wasn't expecting company."

"Yeah. What's with the dress, anyway?" A small smirk tipped the side of his mouth. "It kind of freaks me out."

"Give me ten minutes. I'll change and be right back, then I can whip up breakfast for us. I'm sure you're both tired. That's a long flight."

Evelyn waved her manicured fingers in the air. "It

was nothing like the one you'll be taking to Kenya, darling. Besides, we stayed at a semi-decent hotel last night about forty-five minutes from here. I didn't want to get up this early, but Jacques insisted he couldn't wait another hour to see you." She yawned and daintily tapped her lips. "Oh, to be young and in love again."

"Breakfast is served." Kathy placed three plates on the table along with a steaming plate of pancakes. She'd remembered an old recipe of her *mamm's* and decided to try her hand at it. There wasn't any syrup, but she spread them with butter and sprinkled them with powdered sugar.

Jacques stood next to the coffee pot. He leaned over and sniffed. "Where did these coffee beans come from?"

"Kroger's." Kathy plucked the pot from the warming plate and poured three mugs full, then set them on the table.

Evelyn picked up her fork and glared at the plate of pancakes. "What are these made with?"

"Buckwheat flour. It was my mother's recipe."

"Oh. Well. Then I'll stick with coffee. I'm off gluten now, remember?" She settled back in her seat and smiled. "Actually, there's another reason I flew out besides the need to see how you're doing. When you didn't get back to me about that sweaty farm poet, I got a little antsy."

Jacques looked up from pushing his pancake around his plate. "What sweaty farm poet?"

Evelyn waved him away. "I got tired of waiting to hear from you with a decision. You did say you'd talk him into publishing them, right? Well, anyway, I sent the few pages to McMaster's to get their opinion. Can you believe they already got back to me? I mean, the wheels of publishing typically grind at such a slow rate." She took a sip of her coffee.

Kathy set her cup down hard on the table. "McMasters? What are you talking about? I didn't give you permission—"

"Ta-ta, darling, permission, my foot. I don't really need anyone's permission to show them to someone. Besides, you'll be thrilled to know they loved what they saw. They are salivating over those poems, and they want to see more. You and your friend could be published at the same house, and I'm just the agent to handle it all." She leaned back in her chair with a satisfied expression.

"Evelyn. I told you those were a secret and for your eyes only." Kathy loved her agent, but she could see it had been a huge mistake to trust her with something so sensitive.

Evelyn snickered. "Since when can I keep a secret?"

"You are my agent. You work for me, so aren't you supposed to follow my instructions?"

"No." Evelyn pointed at Kathy while Jacques followed the conversation with his lips pressed in a firm line. "I'm your agent, and it's my job to make you—and me—money. I look for opportunities to do just that." She tapped her nails on the table. "So when I can I meet this Amish hunk?"

Jacques scowled. "What's she talking about, Kath? Have you met someone, and you didn't tell me?"

Kathy wanted to bolt from the table and demand they both leave, but they were her friends and coworkers. She drew in a deep breath, determined to get this dealt with. "No. I—"

The phone buzzed, cutting her off. She glanced at the screen and groaned. "I have to take this." Scooping up the phone, she headed to the living room, then swiped it to accept the call. "Mr. Russo, hello."

"Miss Yoder, I have good news. The papers are all ready to sign. I contacted Miriam and Amos and they are agreeable to taking care of it today. Will that work for you?"

Kathy glanced back toward the kitchen, a sense of reprieve flooding her. "Yes. Definitely. How about in, say, thirty minutes at the farm? That would be the best time for me."

"Oh. Well. I suppose, if that is the only time you can meet me, I can make that work. I might take a few minutes longer, but you can always visit with your sister and family, correct? I will see you there, Miss Yoder."

She switched off the phone and walked back to the kitchen. "Sorry, guys. That was the Amish arbitrator. He needs me to meet him at the farm to sign the papers. My sister and her husband are expecting me."

Jacques pushed to his feet. "I'm sorry, that's not going to work. I need answers. Now."

Evelyn jerked her head in a nod. "Yes, and I expect to meet your barnyard Shakespeare. You can't just run off like this when we've barely arrived."

"I'll try not to be too long, but it takes fifteen minutes to drive there, so make yourself at home while I'm gone. Also, please stay in the house? I only rent it, not the property, and it won't be considerate if you roam around." She gave them her best smile. "I know it was a long trip. Rest. Drink coffee. Eat all the fresh pie you want, it's excellent." She grabbed her keys and waved. "See you soon."

Chapter Twenty-Two

KATHY SETTLED ONTO THE CHAIR ACROSS from Miriam and Amos while Mr. Russo took the seat at the head of the table. Her arrival had been met with what seemed like nervousness on Miriam's part. Did her sister think she'd change her mind at the last minute? Kathy held back a sigh. What would it be like to have a good relationship with her sister again?

Mr. Russo pushed a short stack of papers toward Kathy and another across the table to Miriam. "These are the deeds, the transfer agreement, and everything else needed to accept Mr. Yoder's will and get the farm put in Miriam's name. If each of you will sign, then swap piles, it will expedite the process." He pointed at a yellow arrow on the first page as he looked at Kathy. "Miss Yoder, you will sign each place with the yellow arrow." He pointed to another spot. "Miriam, the green arrows are yours."

Silence engulfed the room while Kathy and Miriam leaned over the table and hurried through the signing. After they'd swapped piles, they went through one more time. Kathy finished first and slid the papers to Mr. Russo.

He gathered up both piles and flipped through each page. "Excellent. It appears we are finished. Congratulations, Miriam, you are now the sole owner of this lovely farm. What are you going to do to celebrate?" He gave them a soft smile. "Although I am sure there is more than enough work around here to keep you busy."

Miriam and Amos smiled at each other and nodded. "Always," Amos said.

Kathy leaned over and plucked her backpack from

the chair where she'd dropped it when she arrived. "Miriam, I have something else for you."

Miriam's eyes widened. "This is enough, Katrina. I told you, we will not take your money for the taxes."

"I know, and this isn't money. I started working on this when I got back, and I thought you might like it." She pulled the still-unfinished quilt out and spread it on the table. "I found it at the *Daadi Haus* the day I arrived. It's not finished yet, but I got a good start on it."

Miriam leaned over the table, touching the starburst pattern with her fingertips. "This is the one you and *Mamm* worked on years ago?"

"Yes. I can keep working on it in the time I have left here, but I thought you might like to do some work on it too, so all three of us would have a part in making it. It's not even a quarter of the way finished, but..."

Miriam chuckled. "I'll say. It is more the size of a towel than a quilt." She picked it up and peered closer. "Did you use one of your *Englisch* sewing machines to get these tight stitches?" A sparkle danced in her eyes.

"Are you kidding? Of course not. Every one of those were put in by hand. I even have a few needle marks in my fingers to prove it. I did this the Amish way."

Miriam dropped her gaze, but not before Kathy saw moisture gathering in her eyes. "*Mamm* would have liked this."

Kathy walked around the table and stood near Miriam's chair, hoping she'd get up. Praying she'd accept a hug from her. "Well, I guess this is goodbye. I'll be at Isaac's or Sarah's for the next couple of weeks, but I'm not sure if I'll have a reason to see you again." She bit her lip, waiting, but Miriam didn't move.

"*Ya*, Katrina. *Gutt-bye.*"

Kathy walked to the door, slinging her backpack

over her shoulder. As she pulled it open, a soft voice behind her said, "*Denke*, Katrina. *Denke*."

Isaac stared at the two people exiting the house Katrina rented from him, wondering where they'd come from and what relationship they had with her. He'd noticed her car pulling out earlier, but the other car remained in the drive. He walked toward them, tipping his head. "*Gutt* morning. May I help you with something?"

The woman strode ahead of the man, who wasn't in a hurry, but the man seemed to be appraising him like a cat watches a toad it plans to pounce on.

Extending her hand, the woman spoke in an almost falsetto-type voice. "I'm Evelyn Arnold, Kathy's agent, and this is Jacques Burly, TV star and"—she glanced back at Jacques—"very good friend of Kathy's. We came for a visit, but she had to run to see her sister and take care of some business, so we decided to take a stroll. Who are you?"

Isaac took off his hat and held it while he shook her hand. "I am Isaac Mast, the owner of this farm and house." He pointed toward his cabin. "That's where my daughter and I live."

"Your daughter?" Evelyn Arnold's brows rose. "I didn't realize you were married. Kathy didn't mention that."

"I have been widowed for three years now." Isaac placed his hat back on his head and turned away. "I'm sorry. I must get back to work. Enjoy your walk."

"Oh, please don't rush away." Evelyn touched his arm. "May we hang out with you for a bit? We'd love to get acquainted with one of Kathy's friends."

He shrugged. "That is fine. I occasionally give

Englischers a tour of my workshop, so if you'd care to do that, I don't mind. Let's go inside." He rolled the doors open to his workshop housed in the barn and beckoned them inside.

The sound of tires on gravel caused Isaac to swing around. Kathy parked her car and jumped out, then headed for the house. He heard her calling her guest's names as she entered the house.

Isaac walked over to join Evelyn and—what was his name? Jack ... something. He shook his head. They stood admiring a table and chairs that he'd recently been working on. Kathy would probably find them out here. "This dining room set received its first coat of lacquer earlier this week. Every piece of furniture I create is custom made and is designed with a specific customer in mind. At the end of the month, I'll ship this set to my client in New York City."

Evelyn gasped. "New York City?" The woman looked at him as though she'd seen him for the first time. "Why am I surprised? You seem to be a man of many talents. I'd kill for something like this." She reached out to touch it, but Isaac stepped in front of her.

"The varnish takes time to completely set. We don't want fingerprints to show up. I'd have to strip the finish, sand it, and do all of it over if that happened. That's why there's no hay or other things you'd typically find in a barn. The horses are kept in a different section that's walled off from my workshop, as I can't have dust or bits of hay floating around in here." Isaac smiled. "And yes, much of my work goes to clients in New York."

Jacques smirked. "So, do you ship ground or horse and buggy?"

Evelyn slapped the man's arm. "Oh, stop that, Jacques. You sound jealous of Mr. Mast's work." She smiled at Isaac. "May I call you Isaac? Mr. Mast sounds so formal among friends."

Isaac heard running footsteps and glanced at the door.

Katrina arrived appearing flustered and out of breath. "What's going on?"

Evelyn waved an airy hand, not seeming to care what Katrina thought. "There you are, darling. Your charming friend was showing us around his workshop."

Katrina hurried forward. "But I asked you to stay in the house until I got back."

Jacques moved closer to her until their shoulders were almost touching. "After you told me about this Renaissance man you were spending all your time with, I had to meet him. When I noticed him walking around outside, we came out to get acquainted."

Katrina grabbed the man's arm. "Jacques, please."

Isaac narrowed his eyes. "Renaissance? I am not sure I know what you mean."

Jacques snorted a semblance of a laugh. "I can see why you wouldn't know what I mean. You live a very rustic life out here, right?"

Evelyn sighed. "That doesn't matter at all, Isaac, at least not for my purposes."

Jacques laughed out loud this time. "Who cares if he builds custom furniture and writes poetry." He jerked his thumb at his chest. "I have my own TV show."

Evelyn dug into the large purse she carried over her arm and pulled out a pen and a few papers. "Don't listen to him, Isaac. What matters most is that we get your wonderful work published. I brought a contract to represent you. All you need to do is read through it. We're planning to spend the night. I'll leave these papers with you, and you can let me know if you have any questions." She thrust the pages toward him. "I'll be happy to walk you through any obstacles that might present themselves. Kathy can tell you what a good job I've done for her."

He swung on Katrina, rage building in his chest, to see her standing next to Jacques with her mouth hanging open and her eyes wide. "What is she talking about? Did you tell them about my poetry?"

She shook her head. "Not exactly…"

Evelyn placed her hand on Isaac's arm. "Let me step in here and explain. I'm Kathy's literary agent. She sent me a sample of your poetry to read. When I saw what you've done, I knew I had a potential bestseller on my hands, what with you being Amish. I spoke to Kathy's publisher, and he's dying to read the rest. Based on the samples alone, he's apt to offer you a contract. More than likely, he's afraid someone else will snap you up. If this book does as well as I expect, you may not have to keep building furniture. You can do it as a hobby in the future or not at all. Won't that be wonderful?" She beamed at him as though somehow her words would make all his dreams come true. "All you need to do is sign a contract with me so I can represent you."

Kathy rounded on her agent, what appeared to be a mix of anger and anguish covering her face. "Evelyn, stop!" Then she looked at Isaac with pleading in her wide eyes. "I may have sent her a couple of your poems to read, but that's not all of the story."

He backed away toward the double doors. "I do not want to hear your story. I can see it all for myself. You have fooled me. You are no longer the young Amish girl I knew years ago, or the friend I remember. You are *Englisch,* and you always will be."

"I didn't lie to you, Isaac. Everything I said is true.

If you'd only let me explain." She threw her arms wide.

"I do not want to hear your excuses. I told you I did not want to share my work. You deceived me, Katrina. Or should I say, Kathy? You are part of their world, not mine. I do not want you here tonight. Please go with your friends to their hotel where you belong."

"If you'd give me a few minutes, Isaac ... please?" Katrina acted as though she were going to grab his arm, but he walked to the doors.

"It is time you all left." He slid open the doors as wide as they'd go and beckoned toward the two cars. "Kathy, you may get your bags now or come back for them tomorrow. It is up to you."

Evelyn gaped at him, the papers still clutched in her hands. "But I flew all this way to see you. Can I at least leave this contract for you to review?"

Jacques placed his arm around Katrina's shoulders and walked her out the doors. "Come on, Kath. This isn't where you belong. Evelyn and I will take care of you, and you'll be back in L.A. before you know it."

Isaac clamped his lips shut. He was thankful Sadie wasn't here to see this. She'd be heartbroken, but it couldn't be helped. It was a good thing he had found out the truth before he'd done something stupid that he'd regret the rest of his life.

Chapter Twenty-Three

ISAAC DIDN'T KNOW IF HE WANTED to break something or sit down and cry. This hurt far more than it was supposed to. It hadn't even hurt this much when Katrina had walked away ten years ago, so why had it hit him so hard now? She hadn't even been back that long, but somehow she'd managed to burrow into his heart. He'd said he should call her Kathy, but that wasn't the truth. She would always be Katrina to him, no matter where she lived or what she did.

She had left an hour ago, and that smug *Englischer* Jacques had climbed into Katrina's car instead of Evelyn's. Why should that matter to him? He'd told her to leave, and she'd done so. Good riddance to all of them.

He needed to go pick up Sadie at Hazel's in a while, so he'd better pull himself together. He closed his workshop doors and headed to his cabin, then stopped at the sight of a buggy coming up his driveway. He shaded his eyes. "Miriam?"

She reined her bay gelding to a stop near the hitching rail, then climbed down, not waiting for him to assist her. "Isaac. Where is Katrina? I need to talk to her." She waved what appeared to be several envelopes in the air. "I found these in the *Daadi Haus,* and they change everything."

"I have no idea what you're talking about, but Katrina isn't here. I asked her to leave."

"What?" Miriam stood right in front of him. "Why? What did you do to cause her to leave?"

He barked a laugh. "What did I do? You were right

all along. She is your typical *Englischer*, not caring at all about others' feelings. She can't be trusted, so I asked her to leave."

Miriam came even closer and thumped him on the chest with her finger. "I found these letters. All these years, I thought she ignored *Daed* and didn't want anything to do with us. He never told me she wrote and sent him money." She waved the envelopes again.

"Why does that matter?" Isaac wasn't taking in what she was saying. Katrina had left years ago, and that's all that mattered. He didn't care whether she'd written to her father or not.

"Why does it matter!" Miriam practically shouted the words, then she jerked a letter out of the envelope and began to read. 'Dear *Daed*, Greetings from South Korea! I love the food here. Yesterday my lunch reminded me so much of the egg noodles *Mamm* used to make when I was a kid.' She stuffed it back into the envelope and pulled out another one. 'Dear *Daed*, I'm back in L.A. after three months touring Europe, getting ready to write my next book. I got a very good advance, and I'm sending you another check. This will help you get through the winter and allow you to take it easy. Please promise me you'll cash this one?' "

Miriam raised her gaze to his. "Each letter is the same, and there are dozens. Dozens! And many of them contain a check that our father never saw fit to cash or tell me or Amos about. Why he did that, I will never understand. All these years, I was certain she had forgotten us—that she'd left me to do all the work, to try to find ways to make enough money to survive—" Her words choked off in a sob. "All this time, I was so wrong about her. I must tell her, Isaac. I must ask her to forgive me. Where is she?"

He shook his head, feeling too numb to take in all that she'd said, but some of her words penetrated. "Her friends from Los Angeles came. I told her to go back with them. I didn't want her here any longer. She left."

Miriam gasped. "She was going to stay out the term of *Daed's* will. Now that the papers are transferred, I don't know that it will matter, but it matters to me." She straightened her shoulders. "She is my sister, Isaac. I want to know what happened. You must tell me."

Isaac drew away from her, not sure what to say. "She betrayed my trust. That is all I will tell you. Now, she is gone with her friends back to the world where she belongs."

"I do not know anything about these *Englisch* friends, or the manner in which Katrina betrayed you. But seeing you two together at the work party—it does not seem to me she would ever hurt you intentionally." Miriam peered at him through narrowed eyes.

"Katrina has changed." Isaac turned his face away, looking at the house where she'd lived for the past week.

"Not as much as you may think. These letters showed me her heart. Not only that, she could have forced me to sell the farm so she could get her half, but she didn't. She signed it all over to me and refused any money. She even offered to pay the taxes for this year." Miriam shook her head. "She is still technically Amish, you know, since she never joined the church."

He gaped at her. "How can you stand here and defend her? Everyone could tell you weren't happy to see her when she came back."

"Yes. Much to my shame. I have much to make up to her, when I see her again." She looked at him one last time, then headed for her buggy. "You seem like a rational man, Isaac Mast, in every way other than where it concerns my sister. You need to put much thought into what you are doing, and maybe even a bit of prayer." She untied her horse, then walked around, climbed into the buggy, and didn't look back as it rolled down the driveway.

Chapter Twenty-Four

NUMBNESS HAD FLOODED THROUGH EVERY NERVE in Kathy's body. She was shocked she could even drive her car out of Cave City. Try as she might, she hadn't been able to block out Jacques's continuous stream of conversation. She adjusted her rearview mirror so she could check behind her. Evelyn's car had stayed with her through the last traffic light.

Jacques reached out and touched her hand on the steering wheel. "You won't regret coming back, Kath. You and I are going to be big hits on the Traveler Channel. I'll bet we'll have one of the most highly rated shows after it breaks. You won't ever have to write another book again."

She gave him a tiny smile, but her heart wasn't in it. "I happen to like writing."

He laughed. "You have to admit, Evelyn offering your farmer friend a contract was amusing. I can't see someone like that completing a book."

She glanced at him. "I don't find that funny."

"Just joking, Kath. You need to chill. You'll feel a lot better once we get out of this hayseed town."

"Honestly, I don't appreciate that kind of talk right now. Actually, I don't think I'd appreciate it any time."

He sobered. "I'm sorry, I was only joking. I know you love this place, but how long would you be happy here? We're adventurous souls who can't be satisfied in one place for long."

"You may be, but I'm not." Suddenly, Kathy knew that was true. She'd had more than her share of traveling—enough to last a lifetime. "You crave adventure, not me."

"So you crave what? Amish pancakes, living without electricity or cell phones? You wouldn't last long in that life. Admit it, we're perfect for each other."

She kept her eyes straight ahead on the road until something caught her eye. It seemed familiar ... she hit the brakes and slowed, then swerved to the left and onto a pullout. Glancing in her mirror, she saw with relief that Evelyn had followed her.

Evelyn swung her legs out of the car, her high heels sinking into the ground. "What do you think you're doing, Kathy? I almost rear-ended you."

Jacques climbed out and leaned on the hood. "Yeah. I thought you were going to put us into the ditch. What gives?"

Kathy stood next to the car, knowing exactly what she needed to do next. "Give me ten minutes, okay? I need to do something." She raced through the small stand of brush and hit the grassy path to the cemetery.

Kathy didn't stop at the tombstones but kept on until she got to the pond. She stood for a moment, drinking in the peace, wondering why she'd ever left this magical spot ten years ago. She searched the ground and picked up a flat rock, then tossed it, watching it skip across the water. Memories flooded back once again—of Isaac standing next to her, holding her hand, asking her not to leave but to join the church and see what their future might hold. If only she'd listened. Now it was too late.

She bowed her head, hoping she'd hear something—anything. As she waited, something soft drifted into her spirit—she couldn't say for sure it was God's voice, but she could sense His presence all around her. Peace enveloped her with such sweetness she wasn't sure she could bear it. She knew what she needed to do now. All she could do was pray God was guiding and would go before her to prepare the way.

Voices sounded behind her, and she turned to see Jacques holding Evelyn's arm as she picked her way down the path, tottering occasionally on those foolish heels she insisted on wearing. "What are you doing?" A slight whine in Evelyn's voice drifted to Kathy's ears.

How had she thought all these years that Evelyn's voice was so sophisticated and polished?

Jacques's voice followed Evelyn's. "Why are you wasting time at this stinky pond? It's going to be dinner time soon."

"I just need another five minutes, all right?"

Jacques deposited Evelyn at the large, flat rock. "Sounds good to me, as long as it isn't much longer. That'll give me time for a cigarette before we have to tramp back up that hideous jungle to the car."

Kathy raised her brows. "Since when did you start smoking again? You know your agent doesn't like it. You told me months ago that you stopped."

He shrugged. "I did stop. Then I started again. Then I stopped. But when I get stressed, I can't help myself."

Evelyn extended her hand to Kathy. "Come on, darling. We need to get back to our hotel and celebrate. The two of you are going to be brilliant on TV."

"I'm staying here." Kathy looked from one to the other, then out over the water, trying to regain the peace she'd felt minutes ago.

"For how long?" Jacques blew a ring of smoke. "Another ten minutes? Fifteen?"

"I'm not going back to L.A."

Evelyn sighed. "Are you going to finish out the terms of that tedious will? That means you want to stay another two weeks? I'll need to get in touch with

Jacques's agent and make arrangements, but I don't think the producer will be happy to hear it."

"No." Kathy shook her head. "Not another two weeks. Hopefully, much longer. I'm staying here in Cave City permanently. Jacques, I'm so sorry. I never meant to lead you along. I guess I always knew your feelings went much deeper than mine. It wasn't right for me not to tell you that. You're always searching for the next adventure. I can't do that any longer. My search ends here. I won't be doing the TV show with you, and I doubt I'll be writing any more bestselling travel books, since I plan to stop traveling."

"Seriously? You're going to ditch me for that Amish guy?" He snorted, then stubbed out his cigarette. "I can't say I'm totally blindsided. I saw how you looked at that farmer. When you flew out here, I was worried this place would get under your skin again and keep you here. I'll miss you, Kath, but I think you're making a huge mistake."

She reached out and gave him a quick hug. "Friends?"

He nodded. "Friends—I suppose. But you're going to miss an amazing adventure—and I think you're going to miss me."

Kathy laughed. "I think I've found my adventure and more. At least, I hope so."

Evelyn rose from the boulder. "What about me? You have a contract for *The Broke Girl's Guide to Kenya*."

Kathy smiled. "Even the Amish do conference calls when they have to, Evelyn. I'll be in touch and we'll see what we can work out. But I'm telling you right now, I'm never doing another contract after this one, and I've lost my drive to write those kinds of books. Maybe we can find something else that would satisfy my publisher."

As Evelyn hobbled up the path hanging onto Jacques's arm, Kathy reached into her pocket and pulled out her cell phone. She hefted it in her hand. More than anything, she wanted to throw this and the rest of her *Englisch* life into the pond, but she'd better wait until she completed her obligations with that life.

She sat on the boulder and unzipped her backpack, removing a small notebook and a pencil that she always carried with her in case inspiration should strike. She leaned over it and began to write.

Chapter Twenty-Five

KATHY STOPPED IN FRONT OF SARAH'S inn, wondering if she'd have room tonight for one more guest. She also wanted to see if her cousin had made any more arrangements about her future with Jeremiah. She smiled. From what she'd witnessed at the hospital, the two wouldn't wait long to marry. At least, only as long as the church decreed.

She slipped from the car with her backpack slung over her arm and headed up the path in the dusk of the evening, wishing she were back at Isaac's. That would have to wait. Besides, she wanted to talk to Sarah first and run an idea past her. Pushing the door open, she stepped over the curb. Silence. No sound of guests chattering or children's footsteps from the last family who had stayed. Good. Maybe everyone was gone.

"Sarah? Are you home?" Kathy walked through the entry and on into the kitchen but didn't find anyone there. She pushed open the back door and stepped out into the yard that bordered the garden area. "Sarah?"

Sarah stood and shaded her eyes. "Katrina? I wasn't expecting you today."

Kathy rushed outside and enveloped Sarah in a hug. "It's so good to see you."

Sarah hugged her in return, then studied Kathy for several long moments. "It is Isaac, *ya*?"

Kathy felt as though she'd been run over by a charging horse. "Why would you possibly guess that?"

Sarah led her over to a set of cedar chairs and beckoned for her to sit. "The last time I saw you together ... well, before the hospital, I wondered. Now I see it in your eyes. Hurt mixed with hope. Am I right?"

Kathy nodded, suddenly unable to form the words she'd come to speak. "*Ya.*"

Sarah reached over and squeezed her hand. "Have you come to some kind of decision?"

"I have. But before I share that, would you tell me what's happening with you and Jeremiah? I haven't seen you since a few days ago in the hospital. How is he doing?"

Rosy color flooded Sarah's cheeks. "They kept him for observation. After the swelling went down, he was out of danger, but they wouldn't allow him to *kumm* home yet."

"But you've had time to talk? To make plans?"

"*Ya.* We have." Sarah put her hands over her cheeks. "It's still all so new, I can hardly take it in. Before the accident, I wasn't sure. I thought I might be coming to care for him—especially after I saw Gabe and knew my heart was at peace about him. Then, when I thought I might lose Jeremiah forever..." She placed one hand over her heart. "I did not think I could live if he did not live. Does that make sense?"

"Perfectly. Now that you're sure, will you be courting for a while?"

"We will court, *ya.* You remember it is not our custom to tell anyone when we are betrothed? Since it is July now, we must announce our intentions this month or next, if we want to marry in the fall."

Kathy nodded. "I do remember, now that you mention it. I guess I've been away for long enough I hadn't thought about that." She leaned close to Sarah. "But you'll tell me, right?"

Sarah giggled. "We will not break tradition. It will be

announced at church when the time is right."

Kathy grinned. "*When* the time is right, not *if*?" She pumped her fist in the air, then realized how very *Englisch* that was. "Okay, I won't push you, but I think you've given me the answer I hoped for. I'm happy for you, Sarah."

"*Denke.* What about you, Katrina? Will you and Isaac...?"

Kathy stilled. Time to share what she was planning with her best friend. "I had guests show up today at Isaac's house, and it's been quite an unsettling few hours, but I came to a decision. I hope you have time for me to fill you in on all the details." She unzipped her backpack and pulled out the little notebook she'd used while sitting at Founder's Pond. "First, read what I wrote, then I'll explain the rest."

Sarah read the words once, then a second time, then raised shining eyes to Kathy. "*Wunderbar.* Lovely. I think this will do it, Cousin. *Ya,* I do."

Isaac tucked the covers tighter under Sadie's chin and leaned down to kiss her. "That's the third story in a row, plus a poem. You must be tired by now?" He'd been peeking at her through the entire last story, expecting to see her lids close any moment.

"*Nein.* I want to know where Miss Katrina went. She isn't at our house. I checked. I knocked and knocked, and she didn't *kumm.*"

"She went home, Sadie."

"I thought she lived here now."

"No. She lives far away in California. She was only here for a visit."

Sadie sat partway up. "Maybe we should go to

California and visit her. She's going to get lonely without us."

"I'm afraid it's too far to drive a buggy, Sadie. I wish you could have told her *gutt-bye*, but she left very suddenly."

Sadie's bottom lip poked out, and Isaac could see a storm building. "Do you want another story?"

"No. I want Miss Katrina."

A knock startled them both and stopped Sadie in the middle of the sob that had slipped partway out between her lips. "It's Miss Katrina! I know it is."

Isaac patted her head. "Don't get your hopes up. She's far away by now."

The knock came again, louder this time. "I know you're in there, Isaac Mast. Open this door right this instant."

Sadie began to giggle. "I told you so. It *is* Miss Katrina. Let her in, Papa!"

Isaac stood, then bent over Sadie. "You be a good girl, and after Miss Katrina leaves, I'll sing you a bedtime song."

Sadie bounced on the bed, making the springs squeak.

Isaac walked with dragging feet to the door and opened it a crack. "Katrina. It is late and I'm putting Sadie to bed. You were supposed to be gone."

She crossed her arms over her chest, her face blanketed in quiet determination. "I came back. I have something to say to you, Isaac, and I'm not leaving until I've said it."

"This is not a *gutt* time, Katrina." Something hit the back of his legs and his knees bent. He looked down, knowing what he'd see.

Sadie grinned up at him, then peered out the door. "Hello, Miss Katrina."

"Hello, Sadie."

"Papa was going to sing me a song. Would you like to come in and hear it?"

"Very much. But I have a poem I'd like to read to your papa instead, if that's all right with you?"

"*Ya.* That sounds *gutt.* I would like to hear your poem. I've heard all of Papa's many times." She wrinkled her nose. "He needs to write new ones."

Kathy bit her lip, but a smile slipped out.

Isaac glared at her. "Since when do you write poetry?" Frustration filled him to the point of boiling over. Hadn't he told her to leave and go back to L.A. with her friends where she belonged? Why was she here, looking so ... adorable. He didn't know if he should grab her and kiss her or run her off the property again.

Sadie hopped up and down, nearly pushing him over since she still had her arms around his legs. "Please, Papa. Please?"

He swung the door wider, curious in spite of himself at what Katrina could be up to. "All right. But only for a few moments, then Sadie must go to bed."

"Yay! *Denke.*" Sadie rushed over and hugged Katrina, then tugged on her hand and drew her to the bed. "You sit on the edge of the bed, Papa will sit in his chair by the bed, and I'll get under the covers. Just a minute." She slipped between the sheets and snuggled down, then patted the spot beside her. "Sit."

Kathy glanced at Isaac and mouthed, "The little dictator."

A soft smile touched his lips, then he smothered it.

He would not allow his emotions to be sent into turmoil by this woman again. It would have been more sensible to send her away, and if not for Sadie's insistence, he would have. Or at least, he thought he would. "All right. Read what you have written." He leaned back in his chair and crossed his arms, hoping to keep a barricade between his heart and hers.

Katrina opened a little notebook and glanced down, then raised her eyes and met his.

"There is a paradise as lovely
As the cliffs of Santorini,
Northern Lights in Norway,
Topaz waters of Tahiti.

Where the air smells like Lilies in the garden of
    Versailles, A place I feel as warm,
As a mountain hot spring in Hokkaido,
Or a summer night in Texas,

I didn't need to trot the globe,
As I've searched my heart and come to find
While seeking high and low
All along my heart was here with you
My paradise is home."

She peeked up at him as though afraid of what he might say.

He barely dared to breathe, unsure if she meant what he hoped she did. He glanced at Sadie, wondering if she'd caught the significance of the last words, but the child's eyes had drifted shut and her breathing was soft and even.

Kathy reached out and took Isaac's hand. She picked up the lantern at the head of the bed and nodded toward the door. "Come. Let's go outside where we can talk and not wake her."

Isaac rose and followed, his mind still spinning with the implications of what he'd heard.

Once they got outside, she faced him. "What did you think?"

He wiped a tear that had spilled over and trailed down his cheek.

"That bad?" She tried to laugh, but it came out a croak.

"*Nein.* It was very touching." He placed two fingers over his heart. "I felt it ... here. But did it mean what it said, or did I misunderstand?"

She drew him down onto a rustic wooden porch swing in the far corner. "I'm so sorry, Isaac. I never meant to betray your trust or hurt you."

She held up her hand when she saw he was about to respond. "Please. I need to say this. I sent Evelyn a few of your poems because they touched me so deeply, I couldn't hold it in. I wanted to share them with someone who would appreciate them as much as I did. I knew it would be a betrayal of your trust to tell Hazel or Sarah, so I chose Evelyn. I told her they were secret, and she couldn't share them with anyone. I also told her you had no interest in having them published. The rest she did on her own. I didn't know she contacted my publisher until after she'd done it." She ducked her head and focused on her hands in her lap.

Isaac reached over and touched one hand, then wrapped it in his large, calloused one.

She leaned closer. "I never understood you before."

"But now you do?"

"I think so. I hope so. I know there's so much more to know, but I want to learn." She squeezed his hand. "I'm not going back to L.A., and I'm not going to Kenya. I'll find another way to fulfill my contract, or I'll return the advance and see if they'll release me. I belong here. I know that now. With you."

This time his grip tightened, and he stroked his thumb over her knuckles. "You would do that for me? Give up what you've worked so long and so hard for? But you are an author. You have spent ten years building this life."

"Yes. I know it won't be easy, but I've also spent the last ten years trying to figure out who I am—what I want to be—and I know now that it's all centered here, with you, with this community. There's a lot I'll have to relearn, like how I talk and dress, but I can do it, if you want me. It will take work, but I know I can do it." She took a shaky breath. "What do you think? You haven't said much."

Isaac glanced at her. She wasn't sure if he thought she was crazy or what, but at least he hadn't let go of her hand or raced for his cabin and slammed the door shut.

"Hey." She shook his hand. "Don't keep a girl waiting in suspense. It wasn't easy for me to come here and say all of this."

"*Ya.* I can see that." A mischievous smile touched his mouth. "I was thinking—you never really left the church—technically speaking—since you didn't officially join."

It took her a moment, but then she giggled, and he began to laugh. He wrapped her in his arms and drew her close. "We had better be quiet if we don't want Sadie out here demanding to know what we're doing."

"Right. Sorry."

"I am not sorry. At all." He tipped up her chin. "I love you, Katrina. With all my heart."

She closed her eyes. "I love you too, Isaac." The sweet feel of his lips touched hers, and she knew her heart had finally come home.

Epilogue

Early November, four months later

KATRINA YODER AND SARAH STOLFZFUS STOOD in the *Daadi Haus* on Miriam's farm where Katrina had lived for the past few months. The bishop had read the names of the couples who planned to marry on the first Sunday in October, and life had been a whirlwind getting ready since then.

Katrina and Sarah had agreed they would marry on the same day, in back-to-back ceremonies, and Miriam had insisted on making both of the brides a new dress, apron, and *Kapp*. Katrina held the lavender gown in front of her. "This is so lovely. I still have to shake myself sometimes to take in how different Miriam treats me. I always longed to have our relationship restored, but I never truly believed it would happen."

"*Ya*, she is like a completely different person than the one who was so angry when you returned in the summer." Sarah stroked the rich blue fabric of her dress as it lay on the bed. "You think it was the letters she found that you wrote to your father?"

Katrina nodded. "*Ya*. I do. She told me how ashamed she was when she read them, that she'd misjudged me all these years, and how badly she felt for how spiteful she acted when I came. I think it was the letters as well as my giving her the farm that finally caused the anger to break, as well as the realization that I was the only other living member of our immediate family. She knew I planned to go back to the West Coast, and after she read those letters, it hit her that she might never see me again. She rushed to

Isaac's house, but I'd already gone. According to Isaac, she gave him an earful and told him to shape up." She laughed. "Well, not in exactly those words, I guess."

Sarah came over and stood beside Katrina. "You are at peace that you have joined the church and are staying here?"

"*Ya.* Very much so. It is truly *wunderbar.* I love Isaac and Sadie. It amazes me all the time that *Gott* is giving me so much in such a short amount of time. And my publisher let me out of my contract for that last book. I think they decided if the book didn't come from my heart, it wouldn't do well. I told them my heart is here, and they somehow understood. Another gift from *Gott*, I would say."

Sarah gazed at Katrina, then shook her head.

"What? Did I say something funny? You act like you're going to laugh. Do I have food stuck in my teeth?" She laughed. "Spill. What's up?"

Sarah began to laugh. "One minute you sound like someone who has never left the Amish life. The next minute, you are speaking like an *Englischer* again. It is a bit funny, I must confess."

"Oh, rats." Katrina threw up her hands. "I've been trying so hard to say things in the right way. I had to study hard before I joined the church, and I've remembered so much. But sometimes the *Englisch* me slips in and takes over again." She smirked. "I did get rid of all my jeans and t-shirts, but I decided to keep my phone for now. Who knows, I might decide to start a business. Then I'll need it."

Sarah giggled. "I'll tell you a secret." She reached into the pocket of her skirt. "I have one too. My friend Annie convinced me I needed one for the inn, after she helped me build a website. I am very careful where I use it, but I must say, it is a comfort sometimes." She sobered. "I'm so glad you and Annie have become friends. She will always be *Englisch*, but she's been a *gutt* friend to me, and with Hunter's help, she understands our ways and has fit in nicely."

"I like her a lot. I think she's helped make my transition back to Amish life easier, since she used to live in L.A. and was part of the TV world. Even though she's not Amish, she's learned to live a much simpler life since she and Hunter married."

"*Ya*. And she has another secret too. Has she told you yet?" Sarah's eyes sparkled with a light that could only mean one thing.

Katrina lowered her voice. "A *bopplie*?"

Sarah nodded. "*Ya*. A *bopplie*. She couldn't be happier, and Hunter is over the moon." A dreamy expression settled on her face. "My Ezra and I never had children, but maybe this time..."

Katrina smiled, feeling the exact same hope herself. "It would be *wunderbar* if we both had children close together and they could grow up as close as we were, *ya*?"

"*Ya*." Sarah drew Katrina into a long hug, then stepped back. "Let's get into these dresses and go see our men. I can't wait to get married and start our new lives."

"Me too." Katrina rushed to don her dress, apron, *Kapp*, long stockings, and high-topped shoes. She didn't even care that it wasn't a white wedding gown. It was what came from the heart that mattered, and right now, hers was so full of love for Isaac that she could barely contain it.

Author Note

My producer Chevonne and I brainstormed the original ideas for Follow Your Heart, but she brought the new idea to me after our initial idea was scrapped. We had hoped to write Sarah's full story—the Sarah from *Runaway Romance*—but it turned out the market favored an *Englischer* as the primary character with Amish as the secondary. I was disappointed, as I felt strongly that Sarah's story needed to be resolved, since we'd left her hanging in *Runaway Romance*.

We put together a brand-new idea for *Follow Your Heart*, but because the books are always longer and contain a secondary thread, I decided this book would be the perfect time to give Sarah her happily-ever-after ending. I'm so glad I had that opportunity, since all three books in this series will have an *Englischer* heroine with Amish in the background. And of course, we can't forget Kathy/Katrina Yoder's happy ending as well.

If you watch the movie and read the book, you'll see the endings are different. My book (the main thread) follows the script as it was originally written. At the last minute, the director decided to change the ending. In case you haven't watched the movie yet, I won't spoil it by telling you how it was changed, but I'd LOVE to hear from you to know which ending you liked the best. Contact me via my newsletter link or my website below.

Also, if you've seen *Runaway Romance* and *Follow Your Heart*, you might notice something else. The actress who played Sarah in *Runaway Romance* played

Kathy/Katrina Yoder in *Follow Your Heart*. I have no say in who gets hired for the various parts, but I was a little concerned over the choice. Not because I didn't love Galadriel Stineman as Sarah—I did. I thought she was perfect. And yes, she was awesome in *Follow Your Heart* too.

It just seemed a bit strange to me to have her play an Amish woman in one and an Amish woman turned *Englischer* in the other. However, as it was explained to me, the movies are not related. UP TV released *Runaway Romance*, so *Follow Your Heart* is not a spin-off, since it was picked up by Hallmark. You will also see another familiar face as the heroine in *Finding Love in Bridal Veil*—with the title from the book changed to *Finding Love in Mountain View* airing on Hallmark in October of 2020.

So much has gone into the journey from the concept of this book to the production of the movie that it's hard to sort out all the pieces. But there's one thing that stands out, and that's how it all began. You would think that would be when I received the call from my (now) producer, Chevonne O'Shaughnessy, in the late spring of 2015, but it started much earlier. In fact, what happened has the definite feel of the Hand of God in bringing it all to pass.

Rewind to early 2011. I had a finished manuscript, an Old West romance set in ranch country outside of Sundance, Wyoming, titled *Outlaw Angel*, that my agent was shopping. I'd written and published three books with Summerside Press, all part of their *Love Finds You* series. In fact, my agent had presented the book set in Sundance as another *Love Finds You* book, but it was turned down as the location had already been assigned to another well-known author. I'd decided the manuscript would become the first in a series of three old west romances, but by that point it hadn't found a home.

My editor with Summerside contacted me in January or February of that year, saying they were in desperate need of a book for that setting for their *Love Finds You* line, and asked if I had sold mine yet. I said no, but my agent was shopping it as a three-book series. Long story short, their author had some kind of setback, and she was unable to fulfill the contract and turn in the book on time. They offered me the contract, but at a lower rate than I or my agent wanted to accept. Finally, I almost reluctantly decided to move forward and give up my dream of it becoming a series. After all, I'd first written it thinking it might be a good fit for the *LFY* line.

The book was published in the late summer of 2011, a very fast turnaround time. A couple of years later, I got word that a Hollywood production company had optioned several of the *LFY* titles, including mine set in Sundance. Three *Love Finds You* movies were made and aired on the UP Channel over the next two years, but nothing more was said about Sundance.

Then, in 2015, I received an email from Chevonne, followed by a phone call. Imagine my surprise when she asked if I'd be willing to write a book for them. They were no longer producing the *Love Finds You* books into movies and were working on a totally different project for UP, a possible three-movie series, and she hoped I might be able to work with them. As anyone would be, I was curious why she'd chosen me. She explained that she'd optioned *Sundance* two or three years earlier and loved it. Of the thirty-five or so titles she'd read of the line, that was her favorite. However, UP didn't want to make historical or Old West movies, so she'd had to shelve it.

During that time period, I'd gotten my rights back to all of my *LFY* books and had retitled them *Finding Love in Last Chance, California*; *Finding Love in Tombstone, Arizona*; and *Finding Love in Bridal Veil, Oregon*. *Sundance* became *Outlaw Angel*, and all four are still in print.

Here's the amazing part. I came very, very close to turning down that contract offer with Summerside for *Sundance*. I was disappointed in the advance and royalty rate, and shortly after they released it, they sold the line to Guideposts, and that company didn't continue the line much longer. Understandably, sales waned on their final releases, and I was disappointed with my sales from that final book as all three of my others had done quite well.

For a long time, I wished I hadn't taken that contract and held out for one with another company for a three-book series. However, had I done that, I doubt *Runaway Romance* would ever have been written. It was *Sundance* that grabbed Chevonne's attention and caused her to contact me. And the rest, as they say, is history.

The UP channel decided to release only the first movie, as at that time, they went in a new direction with reality shows instead of movies. I believe that's changed since then, but in the meantime, Chevonne and George were shopping the other two movies. *Follow Your Heart* and *Finding Love in Mountain View* (Bridal Veil) caught the attention of a Hallmark representative. They watched the trailers for each and loved them, then went on to see the advance movie. I am beyond excited to now have two Hallmark and UP TV channel movies!

I also happen to be the publisher at Mountain Brook Ink, a small Christian press. We have now released over eighty titles, with many more on the way, including award-winning books, two others of which have also been optioned by ACI, Chevonne and George's company. While writing this book, I was juggling two other edits for my authors and staying on top of the numerous emails, putting out small business 'fires', training a new intern, and working with our promotion team and acquisition team. At the age of sixty-six, I'm still going strong and plan to keep writing books and running this company until God says otherwise. Oh, and at Mountain Brook Ink, we also started a new speculative fiction line called Mountain Brook Fire—and, we kicked off a spec fiction writing contest that was in full swing while finalizing this book. Nope, I'm not busy at all!

I didn't get to attend the filming of this movie (*Follow Your Heart*), much to my regret. I missed it as well as *Runaway Romance*, due to other professional and family obligations. However, I did get to attend a full day of filming for my book *Finding Love in Bridal Veil, Oregon*, when it was filmed in Mountain View, Arkansas, in September of 2019. That movie will release in the fall of 2020, with the new title being *Finding Love in Mountain View*. Unfortunately, Bridal

Veil hasn't existed as a town since the 1980s, when the last vestiges of the old buildings were removed. There is still a post office, a couple of houses in the outlying area, and a community center, but nothing of the old town still remains.

My Bridal Veil book is a historical romance, with a lot of real-life history woven in. At my suggestion, since the market isn't making many historical movies, it was turned into a contemporary. That was quite a challenge in itself, but Chevonne, George, and their scriptwriters did a wonderful job pulling it off. I decided not to write a new book or to rewrite the old one, as the basic storyline still (somewhat) exists and can be recognized in the movie. We're saying that the movie was inspired by the book, which it was, but not that it's totally based on the book, since there had to be so many changes. I think you'd enjoy reading the historical version to compare and have the fun of learning so much about the actual small town it was based in.

Getting to be on set for that movie was an amazing experience. Getting to meet the four primary actors was even better—AND I got to hang out with Chevonne and get a hug from George. I have a few pictures of me with the actors as well as a few shots of the filming, if you'd like to check out my website. You can see the link below.

I just finished brainstorming and writing the screen treatment for *When Love Comes Calling*, which (hopefully) will be filmed in the summer or fall of 2020, and release in 2021, but you'll have to watch my author group on Facebook or join my newsletter for more updates on that. And here's a secret that very few know yet. When I finished the write-up for *When Love Comes Calling*, Chevonne informed me we left a secondary character at the perfect place for a sequel. So ... I'm guessing that COULD mean there's going to be a book/movie #4. Again, sign up for my newsletter to stay in the know!

If you'd care to connect with me, you can do so at the following places:

My website/blog and newsletter sign-up:
www.miraleeferrell.com

Facebook Author Group:
www.facebook.com/groups/82316202888/

Instagram: miralee_ferrell_author

Mountain Brook Ink website:
www.mountainbrookink.com

Twitter: www.twitter.com/miraleeferrell

I prefer to interact on FB in my author group, rather than adding more friends, so please connect with me there rather than sending a friend request. Another great way to connect is joining my newsletter, as you can reply to it and the reply will come straight to my email. Thank you all for taking the time to read my newest book, and if you have time, check out some of my other fiction, which you can find by doing a search on Amazon or ChristianBook.com under Miralee Ferrell.

Please consider posting a review if you enjoyed this book and share the book with friends and family. Doing both of those is a wonderful blessing to an author and helps ensure we'll have readers for our books in the future. Hopefully, all three books in this series will also be available on Audible soon, as well. Thank you all!

The prologue and first two chapters of
Finding Love in Bridal Veil, Oregon,
the book that inspired the movie,
Finding Love in Mountain View.

THE TOWN OF BRIDAL VEIL, OREGON, was founded in 1886 in the heart of the beautiful Columbia River Gorge. The town began as a paper mill and soon evolved into a lumber and planing mill. Its sister sawmill lay in nearby Palmer, where the timber was broken down into lumber and transported by flume to the lower mill. A thriving community grew up in both Bridal Veil and nearby Palmer, with the two towns' commerce and social lives intertwined. For over fifty years the towns worked together—until 1936, when fire consumed some of the planer buildings in Bridal Veil. The timber supply was almost depleted, and the company moved out of Palmer. The Kraft Company purchased the existing buildings and equipment and produced moldings and boxes. World War II brought yet more change when women were hired to work at the mill, which produced ammunition boxes. After the war, Kraft expanded its operation, and by 1955 the company and town were booming. The end of the nineteen fifties saw a huge downturn in sales, and in 1960, Kraft made the decision to shut down. Homes and buildings were slowly abandoned, and the mill was never reopened.

Miralee Ferrell

Prologue

Bridal Veil, Oregon
July, 1898

YES.

The simple word staring up at JACOB Garvey from the piece of white paper hit him so hard it nearly knocked him to his knees. He'd been afraid of something like this for weeks. The note tucked in the wooden box lying under the tree confirmed his fears.

Maybe this wasn't what it seemed. Jacob turned the piece of paper over, hoping to find an explanation. His hand trembled as his gaze slid over the words printed in the bold handwriting.

Margaret. I'm leaving town this evening and not coming back. I want to marry you. I'll come for your answer after work. If I find the word Yes, *then I'll meet you here after dark. Only bring what you need. I love you and can't wait to make you my wife—Nathaniel*

P. S. If I don't find your reply, I'll know you can't go through with it.

A soft groan passed Jacob's lips, and he rocked on his heels. His eyes returned to the answer written in his daughter's clear script—willing it to change, willing it to disappear. *Yes.* Margaret was everything to him and had filled the awful void after his dear wife died. His sweet girl deserved so much better. There had to be a way to protect her from her own immaturity.

Why did Margaret persist in seeing Nathaniel

Cooper? To his way of thinking, the man had no prospects and even less ambition. The Garvey family might not have much in the way of money, but they had history—their roots extended back to some of the hardy pioneers who helped settle this land.

What did that young man have? Hopeless dreams and no family—at least, none that Jacob knew of. A drifter with no prospects whom Margaret had met a scant six months ago. From what he'd heard, Cooper jumped from one job to the next, with no thought for the future. He'd lasted less than a year here and was already moving on. Margaret could end up destitute if that ne'er-do-well wasn't careful. Besides, she was only sixteen.

Jacob placed the paper back in the box and stood. He'd hide the box with the note inside until he was sure Margaret's future was safe. When Nathaniel returned for it, he'd think she didn't want to marry him and leave town. He snapped the lid shut and hurried back down the trail, anxious to get home.

The gate hinges squealed when he pushed through into his yard. He paused with a glance at the house, praying Margaret hadn't heard. Now, where to dump this box? Starting a fire might raise questions, with the forest so dry this time of year. His gaze lit on his shovel lying next to an unplanted rosebush bound in burlap. He'd prepared the hole but hadn't unwrapped the roots or set the bush. He glanced at the box in his hand, then back at the hole.

Hurrying over to the small rose bed, he peered over his shoulder, praying Margaret wouldn't offer to help. When no movement showed through the windows on the south side of the house, he bent to his task.

He withdrew a sharp knife from his pocket and cut away the burlap from the roots of the rose, then wrapped the long strip around the box and laid it aside. Quickly he enlarged the hole, creating a side pocket at the base, then slipped the box and its message into the cool grave. The rose took its place in the hole, then he tamped in the soil and watered the rose. Another glance at the house assured him of success. Margaret would never know. His daughter's future was safe.

Chapter One

Four years later
Late May, 1902

MARGARET HURRIED TO THE TWO-STORY HOUSE set against the base of the tree-clad hill, anxiety dogging her steps. Papa had been tired when he'd left the house early this morning, but he'd been working at the mill long hours of late. Nothing to worry about, he'd assured her—he needed the Sabbath to catch up on his rest, and he'd be right as rain. But she didn't believe it. He looked peaked and moved as though weights were attached to his limbs. Best to keep an eye on him, in case he was coming down with the grippe.

"Papa? You home yet?" She flung off her sweater and dumped her books on a nearby table. She'd not meant to stay so long at the school, but little Mark James had thrown one of his temper tantrums and needed a talking to. Then the chores had to be done—the floor swept, the board erased, her desk straightened—all things that didn't normally take much time, but Gertrude Graham had stopped by on her way home from the Company store and slowed her down further. Gertrude was a sweetie, but everyone in town knew her propensity for gossip ran as deep as the nearby Columbia River.

Margaret had at last made her excuses and headed home. Part of her hoped Papa had kept his promise to leave work early and rest, while the other part wanted to light the stove and get supper going before he arrived.

Dusk wouldn't settle in for another hour or so, but

she lit one lamp just the same, wanting a cheerful glow to penetrate the gloom when he made his way down the trail.

An hour later she glanced out the window again, hoping to see his familiar figure trudging up the path. Nothing. She dusted the flour from her hands and finished mixing the dough for the chicken and dumplings, then dropped globs of dough onto the steaming mixture in the pan and covered the large cast-iron skillet with a domed lid. At least the house was warm. In a few minutes the dumplings would rise, filling the room with their fragrance. Her mouth watered at the thought, and her lips tipped up at the happiness that would light Papa's eyes when he stepped through the door.

The front door rattled, and her hand flew to her throat. Papa wouldn't shake the door handle or knock; he'd stride in with his booming greeting and big smile. Margaret stood in the middle of the kitchen frozen by uncertainty—but only for a moment. Could it be a neighbor in need of help or one of the unsavory characters riding the railroad cars of late? Hobos had been increasing in number, and her father had warned her not to open the door to a stranger if he wasn't home.

She reached for the heavy wooden rolling pin resting on the painted countertop Papa had built and gripped it tight. "Who's there?" She took a step toward the door in the nearby living room.

No reply. The knob moved again but this time with less energy. What in the world? She gripped her makeshift weapon tighter and crept to the door.

A quick twist of the round metal knob and a jerk of the door brought her face-to-face with Papa slumped against the doorjamb, his head lolled to the side.

Margaret dropped the pin, and it clattered to the floor. She grasped his shoulders and gave him a small shake. "Papa? Are you sick? Papa!" She ran her gaze over his body, trying to find any sign of what might be wrong.

A low groan escaped his pale mouth, and his head rolled like a broken-necked doll. His eyes opened, and he raised a shaking hand "Not. Feeling well. Help me. Inside."

She slipped her arm around his waist and tried to support his sagging weight, stumbling as his feet barely cleared the threshold. Somehow she managed to half carry, half drag him to the worn couch against a nearby wall. He settled down with a moan and started to shake. Beads of sweat popped out on his forehead, and his breath came in shallow gasps.

"What's wrong, Papa? Where does it hurt? Should I go for Doc Albert?"

Margaret leaned over her prone father and clutched his hand, willing her own to stop trembling.

His eyes fluttered open, and the stark pain in them revealed the effort it took to speak. "Chest. Hurts. Shoulder. Jaw. It's bad. No time."

"Hush, Papa. You've been working too hard, that's all. Let me go for the doc."

He gripped her hand with a sense of urgency and persisted. "No time. You need…to listen."

"No. Don't talk, just rest. You'll be fine." She bit her lip, wanting to race down the path to the doctor's home a quarter mile away but was too terrified to leave him alone. Instead she lifted the knitted afghan off the back of the couch, spread it over his shaking form, and smoothed back his hair.

A movement outside the window caught her attention, and she squeezed his hand. "Hold on, Papa. I'll be right back."

She flew to the door and jerked it open in time to see eight-year-old Harry Waters swinging up the path with a fishing pole over his shoulder. "Harry?"

The boy halted midstride and turned toward her. "Yes, Miss Garvey? You need somethin'?"

"Yes. Run as fast as you can and get Doc Albert. Tell him my father is ill, and we need him to come. Hurry!"

The black hair flopped on his forehead as he nodded in assent. "Yes, ma'am." A flick of his wrist tossed the pole into the nearby brush and the boy was off, racing along the path on the shortcut back toward town.

Margaret rushed inside and sank to her knees next to her father. She drew in a deep breath, suddenly frightened by his face drained of color and his tightly closed eyes. "Papa? Are you awake?"

There was a slight movement of his head. Then something resembling a frown crossed his face, but it could have been a spasm of pain. "Sorry, Beth." His pet name for her slipped out as his eyes struggled to open. "Forgive me."

"Shh, it's all right, Papa. There's nothing to forgive. Rest now."

"No. Shouldn't have done it," he panted. "Tried. To fix it. Forgive me." The words trailed off, but his imploring eyes didn't leave her face.

"Of course I forgive you. Hang on, Papa. Doc Albert will be here any minute."

A deep sigh escaped, and his eyes closed again. Margaret grasped his hand tighter and prayed. God couldn't let her father die. She wouldn't allow it. Mama had died twelve years ago, and her grandfather last year. Between that and losing Nathaniel four years ago... that was enough for one person to bear. Papa had the grippe. He'd be back on his feet soon, laughing and teasing about her temper matching her auburn hair and living up to Mama's Irish heritage.

At that moment her father's body convulsed. The muscles around his mouth tightened, then suddenly relaxed, and the already weak fingers grew limp in her hand.

"Papa?" She gently disengaged her grip and stroked his forehead. "Papa, can you hear me?"

He lay still with not even a twitch of his muscles.

Panic sucked the breath from Margaret's lungs, leaving her dizzy and faint. She shook her head, drew a deep breath, and forced the reaction away. No time for foolishness. Papa needed her strong.

She drew close to his face, praying for movement, hoping for another breath. "Papa. You can't leave me alone." A sob tore at her throat and slipped out in spite of her effort to quell it. "I need you, Papa. Please, please stay with me." She lifted a shaking hand and patted his cheek, hoping and praying he'd respond.

All of a sudden, realization struck her with its deadly truth, and she cried out. Frantically she searched for any sign of life—breathing—a flicker of his eyelids. But there was nothing. Papa was gone. He'd never smile or tease her again. Never enjoy the meal she'd prepared or sit in a church pew beside her on Sunday mornings.

How could she stand it? What would she do now? Oh, why had God seen fit to take him when he was still young, and she had no one else in her life? She dropped her head on his shoulder and sobs welled up from a place so deep, a place so terrified of the pain and loneliness she knew would come. Just like it had with Mother. Just like it had with Grandpa. And just like it had with Nathaniel. No. She'd not wallow in that now.

A knock sounded at the door, and the knob turned. She vaguely felt gentle hands stroking her hair and a strong arm wrapping around her, drawing her away from the still figure on the couch.

Chapter Two

Early July, 1902

MARGARET STILL HADN'T FIGURED OUT WHAT her father had needed her to forgive. She wracked her memory but couldn't imagine what had plagued him so close to his death.

She tapped the nails into the wooden crate, then brushed the drooping lock of hair from her eyes and dusted off her hands. That was the last box, and barely in time, too. The wagon would arrive in an hour. One more walk through the house, and she'd be ready to go.

Everything had happened so fast. One day her father was here, the next he was gone. His sudden death had ripped a hole in her life. So many losses these past years. Her battered emotions had begun to heal after Mama passed, and then Nathaniel disappeared. Now this. Grief swamped her again, and she choked back the need to cry. All she'd done this past five weeks was mourn. No more tears today. She must concentrate on the gift the Lord had given her by allowing her time to tell Papa good-bye.

Margaret shook her head and continued her inspection. The past three years she'd stayed here to help take care of Papa, even though the town fathers preferred she live next to the school. The house belonged to the owners of the Bridal Veil Lumbering Company and would be leased to another tenant now that Papa was gone, leaving her free to occupy the teacher's cabin.

Margaret wandered from the kitchen and headed toward the stairs. One more peek at her bedroom to be sure nothing still hid in a corner. She smiled, thinking about the games she'd played in that room with friends growing up and the times they'd hidden under the covers, certain that monsters hid under the bed.

She trailed her fingers along the fir banister on the way up the stairs and patted the newel post at the top one last time. Regret at parting with her old home hit her again, but she pushed it away. Regret didn't belong in her life, and she'd not let it get a stranglehold over her emotions again. Life should be lived *forward*, and constant time spent looking back brought pain. She'd learned that this past four years.

The schoolmarm's cabin was small, so she'd given some of her furniture to a needy mill family with six children. But she kept the treasured pieces she could never part with—her bed, which her father had fashioned himself, and also the solid pine table and chairs he'd built for her mother.

The creaking of wagon wheels and a jingling harness drew her thoughts back to the present. She looked at the gold watch hanging on a chain around her neck. Julius was right on time.

"Hello, the house," a ringing masculine voice called.

Margaret swung open the front door and stepped onto the small covered porch, shading her eyes from the summer sun's reflection off the nearby Columbia River. "Afternoon, Julius. Your mules are looking good today." She nodded at the matched pair of dark bay mules that were his pride and joy and was rewarded by a beaming grin.

Julius Winston's mouth sported a gap where a tooth used to reside, rumored to have been dislodged by a kick from a disgruntled mule. But that hadn't changed his near worship of the creatures. No one who saw Julius' contagious smile thought long about the missing tooth, as the man's entire face was transformed by his grin. A happier teamster she'd never met, and that was saying a lot in this bustling, growing mill town.

He jumped off the wagon seat and dusted his hands against his pant legs. "Yep—they shore do, don't they, Miss Margaret? Why, t'other day I was tellin' Grant down at the Company store—'Grant,' I said—'don't ya think Molly and Verna is looking spry and sassy this summer? Why, their coats is shining so bright sometimes, they like to hurt m'eyes.'" He chuckled and slapped his leg.

Margaret's spirits lifted a bit at the happy chatter from the older man. With Julius warmed up to his favorite subject she doubted she'd need say more than yes, no, or smile the rest of the time it took to load the wagon.

Julius drew the mules to a halt in front of the cabin and Margaret sat on the hard seat of the wagon, taking in the features of her new home. She and some ladies from church had readied the cabin, giving it a sound cleaning earlier in the week and leaving the doors and windows ajar to air it out for a day. By the time they'd finished scrubbing the floors and windows, it opened its welcoming arms with a freshness and sparkle that brought joy to Margaret's weary heart.

Papa would be happy she'd made the decision to move. He'd always worried about her staying to care for him instead of taking up official residence in the schoolteacher's cabin. The teacher for the upper grades was married and didn't need the little house, so it had stood empty the past two years.

A sense of loss swept over her. Her father, both protective and proud, had loved her with a fierce paternal love that had helped fill the chasm created by the death of her mother when Margaret was young. But now she needed to draw her thoughts away from the past and try to absorb herself in the future.

The cabin sat back from the Columbia River, close to the base of the hill. She wished it were within view of the magnificent Bridal Veil Falls. The awesome pounding of the water and the mist dancing like prisms in the sun were a constant source of pleasure whenever she found time to walk the mile or so to its base.

It was a one-minute walk from her new home to the two-story schoolhouse, recently built to accommodate the growing number of students. Who'd have believed this small town would ever boast nearly forty students, ranging from the first reader to the seventh? Margaret loved teaching, even with the challenges some of the more trying students often presented.

Julius jumped down from the seat and scurried around to reach for her hand. "Help you down, Teacher?"

"I think I'd like to sit for a few moments, if you don't mind. Would you tie the mules, and then I'll join you?"

His expression softened as he glanced from her to the cabin and back, seeming to understand her need for some time alone. She welcomed this move, but sadness also pervaded her heart. Change so often resulted from some type of difficulty. Yes, it could be mixed with joy, but she appreciated the time to make the adjustment.

She loved this two-room cabin in the clearing, built

of lumber sawed at their local mill and lovingly crafted by several of the townspeople. Glass windows, brought by train from Portland, flanked both sides of the sturdy door. The cabin could easily withstand the heavy winds that often blew rain and snow through the Columbia River Gorge, keeping its occupant snug and dry.

Margaret loved the cheerful, multicolored patch of flowers along the front, planted by her students early this spring and tended by a different family each week. A mix of towering fir and maple trees created a welcome spot of shade during the heat of the summer months. And possibly best of all, the cabin boasted a small vegetable garden in the back lot. Her father had been an avid gardener, and Margaret had hated the thought of giving up the summer vegetables—so now she'd grow her own.

Julius hitched the mules to a nearby tree and turned back toward the wagon but halted at the sound of a man's hail a few yards up the path. A young man in his early twenties strode into sight. Sunlight danced on his uncovered, curly brown hair, and his rugged face lit in appreciation when he saw Margaret. "I see I made it in time to help you unload." He stopped several feet from the wagon and grinned.

Margaret's pulse skipped a beat, and her breath quickened. Andrew Browning had started coming around a few weeks before her father's death, and she knew that he'd developed an interest in her, but she hadn't quite decided how she felt about him. Right now her heart felt too sore to think about courting so soon after Papa's passing. Thankfully, Andrew hadn't pushed his suit and seemed content to remain friends. But his appearance today and offer of help warmed her, and she gave him what she hoped was a pleasing smile. "Thank you, Andrew. There isn't much to unload, and

Julius assures me he can handle it without much bother."

Julius' chest puffed out at her words, and his whiskered cheeks turned pink. "Yes, ma'am. No bother a'tall."

Andrew's expression lost some of its excitement, so Margaret hastened to his rescue. "Julius?"

"Yes, Miss Margaret?" He swept off his hat and looked up.

"I know you don't really need any help, but do you suppose Andrew might stay and offer a hand?" She rose from the buckboard seat and grasped the rail, but Julius stepped to the side of the wagon and helped her down.

"Guess it wouldn't hurt, if'n he stays and helps." The wide smile again lit the older man's countenance. "Nothin' here I can't do myself, but it might go faster with another set of hands." He cast a sly glance at the once again grinning Andrew. "Although it do appear he's cleaned up some after workin' at the planer mill—might be a shame to get them nice duds dirty packing in boxes and furniture." Julius winked.

Andrew hurried to the back of the wagon and hoisted a wooden crate onto his muscular shoulder. "Don't you worry about my clothes, Julius. They're not my Sunday best. I didn't want to get planer shavings on Miss Margaret's nice things, so I changed before I came."

Julius patted his mule on the rump as he headed toward the back of the wagon. "Ah-huh. Well, let's get to work, so Miss Margaret is feelin' to home before the sun goes down." He nodded at Margaret. "How 'bout you stand inside and direct where you want these things? No sense you gettin' dirty or hurtin' yourself packin' in heavy boxes."

The next half-hour flew by as the two men toted boxes inside. The furniture she'd brought quickly found a place in her new home, and within a short time she stood at the door and surveyed her small domain. The kitchen was just inside the door, with her pine table and chairs a few feet from the sink that boasted a water pump. The far side of the room contained her comfortable old sofa, a round pine table next to it, and two wing-backed stuffed chairs.

Her bedroom lay beyond the cozy living area. The men had set up her bed, matching dresser, and nightstand. It was now a warm, friendly place with colorful braided rugs, polished pine furniture, and a woodstove for the cold winter months.

Julius stepped up beside her. "Looks like that about does it. Want I should stay and pry the lids off those crates?"

Andrew picked up a hammer and strode to the nearest box. "I can get these, Julius."

"Ah-huh." Julius plucked his hat off the table. "Well, then, I guess I'll go split a little kindlin' before I head home. Wouldn't want the neighbors' tongues waggin', the two of you bein' alone in the house without a chaperone." He grinned on his way out the door.

Margaret leaned against a post on the edge of the porch. "Thank you again, Julius. You're a blessing."

The red crept up his neck and washed across his cheeks, and his infectious grin erupted. "Aw, it were nothin'." He moved past the wagon where the patient mules dozed and headed toward the chopping block.

The screeching of nails reluctantly parting from a crate drew Margaret back inside. "Andrew? I appreciate your help."

"Happy to." His warm smile gave her heart a jolt. He reached for another box and applied the claw of the hammer to a stubborn nail. "Everything out of your house, or do you need more help?"

She sank down onto the nearby sofa and shook her head. "It's all here, and the ladies at church offered to help me clean the old place for the new tenant. I hear he's arriving next week."

Andrew raised sparkling brown eyes that smiled into hers. "Good. I'd hate to see you do that alone." He sat back on his haunches. "Looks like that's the last box. Want me to stay and help you unpack?"

"No, you've done enough. Besides, I'm not sure where I want things to go quite yet. I think I'll sit for a while—maybe rest my feet and decide what I want to put where."

"Sounds like a fine idea." He rose and brushed back the hank of curly hair that insisted on draping over his forehead, then set his hat on his head.

Margaret glanced with appreciation at his well-built frame. He wasn't tall, but had broad shoulders and muscular arms from off-bearing boards at the planer mill. When he grinned two dimples peeked out at the corners of his mouth, giving him a decidedly roguish look.

Her thoughts drifted to another pair of dark, intense eyes and a tall, slender man. Nothing about Andrew reminded her of that other man, but thinking about Nathaniel now caused a thrill of excitement to course through her body. After four years she still remembered how she'd felt any time she'd heard Nathaniel's voice or looked into his eyes.

When Andrew cleared his throat, Margaret pulled her thoughts back with a reluctance that surprised her. She'd left the past behind long ago and had worked hard to put the anger and hurt away as well. It wasn't fair to compare Andrew to Nathaniel. Besides, Andrew seemed too kind and honest to disappear from the life of a girl he'd sworn to love.

"If you're sure you don't need any more help, I'll get to my supper, such as it is." Mischief lit his brown eyes. "Sure would be nice to have someone around who loved cooking."

Margaret's mouth twitched in a smile. "Gertrude was telling me that Sally Mae Kent is looking for a beau. I hear she's a fine cook."

Andrew's face fell. "Oh. I don't think. I mean, I don't want..." He took off his hat and slapped it against his leg.

Margaret stifled a giggle.

Andrew stared at her with a straight face. "Blast it, Margaret, that's not funny."

She shook her head as she tried to contain the first bit of real humor that had sliced through her heart since Papa's passing. Sally Mae was a nice girl, even if she did chatter like a magpie. She latched onto any young man who glanced her way, and Papa used to say she'd marry anything wearing trousers.

"I'm sorry, Andrew. And don't worry, I won't let on to Sally Mae that you're looking for a good cook." She covered her mouth with her hand in hopes of hiding the smirk that wouldn't be stilled. Poor Andrew, he was such fun to tease.

He jammed his hat back on his head and grimaced. "You'd best not." His lips quirked, but for a moment it didn't appear that a smile would win the tug-of-war.

Margaret couldn't hold the laughter back any longer—it spilled out of her mouth. Andrew sat for a full minute, then threw back his head and guffawed, his twin dimples breaking out. "Guess you got me that time," he choked as he tried to catch his breath. Swiping a hand across his eyes, he took a step toward the door. "Well, good night, Margaret. And please let me know if you need anything more. I'll let Julius know he can head on home."

Margaret sensed Andrew's reluctance to leave, but she wasn't in a position to ask him to dinner and wasn't sure she'd want to, even if her kitchen was in order. Her heart had mended after Nathaniel's betrayal, but could she really know that Andrew was different? Besides, hadn't God assured her while seeing Nathaniel that He was in control and her future was secure? Hadn't that meant she had a future with Nathaniel? She shook her head. Trust didn't come easy nowadays—not in her own ability to hear God's voice, nor in a man's ability to keep his word.

She enjoyed Andrew's company but felt in no hurry to be courted. Her married friends didn't understand her hesitation, as many women at the age of twenty-one were married and had a child by now.

Andrew was the first man who'd tempted her to forget Nathaniel. Silly, she knew. It had been four years. For months she'd swung between anger and grief—first furious that he hadn't come to take her away when he'd sworn he loved her, then crushed that he hadn't returned to explain.

"Margaret, did you hear me?" Andrew tentatively touched her arm, and she jumped. "I'm sorry. I didn't mean to startle you."

She shook her head. "No. I was gathering wool for a moment. What were you saying?"

He bent his head and drew a deep breath, then raised his eyes to meet hers. "There's an ice-cream social at the church in two weeks. Would you care to come with me?" His expression was both hopeful and full of doubt.

Margaret's thoughts stilled. She hated to encourage

him but staying trapped in the gloom that had surrounded her for so long didn't set well. "Yes. I'd like that."

His face went from blank amazement to joy in two swift seconds. "You would? Wonderful! Maybe I'll see you at church tomorrow, as well?"

"That would be nice, Andrew." She walked him to the door and watched as he strode down the path. Maybe life would settle down and bring some positive changes. After four years, it was time to move on.

Andrew walked down the path away from Margaret's cabin, a lightness in his step that he hadn't expected. He'd come to her house to help in an effort to keep the promise he'd made to her father a couple of weeks prior to his death. He hadn't expected to find his heart pounding and his palms sweaty when he'd asked Margaret to accompany him to the ice-cream social. Sure, he'd been interested in Margaret since he first saw her. What man wouldn't be? She was a beautiful woman with a generous heart and a quick intellect, although she could also be a bit stubborn and independent when the mood hit her. He glanced over at the quiet mill as he walked past the first large building to his right. With no trains running and the planer mill shut down, you could actually hear the birds singing in the fir trees that lined the path.

He hadn't thought too much of Mr. Garvey's request to watch out for Margaret in the event anything happened—after all, Jacob Garvey was only in his late forties and had appeared to be in good health. But something about the urgency of the request had made Andrew wonder if Jacob knew something he'd not shared, and it seemed that *had* been the case. Now Andrew found himself in a quandary—the woman he'd been somewhat interested in had been placed in his care by her deceased father, and without her knowledge. From what he knew of Margaret, he guessed that she'd be none too happy if she discovered the truth. Of course, with her father gone there'd be no way for her to know, and he'd certainly never willingly share what had passed between Jacob and himself. There was no point in upsetting her or making her doubt that his interest in her was genuine.

If his reaction to her nearness back at the cabin was any indication of the turn his heart had taken, his interest was even stronger than he'd realized when he'd given his word to Margaret's father. He recalled the flush on her cheeks when she'd laughed at his discomfort. Yes, indeed. He was going to enjoy keeping his word to Mr. Garvey.

www.ingramcontent.com/pod-product-compliance
Lightning Source LLC
LaVergne TN
LVHW011932070526
838202LV00054B/4603